EXTREME ATTRACTION

X-TREME LOVE SERIES
BOOK 5

KAY MANIS

To those who battle the demons within. May you find peace.

≈

Do not pray for an easy life, pray for the strength to endure a difficult one.
- Bruce Lee

≈

PROLOGUE

BERK

I PULLED the snowmobile into the garage next to Jaime's car, making sure to kill the engine before she could come out and complain about the exhaust. Lord knew I didn't need another reason to fight with my wife. Arguing seemed like the only way we communicated lately.

Hopefully Jaime was inside napping. She hadn't been sleeping well lately, probably because of me. I pushed away the guilty thoughts, refusing to sink back into the darkness. I'd found clarity on the slopes today and I needed to make amends.

A winter storm had rolled in earlier and the poor visibility on the mountain had ended my training session early. As a professional snowboarder I couldn't afford the down time. Not to mention that now days, I looked for any excuse to stay away from home.

Stopping in the mudroom, I quickly stripped off my boots and clothes before reaching for the back door. Jaime was a neat freak and bitched anytime someone trailed mud and snow into the house.

I twisted the knob, surprised to find the door locked. Jaime never locked the back door when she was home, but she hadn't been acting herself lately, and with good reason. The sleeping pills the doctor had prescribed were making her loopy and she must have locked it by accident.

I pulled a spare key from our hiding spot behind the washer and unlocked the door, walking inside.

"Jaime!" I yelled, tossing the key on a side table. An eerie silence rang through the house. Lately our home had been filled with so many people and so much noise, the calm was unusual, but welcomed.

Walking into the house, I glanced around the living room. The flowers that had once littered our house were gone. Jaime must have thrown them away while I was out. *Thank God.* They were just another reminder of what I'd lost. What *we'd* lost.

The fireplace was turned off, a sign Jaime was definitely sleeping. If she were awake, she would have been curled up on the couch, enjoying the warmth of the fire, especially with a winter storm brewing outside.

I paced around the living room, unable to settle my racing thoughts. I envied Jaime's ability to sleep. Maybe I should take a pill.

Most days I ran myself ragged on the slopes during my training sessions, desperate for the exhaustion, craving a way to mentally and physically shut down. But today my workout had been cut short because of the changing weather. Now I had to find another outlet for my nervous energy.

Everyone on my team was giving me time to lick my wounds but I knew I needed to get my shit together soon. The X Games were approaching, not that I gave a rat's ass. It wasn't like I needed the invitation, or the publicity, but at least training for the competition gave me something else to think about besides the dark thoughts threatening to take me under.

Suddenly my stomach grumbled.

The thought of eating made me nauseous, but my training sessions this week had been brutal and I knew I needed to refuel. I should check on Jaime first, make sure she was all right.

On the slopes today, I'd been able to reflect on the last few weeks, finally realizing that blaming my wife was only making our impossible situation worse. It wasn't all my wife's fault. As soon as Jaime woke from her nap, I'd offer my apologies for being such a prick. Maybe we could start over.

My stomach rumbled again. Food first.

Making my way into the kitchen, I threw open the freezer door, surprised to find it completely empty.

What the hell?

Just last night the fridge had been crammed full of casseroles. I opened the refrigerator, thankful to find a half-filled gallon of milk in the door. At least I could make a protein shake. The thought of preparing a full meal was exhausting.

Reaching into the cabinet above the fridge, I searched for my protein powder but found the shelf empty. What had Jaime done with all my shit? I drew in a deep breath, reminding myself that blaming her for everything wouldn't help us heal.

Taking out my anger on her wasn't fair but I had no one else to lean on. My friends and family couldn't understand the pain I was in, only Jaime truly understood. We were survivors now, forced to walk a dark path neither of us were prepared for.

Sagging into a chair at the kitchen table I noticed a note laying against a vase of wilted flowers The once vibrant petals were dying. How poetic.

The envelope was addressed to me, in Jaime's distinctive hand-writing. She'd probably left me a note to say she'd gone out for a walk. She hadn't been out of the house in days and I knew the fresh Colorado air would help ease her pain. Jaime's doctor warned us that she was in a fragile state right now but fuck, so was I.

My stomach growled again. Maybe when she returned from her walk, I'd take her to dinner. We needed to get out of the house, be with friends and family. We couldn't hide in our remote cabin any longer.

I lifted the envelope and ran my fingers over the paper, remembering how many love notes Jaime had written me when we first met. We could get there again, couldn't we?

I tore open the envelope and pulled out the note, smiling at the cursive monogram printed on the front. It was a left over *thank you* card from our wedding. I'd balked at the idea of her ordering so many when we'd first been engaged, but Jaime assured me she would use them all.

Now, five years later, the only thing she used them for was to leave me sporadic love notes. This was a sign, though, a gesture that said she was trying. The monogram of our joined initials solidified the fact that we were in this together.

Someone pounded on the front door and I jumped. It was probably Jaime. She'd forgotten her key. She was always losing things. Walking to the door, I swung it open, surprised to find Jaime's sister, Jackie, standing on the porch. Behind her was a police car, a uniformed officer leaning against his door.

My chest tightened with fear as my head began to spin. "What's wrong, Jackie?" I asked, my gaze traveling from the officer to her.

She stared at me, tears rolling down her face before her head fell.

I stepped out onto the porch and noticed the snow falling faster now. If Jaime didn't get home soon, she'd be caught in the drift. Fear tightened my gut. "Jackie?" I repeated.

She lifted her head, her hazel eyes meeting mine. She looked so much like Jaime in that moment.

My breath caught in my throat.

"There's been another accident, Berk," she whispered, her words barely audible over the whooshing sound of blood beating in my ears. "You need to come with us." She nodded toward the police officer.

"What kind of accident?" I said through gritted teeth. The

familiar feeling of dread in the pit of my stomach warned me I didn't want to know the answer.

Jackie stared at me, her eyes red-rimmed and full of pain. "It's Jaime," she finally said, her voice hoarse with emotion.

My hands shook and my fists clenched tight around something. I glanced down and realized Jaime's note was still in my hand. Lifting the flap, I held my breath, fearing what she'd written. Her two simple words brought me to my knees.

I'm sorry.

～

Even the knowledge of my own fallibility cannot keep me from making mistakes. Only when I fall do I get up again.
- Vincent Van Gogh

～

CHAPTER 1

GENEVA

THE SUN'S rays cast a welcome blanket of warmth over my exposed skin. The smell of salt air and the calming lull of the waves transported my mind to a distant place where worries no longer existed, and my past was completely absolved. My only desire was to stay locked in this Hawaiian bubble forever. But Dana's cutting words disintegrated the moment like a nuclear bomb.

"Holy motherfucker, guys!"

"What?" Hindley asked.

Even with my eyes closed and covered by dark sunglasses, I could still picture Hindley sitting straight up on her lounger, her face contorted in fear as she scanned the pristine Hawaiian beach, searching for any lurking child predators. I quietly chuckled at what a protective mother she'd become—fierce and strong.

"This time tomorrow I'll be married!" Dana shouted, loud enough for people inside the resort to hear.

"You're just now realizing that?" I laughed, never once opening my eyes or turning to face her.

"Yeah," she answered, as if astonished by her own words, "I guess I am."

"Technically, you're already married," Hindley corrected.

Dana and her husband Peter had already married in a small ceremony back in Austin where we were from. This destination wedding in Hawaii was a bonus.

"Well, yeah," Dana agreed. "But this is different. I mean, the kids will be there."

Dana and Peter were currently fostering three children they hoped to adopt soon. Since she was unable to carry a child, she and her husband had decided to adopt. Thankfully for them, the adoption had come more quickly than expected. I delighted in seeing my friend in her new role as wife and mother.

Hearing a slight quiver in her voice made me realize my friend needed more than just a snarky comeback from me.

I sat up on my lounge chair on the beach, pushing my shades up high on my head. "What's wrong, Dana? Peter loves you. The kids adore you. Tomorrow will be perfect." I reached beside my lounger, grasping for the plastic glass. "Drink this." I held the fruity cocktail out to her.

She took it willingly, chugging the remainder of my pina colada as if she were a college student in a fraternity drinking contest.

"It's just…" Dana stumbled with her words.

"You feel like this is your last night of freedom?" Hindley asked.

"Yeah, I guess," Dana sighed. "Something like that."

"So *now* you want a bachelorette party?" I half yelled, glaring at her. "I offered to throw you one for the last three weeks." I held up three fingers for emphasis. "Now, here we sit on the tropical shores of Kauai, thousands of miles away from the friends I know would want to attend." Her destination wedding was a small affair, just family and close friends. How the hell was I supposed to pull something together?

"But you were sick," Dana pouted.

"It was just a stomach bug," I said. "We still could have gone out."

"It wasn't *just* a stomach bug, Geneva. You were puking up your toenails for over a week," Hindley said.

"You were so sick, I wasn't even sure if you were going to be able to come to Hawaii," Dana said. Her concern for me wasn't surprising, but I still didn't feel worthy of it.

"I would have given you a party back home if that's what you wanted, no matter how sick I was."

"I don't want a party," Dana said with a coy smile.

"Cut the shit, Di Grazio," I said. "Your demure expression does nothing for your face."

"Fuck you, Geneva." She laughed, wadding up the damp napkin under her glass and tossing it in my direction.

"You'd like to." I smirked, snagging the napkin mid-air.

"Actually, no. I think you'd like to fuck *him*." Dana nodded toward something, or rather someone, out in the water.

Curious, Hindley and I followed her gaze and stared, jaws lax, as a man emerged casually out of the water carrying a bright yellow surfboard under one arm. His other hand pushed back long, jet-black hair from his face.

I thumbed through the massive bank of adjectives floating around in my mind but discovered there truly were no words you could use to describe this man.

He wasn't your typical beau-hunk, romance hero, the ones authors wrote about. The kind you fantasize over for days after reading all of their steamy sex scenes with the virginal heroine. At least not the ones I read.

I gazed down at the semi-pornographic cover of the novel sitting beside me on my beach bag. No, the man sauntering toward us looked *nothing* like the blond fox posing semi-naked on the front of my book, but it didn't make this ball-of-hotness walking toward us any less cover model worthy. The man, who had all three of us speechless, was a Greek God, Poseidon, rising from the waters of his home deep within the ocean.

His body was ripped like a Calvin Klein underwear model, his chest hard and dark, in grave contrast to the neon yellow and green board shorts hanging low on his hips. A tingle erupted between my legs and I had to cross my ankles and rub my thighs together for relief.

What the hell was that?

I didn't have to ask. I knew what it was—sexual desire for a complete stranger. Something I was used to, something I would have acted on in my old days. Thankfully these days I was a new girl.

"Holy fuck!" Dana bellowed.

I'm sure her outburst caught the demi-god by surprise, as well as the other guests lounging nearby.

I slammed my eyes shut, denying myself the pleasure of gawking. He was probably used to women ogling his gorgeous body. I pictured his delicious lips curving up into a seductive smile, his long mane of hair dancing in the island breeze—*Stop, Geneva. Stop it.*

I couldn't help it. I hadn't experienced this instant connection, this burning desire for a man, in years. I didn't need that type of relationship, though. Not now.

These types of feelings always ended the same. They started with a tiny spark, but quickly turned into a raging inferno that would destroy everything in its path. Especially me.

I'd survived many sordid relationships before I was married. But after my divorce, I'd closed myself off to those carnal feelings, choosing instead to concentrate on my studies and my new career as a teacher.

I slid my shades down over my eyes and drilled them shut before sinking back in my chair.

"Are you ladies busy this afternoon?"

I shuddered slightly from the sounds of the deep voice above the roar of the waves, his words gliding over my skin like suntan oil. His masculine vibrato was laced with the hint of an island accent, and I didn't have to open my eyes to know it was Poseidon. Instantly, my stomach twisted in knots.

Don't look, don't look.

"Whatcha got in mind, sailor?" Dana giggled.

I'm sure the dude was lost in her hypnotic blue eyes and deep dimples.

Don't look, don't look. It's like the sun. If you look at him, it could blind you.

I couldn't stand the suspense. Against my better judgment, I slowly lifted my lids.

Damn!

Drawing in a deep breath, I tried to appear as unaffected as possible. I didn't want him to see the goose bumps prickling over my skin. Even though they were probably visible from the space station and dotting every surface of my body, despite the warm sun.

"I was wondering if you all might be interested in some surfing lessons today." He was staring straight at me.

I squirmed in discomfort, afraid I might scream from my spontaneous orgasm about to erupt from the rich tenor of his voice. Thinking about straddling a surfboard, my legs gaping wide open with Poseidon poised behind me, his massive erection poking in my back…*Stop!*

I jumped up from my seat, gathered my towel and cover-up and nervously shoved them both into my beach bag. I had to get the hell out of here or this guy was gonna end up underneath me on this lounge chair, screaming out my name in a chant of pure ecstasy, begging for mercy. Yeah, I was that good, and I knew it. Unfortunately, so did half the men in Texas.

"Well, I'm getting married tomorrow," Dana answered, "and I don't want to walk down the aisle with a broken leg. And this one here," she said, motioning her thumb toward Hindley, "she's preggers, so that's a no go."

I knew what Dana was doing. She was setting up Poseidon to put all his surf lesson sales efforts on me. I cut my eyes toward the surfer, surveying his perfect form. When our eyes finally met, I wasn't surprised to find his focus squarely on me. It was as if he hadn't even noticed Dana and Hindley at all.

"What about you?"

His quiet voice had my body humming. This was bad, *really* bad. If I accepted his invitation, it would be over. I would throw him down and fuck him senseless right here on the beach.

It's only a week. What could it hurt?

True. No commitment, no strings. Maybe Poseidon was just what I needed.

"What about me?" I asked.

"Would you like to learn how to ride?"

Dana giggled at the innuendo, always turning the most mundane things into something sexual. My eyes drank him in from top to bottom like the sexual predator I used to be.

His deep, rich tan was not a product of hours in the sun, but God-given, his heritage as a native islander. Jet-black hair hung past his shoulders and moved with the light breeze.

I swallowed the lump in my throat, watching helplessly as he dug his massive hand deep into his scalp. Threading his fingers through the strands of his silky mass, he pulled back the hair that had blown across his face. His face.

Holy fuck!

"Wow." Dana laughed. "That's an offer *any* chick would have to be completely insane or half dead to turn down."

She was right. A woman would have to be a gold-star lesbian not to be affected by this man's sultry invitation.

One problem, though. I was a creature of habit. The turbulent wakes I'd created in my past were constant reminders to stay alert to my natural tendencies. I couldn't afford to surrender now.

Something about Poseidon warned me that if I let him lead me into the ocean and put his body anywhere close to mine, even for something as simple as a surfing lesson, I'd never return. I didn't want a man to have that kind of power over me. I never had. I existed in a bubble for a reason.

"Maybe some other time," I answered nonchalantly, as if his invitation hadn't affected me.

Throwing my bag over my shoulder, I stalked through the sand toward my private cabana, never once looking back at the mythical god of the sea standing behind me. I knew if I did, I'd regret it. But now, walking away from him, I already felt like it was the biggest mistake of my life.

CHAPTER 2

GENEVA

"WHAT THE HELL, GENEVA?" Dana fussed at me as I towel-dried my hair.

"What?" I feigned innocence as I threw the towel over my shoulder and pulled a beer from the refrigerator. I twisted the cap, brought it to my mouth, and took a long swig.

"What?" she huffed in annoyance. "You know what, dumbass. That hottie at the beach. He was practically begging you to hop on his board. Ahhh," she laughed, "his board, get it?"

"With you, Dana," I smiled, "it's very difficult *not* to get it."

"You're just jealous." She smirked, tossing a dishtowel at me.

"Why would I be jealous of you?" I asked the rhetorical question, knowing she was absolutely right. Dana had a past, but not nearly as tainted as mine.

My life had been a complete mess until a few years ago, and now all I truly desired was what Dana and Hindley had—men who adored them and babies they would lay down their own lives for.

"You're jealous because you don't have these."

My gaze swept over to Dana who was standing at the edge of the counter. Her hands gripped her massive breasts, shaking them vigorously as I'm sure her husband, Peter, did every night.

"Geneva doesn't need those," Hindley said. "That dude was eye-balling her like she was his midnight snack and he was a starving, wild coyote."

Dana cupped her mouth and let out a wild howl as her head fell back.

"Whatever." I shook my head and took another gulp of beer.

"She's totally right," Dana added. "I damn near thought the dude was gonna serve you up on his surfboard and eat you out hard."

Just the thought of lying on Poseidon's surfboard, legs splayed open with his face buried in my lady parts, had my clean panties dripping wet.

"Awww," Dana howled as she pointed her petite finger at me. Her raspy voice echoed through my cabana. "You like him. I told you she was scared shitless, Hindley."

"What are you talking about?" I tried to act unaffected, but I knew exactly what she was saying. Dana and I were close, and she always knew when a guy turned me on, mostly because it almost never happened anymore.

"You practically ran away from the poor guy." Hindley laughed. "You should have seen him when you left. He was so miserable looking, like Santa Claus never showed up at his house for Christmas."

"Whatever." I waved a dismissive hand. I surveyed the large open-air villa, my eyes roaming over the cliffs outside that jutted into the deep blue ocean. I was thankful my father had talked me into allowing him to pay for my own private cabana. I could never afford such an extravagance on my teacher's salary. It was amazing to me how I'd gone from citizen high to citizen low in such a short amount of time.

"So, what do you want to do tonight?" I asked Dana, trying to change the subject. "It's your last night of *freedom*." I used air quotes since she was already technically married.

Dana had lived through a difficult time in the last ten years. Not only had her parents been killed in a car wreck as a teenager but she'd also been diagnosed with uterine cancer. Her doctor was forced to perform a complete hysterectomy.

She'd met Peter, a professional freestyle motocross rider, only a few months ago, but they instantly fell in love. It had been difficult for Dana to discuss her illness with him. Having a huge family had been one of Peter's life-long dreams. Her hysterectomy meant she couldn't have children.

Shortly before the wedding, Peter's ex-wife, a bitch crazier than me, kidnapped Dana and her brother Sam and held them for ransom. After her near death experience with the psycho, Dana's decision to adopt was fast-tracked, not only by her and Peter, but by the adoption agency as well.

They'd been fostering two boys, Lucas and Levi and their sister Lilly. The agency had placed the kids with Dana because of her experience with special needs people, her own brother Sam suffering from cerebral palsy and a host of other cognitive disabilities. Lilly was only two, and she had Down syndrome. Taking them into their home was a no-brainer for Peter and Dana. And now they were well on their way to adopting them.

Dana's brother Sam was a doll, and he and I were madly in love, as friends. I was an instructor at Sam's in-home residence, Whispering Oaks, a full-time residential facility for adults with cognitive mental and physical challenges. I protected him almost as fiercely as Dana did.

"Let's go out and get totally hammered," Dana answered, rubbing her hands together.

"Uh, hello." Hindley pointed to her belly.

"You can be our designated driver." Dana laughed.

"You don't want to be hungover walking down the aisle tomorrow, do you?" I asked.

"True, good point, Gen," Dana said.

"What about the kids?" I asked, wondering where they were today.

"Oh, Caroline and Barbara have them. They're at the pool."

Caroline Hagen-Barton was Hindley's mom and was married to my father. She'd been like a mother to me ever since they'd married over fifteen years ago, when Hindley and I were in middle school. Caroline had also been a surrogate mother to Dana, since her parents had died nearly ten years ago.

Barbara Fontenot was Peter's mom, Dana's mother-in-law, and was now engaged to be married herself. Apparently, she'd fallen madly in love with Peter's late father's best friend, while Peter had been estranged from his family…God, it sounded like a plot line from one of my steamy novels. My novel. Oh, shit!

"Has anyone seen my book?" I raced around the villa, searching for my beach bag.

"Calm down, SpongeBob Smutty Pants." Dana cackled. "You and those fucking porno books of yours." She pulled my novel out of her own bag.

I liked this particular book because it was the first novel I'd read about BDSM. I was on board with the bondage and the dominance, but the submission and masochist stuff…not a hundred percent sure on that one. I didn't want some dude leading me around like a dog on a collar. But after reading more, I discovered that was really not what the lifestyle was about. It was based on trust and honesty—two things I had little experience with.

"Where the fuck do you get this shit anyway?" Dana turned the book back and forth in her hand.

I lurched for the novel.

Dana tossed it across the counter to Hindley.

"This dude on the cover is seriously hot." Hindley studied the front of my book.

Typically, I didn't buy the paperback of these steamy novels because the covers were too risqué. Plus, they embarrassed the shit out of me. It wouldn't look good for me to be in the break room at work holding a book that had a half-naked woman on the cover, blindfolded and tied up to a chair, with a shirtless dude donning a riding crop.

This particular series was by one of my favorite authors, though, and it was her first attempt at an erotic book. Turns out, I loved it, so I knew I wanted to have the paperback. I didn't consider myself a fan girl of the author by any means, but I held out hope that maybe one day I would meet V.M. Wilson.

"Is this chick tied up?" Hindley asked, surprisingly unoffended.

She and Rory were into bondage, role-playing stuff, not like in this particular book, though. But everyone knew her husband, Rory, had a dominant personality that Hindley loved, despite her past.

Rory was also a professional extreme sports athlete like Peter— not a motocross rider, but a skateboarder. Who knew there were professional skateboarders in the world? Rory was not only Hindley's husband, but also my brother-in-law. Rory and I had an unfortunate past that we were trying to mend.

"Give it back!" I yelled, snatching it from Hindley's hand. "You're gonna ruin it, drooling over the cover."

Hindley laughed and shrugged me off.

"We're not all as lucky as you two smut bags," I said. "I don't have a real guy eating out my cooch every night like you two skanks. Sue me if I have a few hot book boyfriends to get me off."

"True." Dana smirked, taking a long drink from her beer. "We are some lucky bitches, Hindley."

I rolled my eyes as Hindley got that starry eyed look on her face. *Bitches*.

"So, what are we gonna do tonight?" Dana asked. "Caroline and Barbara are keeping the kids. Sam's with your dad, Hindley. I'm free as a bird, ready to get crazy." She smiled, lifting her beer high above her head, her hips gyrating like she was a stripper. "Ooo, maybe we can find that surfer dude and hook him up with Gen." Dana shot a conspiratorial wink at Hindley.

"Wouldn't that be fun?" Hindley rubbed her hands together, her eyes glowing with a deviant gleam.

"No, thanks," I answered. "I think I'll stick to my book."

Both girls rolled their eyes.

"You're no fun anymore, Gen." Dana frowned.

"Let's go to dinner, then. Maybe later we can hit up some of the local clubs." I stared at Dana, trying to pacify her.

"That sounds highly boring." Dana rolled her eyes.

"You're both married. And moms," I reminded her.

"It doesn't mean I'm fucking dead." Dana perched a hand on her petite hip.

"Yeah," Hindley chimed in. "We're still alive and looking for a good time. We'll live vicariously through you tonight, Geneva."

"What the hell does that mean?" I asked.

"It means we're gonna get you totally fucked up. Do you think we could score some weed tonight?" Dana asked.

What the fuck?

"I mean, we're on a tropical island." Dana waggled her brows.

"You don't even smoke weed, you idiot," I said.

"Fine, all right, Miss Straight Lace Princess." Dana wobbled her head, holding up her hand in a mocking gesture.

"So, dinner and clubbing?" Hindley asked.

I smiled at Hindley, knowing she was pulling me out of a tight spot with Dana.

"Why don't we go to the spa and get a massage this afternoon, before our mani-pedis," Dana said.

It sounded like heaven, but my funds were limited.

My fall from grace several years ago had cost me more than my social status—it had cost me financially. I was no longer a pretty princess sucking up money from my father and ex-husband. Instead, I was a working girl, trying to survive on a measly teacher's salary. But I loved it. I loved the life I had now and reveled in the sacrifices I'd been forced to make.

"My treat!" Dana shouted.

"It's *your* wedding, Dana, you can't treat," I said.

"I'll treat." Hindley stepped forward, jutting out her chest.

"Actually, it's *my* treat." A deep voice rumbled behind us.

We all three turned, our eyes wide with surprise to find Peter and Rory standing in the entryway of my cabana.

"When the hell did you two sneak in?" Dana shot off like a rocket toward her husband.

Peter enveloped her in his warm embrace, leaning down to place a light peck on her head.

I let out a small sigh, pushing away my envious thoughts.

"We knocked twice." Peter hugged Dana tighter. "What were y'all doing in here? And why is your door unlocked, Geneva?" Peter's gaze fell on me, his eyes narrowed in brotherly-like concern.

"Your wife was the last one in, don't blame me, you giant of a man," I answered, pointing to Dana.

It always pissed me off that the little pixie girls got the tall guys, leaving my five-foot, nine-inch Amazon ass with the little midget men.

Peter's brow furrowed as he cast a menacing glance at Dana.

Ever since Peter's ex-wife, Jillian, had kidnapped Dana and beat the shit out of her less than two months ago, Peter had become uber protective of her.

She flashed him her most alluring smile, her deep dimples wiping away all of his anger. *Lucky bitch.*

"What are y'all up to?" Rory asked. He stalked toward Hindley and wrapped his arms around her growing midsection.

Hindley was less than three months along in her pregnancy, but, given the fact she was tall and lean, the baby had nowhere to hide.

"Eww, you stink, baby." Rory wrinkled his nose, pushing Hindley an arm's length away.

"Thanks a lot." She swatted at him.

"Abbi's down with your mom at the pool. I could take you back to our room and give you a shower." One brow cocked high.

Oh, God, not this again. These two were the biggest horndogs on the planet, and they didn't care who saw.

Rory and Hindley's daughter, Abbi, was nearly two years old

and the joy of both their lives. I couldn't believe how fast the time had flown and how big my niece was getting. It seemed like just yesterday Hindley had discovered she was pregnant with her.

Now, here we all stood in Hawaii, Hindley expecting her second, Dana with three kids of her own, and me…all alone.

"What time's our appointment in the spa?" Hindley asked, her eyes never leaving Rory's.

"I made all three of you appointments at eleven for massages," Peter said. "Then they'll serve you a light lunch. After that, you'll all get facials." He stroked Dana's face, the desire in his eyes burning through her clothes.

Oh my God. I had to get the fuck out of here. These love sick assholes were physically making me ill.

"That was so sweet of you, baby." Dana lifted high on her toes and brushed her lips against Peter's.

I escaped to the patio, knowing all four of these fuckwads were gonna start getting porno on me soon. Where was my damn book when I needed it?

I could barely hear the couples speaking behind me over the crash of waves below my room. This villa was magical. And wasted on a single girl like me.

Images of Poseidon entered my mind—his long, lean torso, with those board shorts hanging precariously low, hinting at the treasure that lay in wait underneath.

You could tell from his tanned skin and long, raven colored hair that he was an islander. But his facial bone structure and whiskey-colored eyes hinted that he probably wasn't one hundred percent native to Hawaii. Still, he'd been a sight to see in his own right. The tingle between my thighs returned.

Regret filled my heart, and I wondered why I'd run away from his offer to spend the day on his "board." Trying to wipe away the memories of what could have been, I turned back toward the two couples that were thankfully extricated from one another.

"So, what do you guys have planned tonight?" Hindley asked, looking between Peter and Rory.

"I think we're just going to go have dinner with Paul and AJ, then maybe hang out at the resort's bar by the beach," Peter said.

Paul was my father and the absolute *best* man in the entire world. My mother died when I was eight and for many years it had just been the two of us. But when he met Hindley's mom, the two of them had become inseparable.

In my pre-teen mind, I had been his princess and he was my novel hero. Then, Hindley and her mom came along and everything had been shattered. The once impenetrable bond my father and I had suddenly broke as he made room in his heart and in our home for the new loves of his life.

I'd felt abandoned and betrayed, as if my father had no right to move on with his life without my mother. At least that was what my adolescent mind tried to convince me.

Caroline was wonderful and tried so hard to connect all four of us as a family unit. Right away, I saw my father's pull toward Hindley, which meant my grasp on him was strained. I was jealous of Hindley from the moment I laid eyes on her. I quickly made it my mission in life to make her life as miserable as I possible—a plan I executed very well.

Looking back on my actions, I wondered how Hindley could be in the same room with me now, let alone the same planet. I'd been awful to her, in the worst sort of way, for years. I had hated her and she had known it. Hell, everyone had. The only person who had ever stood up to me and defended her had been Dana, which meant I had hated her, too.

As I stood in my villa and stared at Hindley and Dana, words escaped me. I had no way to explain how grateful I was for their forgiveness. I wasn't sure how or why they'd both extended it to me, but I knew my life would have been shit if they hadn't.

"Dinner is all this guy can handle." Rory laughed, bumping Peter's arm.

"That sounds positively boring." Dana wrinkled her nose.

"What are you guys doing?" Peter asked, cocking his head in suspicion.

"Well, we've got a single lady over here and we plan to live vicariously through her." Dana pointed toward me.

All eyes fell on me. My face heated with the unwanted attention. It was completely unlike me to embarrass so easily.

"She's already got a secret admirer." Hindley smiled.

"Oh, really?" Rory tilted his head, wrapping his arm around his wife. "Who is it?"

"No one," I answered quickly, cutting my eyes at Hindley.

"He's an islander, a local yokel." Dana smirked as she wiggled her brows. "He wanted to give her a ride on his board."

My eyes drilled into her with lethal daggers, which were meant to silence her.

She snorted and buried her face in her husband's massive chest.

Pussy.

"A surfer?" Peter smiled. "Nice, Geneva."

"She said no. Practically ran away from the poor dude. I thought he was going to cry." Hindley giggled.

"Whatever." I shook my head.

"What's up with that, Gen? Nothing wrong with a little island loving." Rory smiled, grinding up against Hindley.

Uggh!

"Go take your shower, you two horndogs," I said to Rory and Hindley, shaking my head. "And you two," I turned toward Dana and Peter, "go do whatever it is you sappy-ass lovebirds do. I'll meet you guys at the spa in an hour."

Unable to stand their lovey-dovey actions for another second, I bolted for my bedroom. As I passed by the kitchen, I noticed my book lying on the counter and snatched it, holding it close to my chest.

"Jealous much?" Dana shouted at me. "Enjoy your erotic sex

book, and your vibrator!" She laughed like a hyena as the others joined in.

I held up my hand, giving her the middle finger before I slammed the bedroom door. The last thing I needed reminding of was how utterly nonexistent my sex life was. If it weren't for battery-operated machinery, I'd probably have cobwebs growing on my cooch by now.

I plopped down on my bed and gazed out of the picturesque window. The gossamer curtains floated with the breeze as the roaring sea below echoed through the massive room. This was a fucking honeymooners' paradise. I turned and stared at the empty spot beside me. Great. All alone. Again.

Peeling back the pages of my book to the spot I had marked earlier, I nestled in with the only partner I had. My sexy book boyfriend.

His calloused hand slides under her lace panties, his fingers delving deep into her core as the paddle strikes CC's ass again. Her bound hands hold her tight. She's unable to protect herself from his erotic blows. Truthfully, she doesn't want protection, though. She wants this, practically begged for it with her earlier defiance. CC is wet with desire for him, but she knows better than to speak of it.

She yanks on the velvet rope that holds her hands firmly in place. CC's back arches in need as her forehead pushes harder against the unforgiving floor. Her nipples pebble into nubs, her pussy is aflame, wet with desire for his dominance, for more of his sensual punishment.

CC bucks against his hand as his fingers sink deeper within her channel. She wants to deliberately disobey him, so that he will strike her again with his punishing hands. How fucked up is that?

His thumb circles her clit, pressing lightly, her throbbing core aching for more. The pulses of light threaten to blind her from the mind-blowing pleasure he brings. He knows her body even better

*than she does. CC pushes further against his hand, mesmerized by
the sexual tension that swirls within her.*

*The paddle strikes again, harder this time. She moans, not from
pain, but from pleasure, and works hard to hide the smile that
threatens to surface. She desires more, needs more of his dominance, but she fears what his more might be.*

*She hears the tearing of fabric, and without warning, his thick
cock slams inside her after another blow from the paddle strikes her
ass cheek.*

*He punishes her with his relentless thrusts. His shaft is so thick
inside her pussy that she cries out in pleasure, and in pain, as her
walls spasm around—*

Uggh, what the fuck had I been I thinking? I couldn't read this shit
right now. My own juices were flowing and I hadn't packed any
vibrators to relieve my ache. I'd been too afraid the airlines would
confiscate them. *Maybe they sell them down in the souvenir shop.*
Highly unlikely.

My mind filled with images of West, the shy but domineering
man from my book, and CC, the seemingly strong woman who had
challenged him. At first, she'd been brave, questioning his authority
and standing chest to chest with him. Before long, though, CC had
completely submitted to West's sexual supremacy, and loved every
minute of it.

I was just like this female heroine, strong and fearless in my
convictions. I wondered if perhaps that was why I was still alone
after all these years of being single.

No, that's not it and you know it.

As my hands traveled under my robe, my fingers traced the lace
of my own panties. My hand was the closest thing I was going to
get to any type of relief from the ache between my legs for the next
seven days.

One image immediately popped up in my mind—Poseidon's

body emerging from the water, his torso splattered with rivulets of water, his hair dripping from the sea's delicious embrace.

My fingers worked their way deeper into my underwear as Poseidon's face filled my mind, images of him tying me up to his surfboard, pushing my legs open wide with his calloused hands as his face sank deep into my thighs. It was painfully obvious—this was as close as I was going to get to a love affair in Hawaii.

CHAPTER 3
GENEVA

WE WERE on our third club of the evening, and Dana was feeling no pain. She wasn't completely wasted, but I needed to stop her intake of alcohol, or she would feel like shit tomorrow at her renewal ceremony.

Dana and Peter had already been married by a judge at the courthouse in Austin two months before. The ceremony had been very moving, the judge's words so sincere and poignant.

I remembered his words. They'd been etched on my heart that day. Mainly because I'd never heard marriage explained the way he had. The judge's truthfulness and wisdom had resounded in us all.

He said the wedding itself was the easy part. Finding someone you were attracted to was natural. The difficult part was the days, weeks, and months following the ceremony when things got tough. That was where you experienced *real* conflicts and emotions. That was when the relationship was tested in the fires of life. He'd explained that your marriage would either grow stronger because of the struggles you faced as a couple, or it would fall apart and disintegrate in the fire.

The judge talked about putting your marriage into the hot coals of life, to make it pliable, molding it to fit one another, then hoping it came back stronger, like a piece of metal forged in a furnace.

"One more bar," Dana slurred as we walked on the boardwalk along the beach.

"I'm calling Peter," I said, looking over at Hindley.

Her slow nod reassured me I was doing the right thing.

Listening intently as the phone rang, I tugged on Dana's arm, pulling her close to steady her.

"Don't tell me, she's totally passed out, and you can't carry her home." Peter laughed.

"Not that bad," I answered with a giggle, "but I think she's done for the evening."

"Is that Peter?" Dana asked, grabbing for my phone. "I love you, Peter!" she shouted. "I want you inside me soooo bad."

Oh, shit. People close by were staring.

"We're at the hotel bar," Peter said. "Can you make it here or should I come get her?" You could hear the care and concern in his voice.

I stared down at Dana. Her eyes were slightly glassed over, her face washed with an expression of sheer contentment. I was happy that my friend had finally gotten the man she deserved.

"Nah, Hindley and I can make it there. The walk will probably do her some good. Are you guys wasted yet?" I asked, knowing neither Rory nor Peter drank.

"Oh, completely." He laughed. "We totally shut down the titty bar and ran the bartender dry."

Peter wasn't always playful like this, but, when he was, it brought a smile to my face. He was the big brother I never had, always protecting everyone close to Dana, similar to the way Rory did for Hindley.

"We should be there in about fifteen or twenty minutes." I winced at the screeching sounds in the background. "What's that horrible noise?" I asked.

"Karaoke night at the bar."

"Ahhh, the wonderful Karaoke." I smiled.

"Karaoke!" Dana shouted. "I love Karaoke! Let's go!"

"Be careful." Peter chuckled.

"We will."

"Please make sure, Geneva." Suddenly, his voice changed and I could sense real fear in his tone.

"I've got her, Peter," I reassured him.

"Kaaaah-reeeee-ooooo-keee!" Dana yelled.

"I wouldn't miss Dana trying to sing Tina Turner, again." I giggled, trying to comfort Peter.

I remembered back to Whispering Oaks. One weekend I'd brought in a karaoke machine, and we'd held our very own *American Idol* competition. Dana had been an entrant. She was horrible and was nearly booed off the stage until Sam stood up in her defense and quieted the unruly crowd.

"Be careful with my bride." I could hear the love in Peter's voice.

"Okay, we'll be there in a few." I looked over at Hindley.

She rolled her eyes in disbelief as she held on tightly to the other side of Dana. "Karaoke?" She scrunched up her face. "Really?"

I shrugged my shoulders, thinking of how awful this was going to turn out. I gazed down at my phone, double-checking my battery life. If I had to endure Dana's squawking, you could guaran-damn-tee I'd be capturing it all on video to embarrass the shit out of her for the rest of her natural born life.

"Don't worry." I waved my phone in the air. "Video."

Hindley laughed. "We'll never let her live it down."

I nodded my head in agreement.

Ten minutes later we were rounding the corner to the Honua Keena Kapu resort. It was a beautiful hotel, nestled on twenty acres of natural, botanical forest on the island of Kauai. The place was just the right mix of tropical jungle meets sophisticated elegance, and I knew as soon as we'd arrived yesterday evening that I'd want to return some day.

"Geneva!" Peter yelled, flagging me down near the breezeway of the bar attached to the main lobby.

"Peeee-terrr!" Dana pulled completely away from our grasp, then half ran, half tripped toward her husband.

The entire sight was adorable, yet a little embarrassing. But they were so in love that none of us really gave a shit. If anyone deserved to be happy, it was Dana Di Grazio.

She flew into Peter's arms, semi-jumping, but mostly falling as he caught her under her ass, laughing as she wrapped her legs around his waist and melted into him.

They sucked face like there was no tomorrow, no shame in their erotic acts. Instantly, I felt fire burn through me as Poseidon's face materialized in my mind, filling my fantasies just as he'd done earlier this morning when my fingers had crept down into no man's land.

I violently shook my head, trying to rid myself of the sexual fantasies coming to life in my mind. I really needed to stop reading those slutty books—they were killing me.

I had no viable potential for a sexual encounter in the near future to relieve my desires. Reading novels about freaky people tying each other up and spanking the shit out of one another was only doing my aching twat more damage than it was worth.

"Karaoke!" Dana shouted.

Peter jerked back, obviously stricken deaf by his wife's cries.

"Not tonight, Dolly." He extricated her from his body, but his eyes held a delicious promise.

Fuck.

"Pleeeease?" Dana begged, her voice so pathetic, unlike the Dana Di Grazio I knew and loved.

"Fine, but only one song." He held up his pointer finger. "You need your beauty rest."

"Are you saying I'm ugly?" Dana pouted, taking his finger and sliding it into her mouth.

Peter's eyes fluttered before he leaned down and whispered something in her ear.

Dana pulled his finger from her mouth and leaned back. "I promise." She crossed her heart with a finger, but the look in her eyes gave a different answer.

I didn't even want to know the question.

"Come on, y'all," Dana waved us on with her hand, "I want to sing. Peter said I can do one song, and then he's gonna fuck me twenty ways 'til Sunday when we get back to our room." She cupped her mouth, her eyes going wide as she realized how loud she'd spoken.

The building crowd, now gathered near the entrance, doubled over in laughter. My gaze panned over to Peter, who stood silent, shaking his head. He already realized the trouble he had entered into when he married Dana, and every bit of him seemed happier than a one-legged prostitute at a prosthetic convention.

Dana's hand yanked on mine, pulling me inside the bar.

I covered my ear with my free hand, trying to protect my hearing from the horrible song being screeched out by the current "singer."

He was trying to sing "I Will Survive" by Gloria Gaynor.

As my eyes panned the bar, it was quite evident by the painful grimaces on every face in sight that we all questioned whether or not *we* would survive this dill hole's butchering of poor Gloria's song.

"He sucks," Dana half shouted.

"Dana!" I yelled. "Shut the fuck up. You're embarrassing us."

"Fuck you, Geneva." She giggled. "I'll shut the fuck up if you sing."

"No way, I'm not singing, not tonight."

"Pleeeease."

"That shit may work on your husband, but not on me."

Peter laughed as he lifted Dana and perched her onto the stool at the table he and Rory had secured.

"You sing, Geneva?" Rory asked.

"Oh, God, does she," Dana answered, suddenly sobering up. "She is ah-maaaay-zing. You have to hear her." Dana turned toward me. "Please, Geneva." She brought her hands together as if she were about to pray and stuck out her bottom lip, pouting like a kid. "Tonight's my last night as a single woman, and it's the only thing I want."

"Hello, dumbass," I corrected, "you're already married, have been for two months now. And, you have three kids."

"Oh, yeah." She giggled.

This Dana—the sappy, love-sick, drunkard—was so unlike the one I knew, that I had to join in with her laughter.

"Fine. One song." I shoved my finger in her face. "Then it's off to bed with you."

"You're sleeping with me tonight, Dana." Peter's words were commanding and hot as hell.

"But it's our wedding night." She stared up at him.

"It's not our wedding night," he corrected with a slight tone of irritation. "We already went through that when you made me stay with Leif the night before our wedding at the courthouse, remember?"

"Oh, yeah." She smiled. "Plus, you promised to fuck me twenty ways—"

Peter's hand slapped across her mouth, silencing her before she could embarrass us more.

"Where is Leif anyway?" Hindley asked, looking around the bar.

"Oh, I think he met someone." Rory laughed, using air quotes.

"Nuh, uh!" Dana shouted. "Who?"

"The guy seemed decent enough," Peter answered, "and Leif acted like he knew the man, so we didn't really question him."

"My boy got him a man!" Dana hollered, as she stood on the rungs of the bar stool, waving her hand above her head in a circle of victory.

Leif was Rory's surrogate brother and best friend. Even though he wasn't an extreme sport athlete himself, he still worked in the industry, designing award-winning skateparks around the world.

Dana and Leif had been best friends since Rory and Hindley married several years ago. It was Dana he'd confided in about his sexuality. She'd accidentally outed him at her own engagement party.

No one in Leif's close-knit circle of family and friends seemed to care half as much that he was gay as Leif thought they would. Hell, we lived in Austin, not only the "Live Music Capital of the World," but the second most densely populated city for gay people in the United States.

"I still can't believe he and Luis broke up." Hindley shook her head.

Luis was Rory's agent and had worked with Hindley in her law firm when she first represented Rory herself. Luis and Leif had been a couple for several months, but just a few weeks after Leif was outed and their relationship made public, Luis and he split up.

Leif had never really talked about why, not even to Dana or Rory. He hadn't even wanted to come to Hawaii, but Dana begged him to.

"Well, I hope the man *is* decent," I said. "Maybe one of you guys should go back and check on him here in a bit."

Rory and Peter shared a knowing look and a sideways smirk, indicating they knew more than they were letting on.

"I think I'll have my hands pretty full with this saucy dynamo tonight." Peter smiled, reaching down to nuzzle his face in Dana's neck.

Her eyes rolled up in the back of her head at the promise of things to come.

I wanted to hate them, but history had taught me that envy and jealousy weren't emotions that were well suited for long-term happiness. "Get a room," I pouted.

"Got one already." Peter laughed.

"Oh, God, Peter!" Dana shouted out in a garbled moan that sounded like she was climaxing right here in front of God, her friends, and half the resort.

"Dana," Peter reprimanded with a grin that was contradictory to his tone.

"Fuck, Peter, I want you so bad," she moaned.

"Oh my God, will you shut the hell up!" I yelled, looking anxiously around the bar.

"Sing for me, please," Dana begged me.

I leaned into her, whispering in her ear. "If I promise to sing, do you swear to shut up and go back to your room with Peter for the rest of the night and do whatever it is you two fuck monkeys have planned?"

Her eyes grew wide, and she nodded like an eager dog waiting on its next treat.

"Fine," I blew out, exasperated, and scared shitless. "Where do I sign up?"

"I think it's up at the stage," Peter answered.

Pushing my way through the crowded bar, I made it to the front. Apparently, Karaoke night was a bigger deal here than I'd imagined, and suddenly my stomach cramped in fear.

I hated singing in front of people. I rarely did it, if at all. Even singing in front of the residents at Whispering Oaks had been terrifying for me. But I knew Dana needed to get to bed if she stood a chance of looking halfway decent tomorrow. So, I fought through my own fears and, with a trembling hand, signed up for the list of would-be singers.

A thought popped into my mind. *Liquid courage.* That was what I needed right now. Instead of making my way back to our table, I stopped at the bar to buy a little bravery in the form of a mixed drink.

"Good evening," the handsome bartender said to me, his eyes migrating south toward my chest.

I looked down, having no idea what I'd worn tonight. I was

surprised to see it was a strapless sundress that really didn't reveal much in the way of cleavage.

"I love your necklace," he said.

Instinctively my hand clutched the chain around my neck. Of course, that was what he'd been looking at.

It was a star pendent covered in small diamonds. My father had given it to me shortly after my mother passed away, almost twenty years ago. It had been a present to her from my father on their wedding day.

I thought it strange that a guy would notice the piece of jewelry. Usually, it was girls who complimented me.

"Thanks," I replied, rubbing nervously on the pendant.

"Signed up to sing?" He nodded toward the stage as he wiped down the bar.

"Yes, but I'm afraid I need a little flowing fortitude to help me, if you know what I mean."

"I sure do." He winked.

His eyes were dark brown, almost black, and matched his thick hair. His face was a deep bronze color, a native Hawaiian no doubt, his bone structure firm and menacing. But his actions and his words were in stark contrast to his physical form.

"What will it be?" He raised a brow that seemed to ask me more than just what kind of drink I wanted.

"Something that will take the edge off," I answered. "What would you suggest?"

"For Karaoke nerves?" He rubbed his stubble-ridden face, his eyes rolling up to the sky. "Definitely tequila."

"Oh, not tequila," I moaned.

"Bad experience?"

"The worst."

"Let me guess." He laughed. "Fraternity party, senior year in college, you entered a wet T-shirt contest and the prize was a fifth of Patron."

I laughed at his suggestion. "No. More like high school senior trip, Señor Frog's in Cancun."

"Ahhh, yes, the illustrious Señor Frog's tequila bar and hangover haven." He smiled with a nod.

I smiled at his remark. He was good company. Part of me wondered if maybe there could be more.

Without warning, an image of Poseidon emerging from his watery confines, board shorts hanging low on his hips, flashed through my mind.

"So, no tequila for you then. How about a shot of Sex on the Beach?"

Well, how poetic.

"Is that an offer or a drink?" I laughed nervously.

"Both." He smirked.

"All right, we'll start with the drink first. I'm a good girl. But don't tell the others." I nodded toward my friends.

"Never. Your secret's safe with me." He patted his chest and laughed before strolling down the bar to prepare my drink.

My gaze combed the bar, which was now full of people mixing and mingling. My stomach churned, and I wondered if the drink was a good idea after all. I wobbled on my legs and reached out for the stool as I watched the next Karaoke victim take the stage. Taking a seat, I wondered how on earth I was going to get through my song without completely hurling on the front row.

"Did you order a Sex on the Beach?" a deep voice asked behind me.

I turned on my bar stool, and my breath caught in my throat. He wasn't the man who'd taken my order earlier. This guy was taller, broader, and much more brooding. His light brown eyes bore into mine as his massive man hand held my drink out in front of me.

I sat in stunned silence, staring at the real-life man who'd been the object of my fantasies as I'd brought myself to orgasm earlier today. Standing in front of me, holding my drink, was Poseidon.

No matter how dark the night, morning always comes, and our journey begins anew.

-Lula, Final Factory X

CHAPTER 4

BERK

BEER BOTTLES CLANKED TOGETHER inside their cardboard case, the sound echoing in the small storage room of the bar as I hefted them onto the top shelf. I wasn't sure why I'd agreed to switch shifts with my brother Rhen. I hated working at the bar, especially on Karaoke night.

"Shit!" Okie yelled as he barreled through the swinging door into the small storage area, a bar towel wrapped around his thumb.

"What the hell happened?" I asked my cousin, Okalani. He was forever hurting himself at our family's resort.

"I fuckin' sliced the shit out of my thumb, trying to crack open a bottle of vodka."

"Most people cut off their thumb slicing up limes or oranges, but not you, Okie. You manage to do it on a bottle of vodka. How is that even possible anyway?"

Okie pulled the blood-soaked towel off his thumb and held it under the running water.

Peering over his shoulder, I saw it was still bleeding, but the cut wasn't deep. With a few bandages, he'd be back to new in a few minutes, slinging bullshit at the bar as usual.

"Do me a favor, man?" he asked as he scrubbed the wound.

"There's an almost finished Sex on the Beach sitting under the counter. Just add in the vodka and hand it to the hottie sitting at the end of the bar."

"No fuckin' way, man. I'm not going out there, not on Karaoke night."

"Fuck off, man, and get over it. It was one night, and the chicks were totally wasted."

"I don't give a shit. They pulled me onto the stage and practically tore my fucking clothes off, man. I don't even like being back here in the store room, let alone behind the counter."

"She's super-hot." Okie wiggled his eyebrows.

I rolled my eyes. "You say that about all the guests."

Okie was a known horndog and hooked up with at least four or five chicks a month, completely breaking the cardinal rule of our family's resort—no fraternizing with the guests.

He was a decent looking guy, but I was still surprised at the number of women he could catch with his line of bullshit. He told me he was *helping* the guests live out their vacation fantasies by letting them screw an island native. For Okie, it meant fucking them relentlessly during their vacation, then tossing their shit on a luggage cart the day of check-out without so much as a "thanks for the screw."

"I'm serious about this one, dude," Okie continued. "I'm gonna try to work my way into her lace thong as soon as I get this mother-fucker to stop bleeding."

I cringed as he held up his thumb that was still oozing blood like a crimson river. "Fine, whatever," I sighed, knowing I'd never hear the end of it. Plus, Okie was all alone tending the bar tonight, and I felt sorry for the dipshit. Our regular bartender had called in sick at the last minute.

"You won't regret it, dude. She's fucking hot," he called over his shoulder.

I pushed on the swinging door that led to the main bar of the resort.

"But her pussy's all mine, man, so don't get any ideas in that fat head of yours!" he shouted.

I shook my head, trying to erase his words. I had no intention of getting anyone's "pussy" tonight. Especially not one that had already been claimed by my sex-addicted cousin, whether the poor girl knew it or not.

"I prefer my women sober, you idiot!" I yelled back. *My women?* Where the hell had that come from?

His deep chuckle clambered over the wailing of the current singer, who was belting out a Mariah Carey song like she was on one of those God-awful singing competition shows you find on television.

I searched the under-bar for the drink Okie had made. Sure enough, there it sat on the ice machine, only *half* full. I couldn't believe my motherfucking cousin was actually going to fill up the rest of the drink with vodka. Sex on the Beach was a staple drink for the guests who frequented the bar. I was no mixologist, but even *I* knew how potent half a tumbler of vodka could be on an unsus-pecting customer.

Grasping the bottle of vodka I assumed Okie had cut his thumb on, I wrapped a towel around the top and twisted it open with ease. It was official. My cousin was a complete dumbass. Pouring a two-count of vodka into the tumbler, I pulled the orange juice from the refrigerator and filled the rest of the drink with the fruity mix.

The decrease in alcohol would, at least, ensure the woman's safety from the sexual prowess of my cousin. Sinking a twizzle straw into the glass, I inspected the drink in my hand. It looked decent enough.

I sauntered down the bar to deliver the drink and spotted the guest Okie had titled as his next "pussy" conquest. I offered a silent prayer of thanks to the island Gods, that they'd allowed me to inter-vene on behalf of this poor, unsuspecting woman. An unwarranted need to protect her heated my skin.

Her hair was flaxen blonde and the silken strands hung in loose curls just above her shoulders. Her golden tresses swayed as her head moved with each beat of the song, keeping perfect time with the music blaring from the Karaoke machine. As I approached, I noticed a traditional hibiscus flower tucked behind her ear, revealing a single solitaire diamond stud that was almost as big as my thumb, and probably worth more than six months of my salary.

She's a guest here, you idiot. Of course, she's loaded.

Guests were off limits to employees, and to me, as a personal rule. But for some inexplicable reason, I couldn't shake the uneasy spark flickering through my bones that warned me this girl needed protection from the snare of my cousin's sordid sexual web.

"Did you order a Sex on the Beach?" I asked, trying to tame the emotion in my voice.

She slowly turned toward me.

My eyes drank in her form. I tried to steady the erratic beat of my heart. Why was I so fucking nervous, all of a sudden?

Because Okie was right, she's hot.

No, that wasn't it. Beautiful women floated in and out of the resort every week. This woman was different, eerily familiar. Suddenly, that same urgency to protect her surfaced inside me, a compulsion I hadn't felt since before I'd returned to my island home, almost three years ago.

I buried my caveman-like tendencies, knowing if I acted on them, they'd only destroy me like they had in the past.

I held the drink mid-air, staring at her, entranced by the vision in front of me. Her blonde hair swung gently in the breeze, caressing her sun-kissed shoulders and dusting her slim neck. Fuck, if I didn't want to lick up and down the slender column that led to her beautiful face.

My eyes widened in surprise when I finally recognized her. She was the chick from the beach, the woman I'd offered surfing lessons to. She'd gawked at me at the time, like I was a leper, and then bolted up from her lounger faster than I could wax my board. After she'd shoved her shit into her bag, she made a beeline back to the resort. Her dismissive words, "Maybe some other time," rang through my head and splashed my face, and my dick, with cold water.

The last thing I needed to think about was her face—which was illuminated like a celestial creature, aglow from the flickering light of the tiki torches littering the bar. Yeah, I needed to forget her.

Her eyes went wide with surprise, and her mouth fell lax as she focused on me, staring as if I was a display at the zoo, and she couldn't figure out whether to be fascinated or afraid.

I slammed the drink down on the bar to jar her. The loud bang of the tumbler meeting with the hard wood of the counter made her jump.

I stared, curious, as her eyes blinked rapidly and her head shook, taking her blonde hair with it. Drawing in a deep breath, taken aback by her natural beauty, my body was assaulted by the delicious aromas of the hibiscus flower nestled behind her petite ear. That mixed with the erotic fragrance of her musky perfume had my senses heating.

"Geneva," Ralph called from the stage in an irritated tone.

Her eyes went wide with panic. She snapped her gaze to the sound of his voice and slowly raised one hand. Apparently, *she* was Geneva, and next in line to sing.

"It's your turn, sweetheart," he announced.

Sweetheart? My fists clenched at Ralph's term of endearment.

Shouts erupted from the center of the room.

"Come on, bitch, get on the stage!" someone yelled.

Glancing across the bar, I spotted a small table crowded with people. The derogatory words were spewing from the mouth of a petite woman with long, curly black hair, standing up on the railings of her bar stool. She continued to encourage Geneva, pumping her fist wildly in the air. It was her friend from the beach I'd met earlier. The sassy one.

The woman sitting on the stool in front of me turned around, her eyes locking on mine as if begging me for help.

I stood there, motionless, unable to offer her any words of encouragement.

She grabbed her drink and yanked the straw out, throwing it haphazardly at me before bringing the glass up to her pouty lips.

Her actions reminded me that, in her eyes, I was a peon, only worthy of picking up her trash. The realization pissed the shit out of me.

"There's a trash can at the end of the bar," I huffed, holding the straw up to her face before depositing it in the receptacle behind me.

"Oh, I'm so sorry," she offered with genuine remorse. "I have the worst aim."

Her soft, velvety voice had my dick swelling. *What the fuck?*

Before I could say another word, she sucked down the entire drink in three gulps, then slammed the glass back down on the bar with a thud. She grabbed a few napkins and dabbed her lips.

"I'm just really nervous," she explained, fear racing in her tone.

"Geneva!" Ralph shouted again. "Get your sweet little ass up here, girl."

My arms tensed at Ralph's innocent, yet derogatory, comment.

"Come on, everybody, let's give Geneva a hand as she sucks down her liquid courage!" Ralph shouted.

The growing crowd turned toward Geneva and began to shout and offer words of encouragement.

She panned the bar, her eyes wide with fear. Ralph's attempt to encourage her was backfiring.

I could see she was scared shitless, and I wondered why in the world she was going to put herself through this humiliating shit.

"You'll do fine," I offered, having no idea why I felt the need to comfort her.

She shrugged.

Her table of friends erupted in more screams, chanting her name. She turned to face them.

"Ge-ne-va! Ge-ne-va!" they shouted. Their actions seemed to

strengthen her, fortifying her with more courage than the drink I'd just delivered.

Turning back to gaze at me over her bare shoulder, her red lips curved into a smile that displayed the same trepidation mine always did.

"Here goes nothing." She laughed nervously.

Her face was flawless, a classic beauty, her skin soft and supple, kissed by the Hawaiian sun from earlier today. Her lips parted, revealing perfectly straight, gleaming white teeth—the kind you see on a dental hygiene commercial. Her cheeks were stained with a hint of pink as she blushed, her nervousness apparent. Part of me felt a little sorry for the woman as she slid off the bar stool and cautiously walked toward the stage.

Cutting through the massive crowd like a knife through softened butter, her tall form cast an air of supremacy. There was no doubt this chick came from money. Even her walk was regal. There was something in her gait that struck me as odd, though. Even in her state of majestic elegance, she seemed vulnerable, as if she were unworthy of the attention which she garnered so easily from others.

Ralph extended his hand and hoisted her up onto the small stage as she fidgeted with the material of her red, strapless dress. The fabric, littered with the same type of hibiscus flowers that adorned her hair, hung loose on her body and pooled at her feet, revealing nothing of the amazing body I'd seen earlier on the beach. She was visibly shaking, and it was more than obvious to everyone in the bar that this chick was a nervous, fucking wreck.

The music began to play, and part of me cringed inside as I recognized "A Moment Like This" by Kelly Clarkson. Really? I'd heard many a woman, and a few dudes, go down in flames, trying to mimic the American Idol's classic song. My heart sank for Geneva, knowing full well she was probably going to tank tonight and become yet another casualty of the Karaoke gods.

Geneva hesitantly began singing the opening lyrics, but I could hear the promise in her voice, which surprised me. At least she wasn't going to *totally* suck donkey balls. My body sank in relief as I pushed out the heavy breath I didn't even know I'd been holding.

With each verse she sang, Geneva's voice became more confident, until finally, when she hit the chorus, her body opened up, and she became part of the song. Her voice was like heaven, a sweet mix of satin and velvet, raspy but controlled. This girl could fucking sing. Maybe even *better* than Kelly Clarkson.

"Holy shit," Okie whispered behind me. "This chick's got skills. Finally, someone who doesn't sound like a groupie at a Marilyn Manson concert. Or look like one," he snorted, elbowing me in the ribs.

"Shhh," I reprimanded, wanting to enjoy every nuance and note of Geneva's performance.

"Chill, Kahuna."

I ignored his pestering, totally captivated by Geneva's siren refrain.

The song was building and the big finish looming. My stomach seized with apprehension, praying, for Geneva's sake, that her voice wouldn't crack at the most inopportune time and cause the audience to castigate her with boos and sneers. As her deep tone reached higher, her voice grew stronger, with more vibrato. She belted out the last of the song, stronger than any professional singer I'd ever heard, hitting the last note with ease. She held on to it like a seasoned star as the music faded into nothing.

The bar fell silent. The only noise audible was the hissing of the stereo speakers behind her. Everyone was in awe of her, including me. It was a moving performance. The silence of the crowd after she'd finished was evidence that Geneva had bewitched us all. We'd been unexpectedly enraptured, mesmerized by this beautiful enchantress whose voice had taken us on a magical journey none of us wanted to end.

"Fuck yeah!" Okie shouted behind me.

Geneva's eyes snapped to mine, her expression revealing that she thought the words had come from me.

Before I could respond, the entire bar erupted in cheers of adoration for this would-be star. Her bronze skin flushed red with embarrassment, and for some reason, her reaction surprised me.

She quickly skidded off the stage and into the arms of her adoring fans. As she made her way back to her table of friends, patrons congratulated her, shaking her hand and kissing her politely on the cheek, palms groping her bare shoulders.

My unexplained protectiveness over her had my heart racing. I didn't like people mauling her. I saw the fear in her eyes. Neither did she.

When she finally reached her friends, they took her in, hugging her like only close allies do. One man parted the crowd and took her shoulders in a loving embrace, peering down at her in the most adoring way, before grazing her cheek with his puckered lips and taking her fully into his embrace.

A small stab of pain burned in my chest as I watched Geneva's long, slender arms wrap around the man's waist and her face nuzzle comfortably into his massive chest as if it were home.

"Oh, well, guess that one's a no-go," Okie sighed next to me as he adjusted his bandage.

"What do you mean?"

He pointed toward Geneva's table, towel still in hand. "She's obviously taken."

"Maybe he's just a friend," I suggested, knowing it probably wasn't true. The dude was looking at her way too lovingly. He was either gay as a lark or totally in love with her.

"Look at her flower, man."

Instantly, the pain in the middle of my shorts lessened as I saw what Okie was talking about. Her flower was on the left side of her face, a traditional island indicator that she was taken. I suppressed my disappointment, not even sure when it was I'd actually gotten excited about the prospects of this girl. She'd been off limits from the get-go.

Before I could turn away, she peered over her boyfriend's shoulder, her blue eyes latching on to mine. We were paralyzed, caught in a trance of sorts that I didn't recognize. Well, I recognized it, but I hadn't felt this way in a long time.

The electricity shooting through my body scared the shit out of me. As much as I wanted to pull away from her gaze, I couldn't. She was ethereal and elegant, and I realized I'd been wrong in my first assessment of her. She wasn't a judgmental, snotty rich girl like I thought.

Her full red lips spread wide as she mouthed the words, "Thank you."

My gaze cut behind me like an idiot, making sure it was really me she was giving her words of gratitude to. I wasn't surprised to find Okie had completely disappeared. My gaze returned to hers, lost in her hypnotic stare as I returned her smile.

"You're welcome," I mouthed back, meaning every word.

CHAPTER 5

BERK

THE OCEAN BREEZE fanned through the bushes lining my back porch as I sipped on another cup of local coffee. I could never go to sleep after a late shift at the resort without having a cup of coffee from my native island. People always found it strange that I could sleep after drinking caffeine at night, but, for me, it had been a ritual for years, an experience that held precious memories. It wasn't like I slept that well, anyway.

As I gazed out over the rolling waves before me, the echoes of each one crashing into the surf lulled me into a trance. The storm clouds from earlier had dissipated, revealing clusters of flashing stars in the midnight sky. Their heavenly glow was like a blanket over my world, tucking me in safely as I tried to process the events of the evening that had left me feeling so restless.

Shortly after the talented songstress and her friends disappeared from the bar, my cousin Leilani discovered the woman's name was Geneva Barton. Unfortunately, Leilani, who was the assistant manager of our family's resort—and Okie's sister—had been unable to retrieve any more information.

Just as well. I mentally beat myself up for wanting to know more about her. I was never like this with a resort guest, or anyone, for that matter. It had been my policy since my return—no fraternizing with the guests. Especially *this* guest.

I rose from the chair on my back porch. My tiny shack of a home was secluded, far enough away from the main resort to give me privacy, but not so far that I couldn't get there by foot in a matter of minutes.

The house had been my great-grandparents' original home when they bought the property shortly after World War II, almost seventy years ago.

I loved living in the tropical jungle of Kauai, thankful that my great-grandparents had stopped the "white man's desolation of the earth," as they had called it. Actually, my great-grandfather had served in the Army Corp of Engineers during World War II and was given a special deal as a veteran to buy this parcel of lush, tropical land—or "honua," as islanders referred to Mother Earth.

My grandmother, who had inherited the land when my great-grandfather died many years ago, built the resort that now took up almost three quarters of the original thirty acres. She named the resort Honua Keena Kapu, translated loosely as Earth's Sanctuary.

The resort was located on the west coast of Kauai, a fully sustainable, eco-friendly paradise, as the brochure called it. Local islanders were against the build at first, but once they realized it would incorporate the best of the island's resources and employ nearly half of the citizens, they came around.

The island property of my grandparents served its purpose well for me, becoming my escape from the mainland, almost three years ago. My family still worried about my mental health, no matter how much I assured them my heart was healing. Some days my guilt was overwhelming, crushing me, choking me with an over-powering shadow that threatened to consume me.

My family knew that my losses were great. Hell, I'd even walked away from a successful career as a professional snowboarder to escape my misery back home in Colorado. It seemed like a viable solution at the time, but I was just fooling myself, believing

I could run far enough away to escape the demons that haunted me. Not even the beauty of the Hawaiian island I grew up on could quiet them. Especially at night, when I was home alone.

Most people were blown away that a native Hawaiian surfer would turn his sights toward snowboarding. But we hadn't had much say in the matter when my mother whisked our entire family away to the mainland to finish up her doctorate of chemistry at the University of Colorado when I was only twelve.

At first, I hated the cold, loathed it, and begged my mother to let me go back and live with my grandparents in Hawaii. She dismissed me but allowed my brother and sister and me to return to Kauai on school holidays and summer breaks. Before long, I grew tired of the travel and settled into life as a Coloradan, opting to embrace my new surroundings and try winter sports instead.

My first experience on skis was disastrous. As I lay shivering in the snow, my only wish was to be back on my surfboard, riding the great waves of Hawaii. Then, a friend from school introduced me to snowboarding. The board felt like home, and I fell in love with the sport.

My background and technique in surfing had almost been my undoing, though. The two sports were *completely* different in footing and style. Eventually, I caught on and garnered the attention of colleges out scouting the Rocky Mountain trails.

Instead of college, though, much to my mother's disapproval, I'd opted to go pro straight from high school. Up until almost three years ago, my life had been a dream. Fate had dealt me a shitty hand, though, and forced me to leave the sport I loved and return to my native roots to lick my wounds in the confines and safety of the island jungle. I hid my shame behind the mask of the lush greenery, thankful that my family had welcomed me home in spite of my sins.

Leaning over the railing of my small house, I closed my eyes and breathed in the salt air. I let the sea breeze fill my lungs and rid my mind of the dark memories from my past. I loved Hawaii and hadn't realized how much I'd missed it until I'd returned.

My eyes rolled open, and movement close to the water's edge broke my thoughts as a vision caught my gaze. Someone was walking along the beach. I glanced down at my watch, noting the late hour, surprised anyone would be out wandering along the shore at one o'clock in the morning.

I squinted my eyes, trying to make out the form, not sure if it was a man or a woman. The resort property was safe, but if it were a woman, I'd be surprised that she'd feel comfortable being alone at this hour. Most of the guests were from the contiguous forty-eight states, where crime was much higher than on this sparsely populated side of Kauai.

As my vision focused, I could tell this form was a woman, definitely a woman. She was wearing a long dress, and my eyes went wide with surprise as she grabbed a wad of material mid-thigh and dragged it up her long, lean body, exposing her tan, buffed legs.

Before I could process another thought, her dress was completely off her body. She was definitely *not* wearing a bra. Shit! Well, at least she was wearing underwear, skimpy as they were.

As her red dress wafted in the air and fell on the sand a few feet away, she turned her head to gaze up and down the shore.

My breath caught in my throat, and a pain ricocheted through my chest when I recognized the sultry woman standing just yards away from me.

Geneva. Oh, fuck!

I rubbed my fingers through my hair, willing her to stay on the shore.

Her thumbs hooked into her underwear.

My breath quickened at what was about to happen. I turned my back, not wanting to feel like the pervert voyeur I was becoming, but my body went into a full-scale panic attack as I finally realized she was actually going to go into the water for a fucking midnight dip in the Pacific Ocean. All alone. What a fool. This was *not* going to end well.

As I spun on my heel, my long hair battered my face. I pushed it back in one whisk, focusing on the scene before me. Thankfully, her body was now submerged in the deep, blue water and hidden from my ogling eyes, but I had no desire to perform a search and rescue mission tonight.

Please don't let her venture out further.

My hands broke out in a sweat as my chest burned with fire. My head pounded with every beat of my heart. A familiar numbness pricked my fingertips when I saw her body dive into the crashing waves. Oh, fuck.

Before I could even think, I tore off my shirt and shot over the railing of my back porch, my bare feet landing in the soft sand with a thud as I launched toward the open water.

Bile rose to my mouth when I didn't see her surface. One…two…three…I counted. Still nothing. Shit! The full moon cast an eerie glow on the water and reminded me of the high tide pull it had on the turbulent seas. The waves would be higher and the undertow stronger. Worse yet, a rip tide could take her out, making it virtually impossible for anyone to find her. Four…five…six…I continued to count, but still no Geneva. Fuck!

My feet hit the water with a splash as my legs cleared each wave, and I catapulted through the surf. I followed a path in a left-ward direction from her dress, knowing the current would have taken her that way. When I reached the distance at which I'd last seen her, I dove under the water, my body pummeled by a huge wave. The force that hit my stout body was no surprise to me. I surfed these waters nearly every day. She didn't. These waves would likely take her under and keep her there.

I sunk my legs into the sand, steadying my body as my hands reached out in front of me, blindly searching for something, anything.

I was an avid swimmer and could handle the undercurrent, so I stayed beneath the water in search of her. I reached beyond me as far as I could, my palms dusting along the sandy bottom of the ocean floor as I felt for her.

A band of steel wrapped around my chest as adrenaline flooded my veins. The familiar burning erupted from my center, spreading like an inferno, burning me from the inside out.

Haunting images from my past flashed through my mind as I searched for Geneva, knowing she was just beyond my reach. I was losing her. This could not be happening again. I wouldn't let it.

My lungs burned from the lack of oxygen and the intake of salt water, and I was forced to the surface, shaking my head to rid my face of my long hair.

I drew in a deep breath, readying myself for another dive when, suddenly, I heard a blood-curdling scream ring out in the night air. I wasn't sure if I was thankful or scared shitless. As my eyes focused, I realized Geneva was treading water a few feet away from me.

"What the fuck!" she screamed, splashing me with water.

"I'm not going to hurt you. Stop screaming."

"Get the fuck away from me!"

I watched with amusement as she tried to swim backward. She'd never make it with such a silly stroke.

I lunged for her as a huge wave crashed down, tugging us both below the surface. Wrapping my arm tightly around her body, I tried to keep ahold of her so I wouldn't lose her, but her constant kicking and scratching was making it more difficult. Even buried eight feet under the ocean, I could still hear her muffled cries for help through the water.

Finally, the wave passed, and I kicked us to the surface, my hands useless as they still clung to her, acutely aware that her naked body was now pressed to mine. The sensation of her skin rubbing against mine did something deep inside, things I wasn't comfortable with. My mind told me to release her, but I couldn't. I had to take her to shore and make sure she was safe.

"Let me go!" she screamed as our bodies breached the surface. Her voice was lower now as she coughed and sputtered, trying to expel the large amounts of water she'd ingested, thanks to her refusal to hold her mouth shut under water. Her dagger-like fingernails dug into my skin as her legs kicked at me, but I refused to let her go. I knew what these waters could do to an inexperienced swimmer.

"I'm not going to hurt you," I spoke. "You shouldn't be out in the surf at night by yourself. The current is stronger, especially with a full moon." I nodded toward the sky.

Slowly, her body calmed its assault on me as her eyes rolled up to the sky.

I released my hold but grabbed her hand to secure her like a dingy to a steamboat.

She yanked on her hand, trying to break my hold.

I gripped tighter and pulled her toward me, thankful the water was covering her body. I was able to touch the bottom of the ocean floor because I was six feet three, but I wasn't so sure she could.

The moon above cast a glow on her face that literally took my breath away. I'd heard people say goofy shit like that in movies and heard it had been written in books, but until this very moment, I thought they were lying, a dramatic combination of words concocted to sell tickets and books. Now I could see the words were real, not just made-up shit for some sappy-ass romance novels.

Her gaze drifted to mine, her brows furrowing as if she were studying a strange picture.

"Poseidon?" she questioned, all trace of fight gone.

"What?"

She shook her head as if in a daze before staring at me again. Her eyes penetrated through me as if she were seeing straight into my soul, discovering all my deepest, darkest secrets.

She made me nervous, scared me shitless. I didn't want *anyone* seeing into my soul. As much as I wanted to stare at her lovely face, I broke our gaze, tugging on her hand as I made my way toward the shore.

"Wait!" she shrieked, pulling on my hand.

I peered over my shoulder, and it finally hit me. The water was shallower now, and she was naked. I dropped her hand, but feared she might turn and swim back into the sea. "Wait right here," I ordered, then nodded past her shoulder to the ocean. "Do *not* go back out there."

Her eyes grew wide, as if she wasn't used to such reprimands, but she nodded her head once, acknowledging she would obey my instructions.

I ran through the surf to retrieve her clothes, knowing she might decide to wander back into the unforgiving sea. She seemed like a defiant woman, and strangely enough, I liked that about her.

Scooping up her dress from the sand, I turned back toward the surf, half surprised to find her where I'd left her. For the second time in less than a minute, my breath caught in my throat at the sight of her. The rise in my shorts had me pissed off. What was I, some horny teenager in lust with the head cheerleader?

My legs cleared the waves with ease as I jogged back toward her, until I was standing in chest high water directly in front of her. My eyes surveyed this beautiful woman, who, thankfully, was now calmed from her earlier distress. Her hair was slicked back from her face, revealing light blue eyes that shone bright from the dazzling light cast down from the moon above. Her flawless skin glistened with shimmering beads of water.

My dick pressed hard against the inseam of my shorts, and I cursed myself for being such a man.

I looked down at her dress that was dripping with water. "Sorry, it got wet."

She took the garment out of my hands. "Would you turn around, please?" she asked quietly.

Not understanding her request, my brows furrowed.

"I need to put my dress on. Even though now it's completely ruined."

In spite of the crashing of the waves around us, I heard the biting tone in her words. It was a dig meant for me. Suddenly, a fire of irritation raged within me. My menacing eyes roamed over her bare shoulders, traveling slowly up to her face before finally coming to rest on the solitaire diamonds still adorning her petite earlobes.

Spoiled brat. She's nothing more than a spoiled little rich girl, used to getting her own way. Typical tourist.

My need to protect her faded like invisible ink on paper, and I turned away, stalking back toward the beach. Normally, I would have stood at the water's edge and watched the unique ebb and flow of the tide. It was my favorite place to exist. But not tonight. Tonight I was pissed. I'd put myself in harm's way to rescue this ungrateful woman. When would I learn?

Without a glance behind me, I dragged my feet through the sand and marched toward my cottage that was nestled within the lush, tropical forest. From the shore, my home was barely noticeable. Only someone who knew of its existence would ever find it.

"I'm sorry." Her voice rang out behind me.

I was in no mood for apologies. The shutters inside me had already descended like an eclipse of the full moon overhead. I glanced behind me to make sure she was safe. I mean, I wasn't a total dick.

The sight I beheld didn't surprise me.

Although her gorgeous body was now fully dressed, she was just as beautiful as ever, and I cursed my cock for noticing.

Her dress was dripping wet and clung to her like cellophane, her body shaking from the cool evening breeze as her hands ran up and down her arms for warmth. I could almost hear her teeth chattering. Shit! Why did I have to care?

I drew in a deep breath, slowly releasing it before I decided to help her one more time. "Do you want to dry off? I have some towels up at my house."

Her doubting eyes squinted as she tried to focus beyond me, causing a small wrinkle between her brows as she searched for my house through the jungle.

Her expression was endearing to me, and I felt my disdain for her slipping.

"There's a house back there?" she asked quietly.

I nodded in silent response.

"Wow." She approached me, marvel etched across her face.

As she drew nearer, I saw her lips were a deeper red, almost purple. Her jaw was clenched to try to stop the chattering of her teeth.

I didn't think the summer air was *that* cool, but apparently it was affecting her. My eyes roamed over her body, her skin pebbled with chill bumps, glistening with water in the moon's bright beams. There was no denying, she was a gorgeous creature.

"Come on." I nodded. I walked the short path lined with tropical plants and flowers that led to my back porch.

"Wow," she repeated.

I looked behind me and noticed she was standing still, her eyes canvasing my small cottage. I stood silently, waiting for her criticism, but it never came.

"This is amazing," she said to no one in particular, her breath wafting from her lungs like the cool night air.

"Really?"

"Oh, yeah." She nodded, her entire body loosening, as if she felt more at ease. "It's incredible, so secluded, yet so accessible." Her words were foreign to me, disjointed from the pretentious woman I'd seen earlier in the water.

"Come on up." I extended my hand to help her up the steps. Her tall frame was shivering again, and I felt like an ass for even thinking of leaving her behind earlier. I didn't want to care, but I did.

"Are you cold?" I asked.

"A little," she answered through chattering teeth.

"Do you want to take a hot shower to warm up before you go?"

No, no, no, don't invite her in, you moron.

One delicious brow rose in question as a small smirk donned her pouty lips.

Fuck! Instantly my dick went rock hard. She wanted me, and my body was responding.

"Or," I said, "I could give you a lift back to the resort so you don't have to walk?" *Yeah, take her back. Get her the fuck off your property, like now!*

Before I could garner another response, her entire body morphed into a predator, the trembling woman from before gone. Her arms fell loose by her sides, and her blue eyes grew darker. Her lips fell from the smirk into a seductive smile.

Now *my* body was shaking, and not from the cold, but from the blood pulsating through my body.

"Is that an invitation?" she asked, her voice smooth and sultry.

I gulped, nearly choking on my swollen tongue.

Her lithe body moved slowly toward me.

I stepped back, stumbling over one of the patio chairs.

She smiled at my mishap. She knew *exactly* the effect she was having on me. Somewhere between the beach and my porch, this woman had changed.

"Uhh…" What could I say? I hadn't been this aroused by a woman in—

Don't say it. Don't you dare give another fucking countdown of how long you've been alone.

It was true, though. It had been a long time since desire like this burned inside me. The feeling scared the shit out of me. Thinking about her gorgeous body, naked in my shower, my frame pressed against hers, did something to me. I mean, shit, I was still a man, wasn't I?

Before I could process any more reasons why I *shouldn't* do this, I snaked my arm around her waist and drew her against me. Whipping us around, I pinned her up against the wall. My lips found hers, crashing down like the waves behind us, the current of our lust rippling through me.

The moans at the back of her throat were my undoing.

My hand gripped the thick hair at the back of her neck as my hips ground into hers of their own free will.

Her hands roamed all over my body as if she were blind and I were an open book written in Braille.

To open myself up to a woman again was gut wrenching, heart stopping, and nearly prevented me from continuing the kiss. I didn't want to think, though, not tonight. I just wanted to feel something besides shame and guilt.

My lungs burned from the lack of oxygen, and I pulled away to catch my breath. Peering down at her, I tried to gauge her reaction.

Her face was aglow with desire and need as a smile spread across her face.

I couldn't help myself. I barreled down on her lips again like a starved man devouring his first meal in years. The vibrations of her mouth on mine as she moaned had my one-eyed trouser snake up from hibernation. I wanted her.

"Shower?" she murmured against my lips.

Shower? I broke our embrace. "Oh, yeah, a shower." I laughed. I slid my hand into hers, pulling her inside my tiny cottage. Her skin was silky smooth, not rough like mine, and I knew she didn't do much manual labor like I did. She was a snotty, rich mainlander, but I didn't give a shit right now.

Peeking over my shoulder to judge her reaction to my meager dwellings, I saw her eyes roaming over the room. The awe and delight on her face surprised me.

Her gaze fell on me, her expression returning to a deep desire I hadn't seen in a long time, if ever. She wanted me.

My throbbing cock was now swelling to painful limits. I had to get my shorts off.

I led her down the hall and into the bathroom that barely fit both of us. I opened the stall door and turned on the water. As we waited for it to warm, I stared down at her, giving her one last chance to say no. Our mouths were so close, I could feel her breath on my lips. She needed to meet me halfway, though. It was her choice now, her time to accept my invitation.

Without hesitation, her hands slid up over my arms. Her touch sent shivers across my skin as they skimmed over my biceps and along my shoulders. She worked her way up my neck until her fingers slowly slid into my hair, massaging my scalp. Her fists closed tightly, gripping a handful of my hair as she pulled my face into hers, her mouth devouring me.

I'd never experienced a woman so brazen, taking what she wanted with no reservations. It turned me on more than it should. Her kiss was both pleasurable and painful. I was going to shoot a load right here in my shorts if I didn't get inside her soon.

My hands skimmed her upper back, my fingers tugging at the top of her dress that clung, wet and cold, to her body. She pulled away from me. Instantly, I felt lost and alone, but her expression promised me there would be more.

My breath hitched as she grabbed a wad of material at her thighs, just like she had at the beach, and lifted her dress up over her hips.

The unruly pounding in my chest—and my dick—overtook all reason, and I tugged the dress the remainder of the way off her body and cast it aside in a wet lump next to the door. Leaning back, my eyes raked over her delicious body. She was stunning, a sex goddess, standing in such an enticing pose, one knee bent slightly over the other, creating an even more alluring hour glass figure.

"Your turn." She smiled, her eyes roaming up and down my body like a predator about to devour his prey. Her hands reached for the button on my board shorts, and her fingers worked slowly, but deliberately, as she lowered the zipper, her tongue licking her plump lips.

Fuck!

My cock throbbed in pain and fell free, my erection jutting out like a long pier into the ocean.

Her eyes sparked in surprise as she stared at my dick.

For a paralyzing moment, I wondered if she was disappointed.

No matter what a guy said in public, the size of his dick was a concern every man had.

I watched as she knelt in front of me, appearing to utter up praise and prayer. Then her long lashes lifted and her gaze met mine. The expression she wore told me everything I needed to know. I was more than enough for her.

My hands reached for the counter as I felt her hot breath graze across my midsection. I steadied myself, and my eyes came back into focus as her tongue wound its way around the head of my dick. My hips took on a life of their own as they thrust toward her like a hungry animal begging for more.

Instead of being offended that I was, basically, trying to mouth fuck her, her hands wound around to my ass, drawing me even further into her mouth, taking me completely in with one sweet, slow motion.

Holy motherfucker! I wouldn't last long at this rate. *Think of something else.* I drew in a deep breath through my nose, combing through my memory bank, searching for anything that would keep me from blowing a wad within the next thirty seconds.

What about that guest who was here a few weeks ago? She had burly man legs, a unibrow, and a mustache thicker than Tom Selleck. Okay, that seemed to be doing it—at least my orgasm wasn't completely on the verge of blowing up in her face.

As if sensing my pain, she pulled her lips from my dick. The cool air that blew over the moisture left by her mouth had me back at a manageable hard-on.

"Shower?" She nodded toward the stall that was now completely engulfed in steam.

If we stepped inside that shower, we'd have sex, and I wasn't entirely sure how to broach the whole subject of contraception. I'd had casual sex before, but it had been a while, and I wasn't sure how much things had changed over the years. Did I ask her about protection? Did she ask me? Was she a slut? Should I be concerned?

Without even trying, my chubby diminished in size, and I cursed myself.

"I'm not really sure how all this works now," I admitted sheepishly.

She tilted her head, her brows furrowing in that adorable way I was already growing to love.

"Well," she began, "we step into the shower, I wash you, you wash me, the order really isn't important."

I laughed at her answer. "No, I meant..." God, how did I ask? Just blurt it out. "Protection, I mean."

"Oh," she answered, seemingly surprised that I'd asked.

"I don't have any condoms, but I'm clean," I said. God, how stupid was that statement? Of course, a dick-headed guy would say he was clean just to get the chance to drive his woodpile into a hot chick like Geneva.

"I'm clean, too," she admitted. "And I'm on the pill."

My shoulders sagged in relief as blood began to flow freely back into my midsection.

"But, if you don't mind..." She leaned down and picked up her dress, still dripping with water, and reached into a pocket, producing three familiar packets. Condoms. Oh, shit, this girl was carrying protection on her.

This would only be a vacation fuck for her and something deep inside me ached.

"No," she pleaded as if understanding my silent thoughts. "It's not like that. I'm not a slut. Well, not anymore."

Not anymore? What the fuck did that mean?

"I don't go around carrying condoms with me everywhere." Her voice cracked with nervousness. "It's my friend, the one who's getting married tomorrow. She and her sister-in-law...Oh, and my stepsister, too."

God, she was so nervous. I found her irresistible. I leaned back against the counter, watching her squirm.

"They, uh, they shoved them in my pocket tonight. As a joke."

She held up a hand with the foil packets, shrugging her shoulders, her face wrinkled with concern.

She was worried about what I thought of her. In this moment, no matter what her past may have been, she was telling the truth. I'd never been more thankful for condoms in all my life.

Our eyes locked on each other, and I sensed she was searching, looking for an answer, asking me for understanding and permission. Did this girl really need my consent to have sex?

My hands snaked around her waist and tugged her tight against me as my lips gently rubbed against hers.

Her hands slid into my hair, tugging gently to bring my face closer to hers.

I pressed our naked bodies against the wall, my dick precariously close to her core. My lips began a sexual assault on her mouth, licking and sucking, asking silently for my own permission.

Without hesitation, her lips parted, and her tongue found mine. Our bodies intertwined in a way that felt so natural, it seized my heart with pain.

I hadn't felt this way in years. I fought memories that threatened to hold me back. I wanted this. I wanted Geneva in a way I hadn't wanted a woman in a long time.

"The shower," she murmured against my lips.

Never removing my mouth from hers, my eyes cut toward the stall, the steam now nonexistent.

She extricated herself from me, a smile covering her face as she glanced at the shower. "I think we're out of hot water."

I yanked open the stall door and depressed the knob, cutting off the water. Slamming the door with more force than I'd intended, I scooped Geneva up with ease. Her excited "yipe" let me know she was just as eager as I was.

"Condoms." She nodded toward the counter.

I watched expectantly as her long arm reached out and took all three into her grasp. Strolling down the short hall to my bedroom, I smiled down at her as I entered. No woman had ever been inside these four walls.

I gazed down at her face, her eyes focused on mine, lost in her own haze of sexual desire. I tossed her onto the bed with ease, mesmerized as her naked body bounced several times, her hair tousled and her perky breasts rippling like the waves in the ocean outside.

My eyes perused her physique, from the thick, golden hair on her head to the manicured patch between her legs. The thin strip of hair inches below her delectable bellybutton led down to the delicious V between her legs and formed an arrow of sorts that directed me to the Promised Land.

She moved her legs from side to side, forming sexy poses for me, her long arms stretching out, covering the width of the mattress, her desire for me thick like morning fog.

I lowered myself to the bed, my dick now jutting out at full attention and ever growing as I drank in her sensual form. God, this woman was beautiful, and looking into her bright blue eyes, I could see it came from the inside.

Despite what she'd been through in life—and something told me it was just as dark and sordid as mine—she'd come through a better person, unlike me. I pushed aside the thought. Self-admonition would come soon enough.

I crawled up her body like a ladder to a burning building, sensing that tonight we both needed to be saved from the raging inferno that blazed deep within us.

Her long, lean legs opened wide in invitation as her mouth spread into a devious smile. The tip of her tongue slid out, licking her lips. Lifting her hand, she produced a small packet in front of my face. The condom. She waited, holding it between us as if she were a bit nervous.

"Put it on," I growled. My words sounded foreign. I wasn't a forceful man in bed.

Her smile spread even wider as her teeth gripped the packet and ripped it open.

I nearly came from that one sexy maneuver. She obviously liked my dominant side.

Silent fascination paralyzed me as her nimble fingers pulled the condom out of its packet. She took my dick firmly in her hand, and I gasped as a volt of electricity surged through my body. It had been a long time since a woman had held any part of me intimately, and I didn't realize how much I'd longed for it.

How had we gotten here? How had this golden goddess gone from singing her siren call in our bar just a few hours ago to being spread eagle below me in my bed? A bed that had never seen a woman before.

I didn't know, and, at this exact moment, I didn't really give a shit. I wanted her. And if her lustful expression was any indicator, she wanted me just as much.

≈

*If you can't handle me at my worst, then you sure as hell don't
deserve me at my best.*
- Marilyn Monroe

≈

CHAPTER 6
GENEVA

His rough hands set my skin on fire and brought blood to the surface, reminding me that I was still alive despite what my past tried to tell me. I gazed into his eyes, asking for permission. It was so unlike me to wait for approval from a man.

His lopsided grin set my heart fluttering. He was so handsome, I had to catch my breath. His jet-black hair fell forward and framed his face like a portrait.

Without any further thought, I rolled on the condom and stared up at him in anticipation.

His slid between my legs, coating himself as his hungry gaze landed on me.

I was already wet and ready for him, but I could sense what he was doing. He was preparing me, not wanting to slam into me with a dry condom like a lot of guys did. His consideration for my pleasure made me grin.

"You have a beautiful smile," he whispered. His luscious lips curled up in a salacious smirk, small dimples framing the corners of his mouth.

Oh, swoon, dude. This guy was the epitome of a romance novel cover model. The hint of desire in his eyes left no doubt of what he wanted—me.

But wait. I didn't even know this guy's name. But did I really want to? This was a vacation. He was a vacation fuck, right?

If that were true, then why did it feel more intimate than that, too special for just a one-time screw? Lord knew, I'd had plenty of those in my time to know the difference.

He slid inside me, and my heart slammed into my chest as fire scorched across my skin. This may be a one-night thing for both of us, but something told me the memories of this night would stay with me for a lifetime.

His movement was slow and gentle, as if I was fine china and he wanted to protect me and savor my rarity all at the same time.

My legs spread further to accommodate his wide hips.

His moans of approval rippled across my neck as he drove in deeper, his face nestling into the crevice of my shoulder.

I arched my head back, giving him access, closing my eyes as I savored the feel of his tongue lapping across my skin, moving up to my ear. God, I loved it when guys sucked on my ear. I tilted my head, begging for more, hoping my own sounds of pleasure would spur him on.

My need for this man was frightening me. I wanted him, hard and fast, but he wasn't going to fulfill all my needs, not tonight.

Not tonight?

Would there be others if this was just a vacation fuck?

His lips roamed over my body as if he were visiting something sacred and wanted to take in every nuance. The slow, but deep, thrusts of his hips and the angle of his body above mine were igniting a spark in my core that was growing into a full-fledged fire.

He rose above me, one forearm stabilizing his power position, the other snaking up under my hips, raising my ass higher.

Oh, shit! While still technically on top of me, this new angle changed *everything*.

His dick was hitting me square on the spot that made me moan out loud. My arms spread wide as I searched for something, *anything*, to steady myself even though I was pinned under this massive God of the Underwater.

My eyes roamed over his naked body before finally coming to rest at the sight where our bodies were joined. His dick was so far up inside me, I was pretty sure he could count the eggs in my ovaries. He was filling me in a way that was much more than physical, and it felt amazing. The swirling, erotic sensation started at the point where we were connected and spun all the way down to my toes.

Slowly, he lowered himself fully onto my body, his chest rubbing against my hardened nipples. Every nerve ending in my body was raw with desire. My core burned and ached for more pressure.

"Harder," I pleaded.

His gaze held mine with a wanton expression that made me feel exposed but revered.

"Oh, no." He smiled wickedly as he moved slowly out of me, rubbing gently against my aching flesh.

I rocked my hips, trying to gain more friction.

"You feel too good to go fast. I want to savor you, Geneva."

Oh, fuck. He knew my name, and it sounded like warm, hot fudge drizzling over frozen ice cream as it rolled off his tongue.

The angle of this new position, the slow, yet erotic sliding of his erection hitting every erogenous spot between my legs, had me panting, *literally* panting, like a dog. It was actually kind of embarrassing. His returning smirk indicated that he quite enjoyed the reaction he was getting from me.

"Come for me, Geneva," he whispered next to my ear.

This was so textbook romance novel, but, oh my God, if it wasn't working.

His low, guttural command mixed with the growl of his deep voice was my undoing, and I willingly obeyed. I came. Hard. Harder than I had in a long time.

My body arched into him, and my legs seized in glorious delight as I spasmed around him. The delicious tingles started at my belly and shot through my entire being like molten lava spewing from a live volcano. A blinding light hit my eyes, and I clenched my eyes closed as my orgasm rolled on.

He continued to ride me, faster now, releasing my hips as he pumped harder and deeper.

It was all too much, the sensations, the passion, the emotions he was causing deep within me. I wanted to push him off. I was frightened by the deep feelings he evoked inside me.

My eyes burned with unshed tears. I couldn't believe the effect he was having on me. As much as my mind said kick him off, my body wouldn't let me. The sensations were overwhelming, but wildly intoxicating, and I wasn't willing or able to let him go. Not yet.

I wrapped my legs around his ass, my heels pushing him further inside me and snaked my arms around his shoulders, riding out another onslaught of pleasure while simultaneously trying to help him reach his own release.

Before I could take my next breath, the room spun. When I finally righted, I realized he'd whipped us both around in the small bed. I was now straddled atop him, his dick never leaving me. Instead, it was deeper in me, stretching me to capacity.

"Ride me," he whispered.

Oh, goddamn. He still wasn't done with me. Not by a long shot. I didn't know whether to be thankful or scared shitless.

"Now," he growled.

I decided to go with *thankful*, and tucked my legs underneath me, rocking into him. I rode his huge cock like a champion steer, pushing him further inside me, feeling every glorious inch as he filled my still spasming core.

"That's it, Geneva," he moaned.

I'd never heard my name spoken so beautifully in all my life. It was like a song being offered up by an angel in prayer.

His rough hands slid up my thighs, moving toward the spot

where we were joined. "Geneva?" he called softly, the effect doing strange things to my heart. His finger pressed against me.

Sharp tingles rolled up my spine. I couldn't find my voice. My body was still trembling from my previous orgasm, and now he was pushing me closer to another one. "Yes," I finally squeaked out.

"Come for me again."

Oh, shit. Multiple orgasms mere minutes apart? For some reason, his directive scared me.

His body lifted my hips high into the air, his arm wrapping around my waist to keep me in place atop his erection as I continued to rock against him.

Suddenly, he was sitting straight up in the bed, his tongue licking my nipples. And there it was again. With the change in angle, his rock-hard dick was perfectly lined up with that G spot every guy searched for his whole life but rarely found.

Part of me wondered how on earth he could sit straight up while still holding onto me, but in that moment, I couldn't give a shit less. This was the most amazing feeling I'd ever experienced. Ever. It was just like all my romance novels. I knew, without a doubt, I was going to come again. Just as hard and just as long.

His mouth took in my nipple, and sparks flew from every point of contact. I threw my head back in pleasure, my hands bracing behind me, fingers digging into his long, lean legs. Small sobs of sexual delight escaped my throat.

His teeth tugged on my nipple, then lapped and sucked it into his mouth.

Supercharged volts of electricity shot between my legs, pulsating out to every limb.

"Come, Geneva," he murmured against my skin.

With no warning for either of us, I came. Again. Harder this time, if that were possible, screaming out garbled words of something incoherent. My insides clenched around him, drawing him deeper inside me.

His dick swelled, filling me completely. His body tensed underneath me as we rode one another, grasping for body parts, enjoying the last bit of ecstasy as we floated back to earth.

Okay, this was *just* like the novels. Maybe they didn't make that shit up after all. They always said real-life was better than fiction, and this was definitely the case.

My body was on sensory overload, and I tried to squirm away, but he wouldn't let me. Instead, he flipped us over so he was lying on top of me again, his forehead covered in a thin sheen of sweat, the edge of his thick, raven hair lined with dampness from our exertions.

God, he was gorgeous.

I dragged my fingers through his hair, pushing the long strands back to reveal his glorious face. He truly did take my breath away. I knew that sounded cheesy, but hell, that was what his face did to me. Not just because he was gorgeous in a tropical sort of way, but because of his expression.

His lopsided smile had returned, and his eyes were bright with mischief, as if he had a surprise for me and he knew I would love it. Slowly, I pulled his face to mine, lifting my head the few inches necessary for our lips to connect. This time our kiss wasn't carnal, like before. It was gentle, and beautiful, if a kiss could be beautiful.

When he finally pulled away, he tilted his head slightly, his eyes aglow with adoration.

I rubbed my thumbs along the prominent bones of his cheeks, trying to commit everything about him to memory. Because this was a vacation fuck. Wasn't it?

"Stay right here." He placed a kiss on my nose before pulling out of me completely.

I yelped with exquisite pain, missing him already. How corny was that?

"I'm sorry." He frowned.

"I'm fine." I caressed the stubble on his face, trying to reassure him.

He leaned down and gave me a chaste kiss, then left the room.

Oh. My. God. What had I just done?

I'd had multiple orgasms, some of the best in my life, with a nameless dude, that was what I'd just done. I waited for the guilt to overwhelm me but nothing happened.

I'd changed my ways, turned my life around over the past three years, and abandoned these slutty ways. This seemed like something a slut would do—sleep with a random dude from the beach. But it didn't *feel* slutty. None of it did. This time was different.

The shower turned on in the bathroom. I stretched my hands high above my head, searching for relief from my already aching muscles. I wasn't used to this kind of exertion.

"Shower?" he called.

I turned to the sound of his voice.

He was standing completely nude in the doorway. His hands were above his head, holding onto the door frame, his hardening arousal prominently on display.

This was definitely a novel in the making. Gazing down at his thick erection, I was glad I had two more condoms.

CHAPTER 7

GENEVA

I PRIED my eyes open but immediately slammed them shut at the light streaming in through the window. Blinking until I adjusted to the brightness, I noticed the sheer curtains wafting in the breeze from the open window. I inhaled the fresh scents of fruit and wild flowers, which grew outside his house. *His* house. Oh, shit. I still didn't even know *his* name. What a slut bag.

Just like you used to be.

Sitting up slowly, I noticed the room was painted a light blue, the same color as the sky outside. The walls were devoid of any art or photos, giving the room a feeling of remoteness. One side table sat next to the small bed that barely contained both of us. No other furniture existed in this barren room.

Peeking under the thin sheet, I confirmed what I already knew. I was nude. Casting my gaze to the perfect form lying next to me, I noticed *he* was as well.

What was his name? Think, Geneva. There had to be *something* here, *anything* that would have his name on it.

What about a wallet?

I searched the table top next to me but found no identifying documents. The space felt like a hotel room, devoid of any sentiment or personal belongings. I was tempted to open the drawer just to see if a Gideon Bible lay inside but decided against it. I didn't want the dude to think I was a total psycho.

My eyes shot open wide when I finally focused on the one thing he *did* have on his table. An alarm clock. The time couldn't be right. Dana's bridal brunch was in twenty minutes, and I knew it would take me ten to make my way back to the resort.

I lifted the sheet, careful not to wake my Poseidon. We'd stayed up half the night, using up the remaining two condoms before resorting to our imagination to fill the rest of the night with our love making. *Love making?*

A huge smile spread across my face as I recalled all the orgasms we'd shared. He'd been kind and gentle with me, ensuring my needs were met first. Just thinking about his guttural moans of ecstasy from last night, as I had roamed his body with my hands and mouth, had me wet with desire. Last night had been my novel night.

I stood and stretched my arms above my head, admiring the gorgeous man still sound asleep. He really was beautiful. I'd been with a lot of men, gorgeous men, but Poseidon had something that put him in a league of his own.

His perfectly bronzed skin laid in stark contrast to the light blue sheet bunched around his midsection.

He was lying belly-side down, arms wrapped around his pillow as if it were his childhood teddy bear. His pouty, rose-colored lips were slightly parted, and I could see a hint of perfect white teeth. Jet-black hair, longer than my own, fanned over his face and pillow.

That wasn't something that usually attracted me, long rocker-style hair, but on Poseidon, it was perfect. I wanted to run my fingers through the silken mess, but I knew I didn't have time.

Instead, I tiptoed to the bathroom and relieved my bladder. I drew in a sigh of relief when I saw my red dress crumpled up on the floor next to the shower.

The shower. Holy hell, had that been hot. I'd had sex in showers before. After all, I was no saint. But Poseidon's was so small we had to mold into one person to fit both of our long bodies inside, leaving us little room for sex. Instead, he'd showered me with kisses as his fingers had worked magic. Oh, God, his fingers . . .

Suddenly remembering Dana's wedding, I pulled the semi-wet dress over my head and shivered from the dampness. Hawaii was a beautiful land, and its weather was gorgeous by anyone's standards, but I was used to the scorching Texas sun. The cool breeze wafting through Poseidon's house had me shivering all over again. I wished for the warmth of his body and fought the urge to slink back into his bed.

Checking myself in the mirror, I finger-combed my hair and rubbed away the leftover eye makeup from the night before. I nodded once in approval. This was as good as a morning-after makeover could get.

As I entered the tiny living room, I searched for anything to write him a note. I didn't want to wake my sleeping giant. Besides, what would I say? "Good-bye, guy whose name I don't know but sucked on every part of your body." No, I'd leave him a note with *my* info, and when he woke up *he* could decide whether or not to contact me again.

I'm sure I was just another resort fuck for him, anyway. The thought stung a little, but I wasn't going to get all pissy about it. The night had been everything I'd wanted and needed. I would leave it at that. Yeah, another night or two with my Sea God would be nice, but I was under no illusions that this was his first go around with a resort guest.

I noticed his cabana was smaller than my villa. Even in the early light of morning, I could tell his surroundings were sparse, as if he were only staying here for a night or two and didn't want to make this house his home.

About ready to give up finding paper, I finally spotted a stack of napkins on the counter. I located a pen that worked and sat down to write a note.

What should I say? Thanks for the best night of my life? No.

That was cheesy. Besides, had it been the best night of my life? I could definitely say it was in the top five, for sure, even though no other memories came to mind currently.

Scribbling furiously, I wrote down my name and villa number and thanked him for saving me in the ocean. That seemed appropriate—thanking the man for saving my life. Feeling satisfied with my note, I placed it on the stack of napkins with the pen on top and returned to the bedroom for one last look at this mythical creature. I had to make sure he was real.

I knelt beside him and catalogued every nuance of his face, committing each detail to memory, in case I never saw him again. The prospect hurt my heart but I was a big girl and lived in the real world. One-night stands were a fact of life.

My fingers combed through his thick, black hair and roamed down his cheek. I skimmed the morning stubble that littered his strong jaw. My skin had always been a golden tan, but with my fingers splayed across his skin, I appeared as pasty white as Hindley.

Hindley! Dana! Shit!

Poseidon moaned at my touch, stretching his lean body.

I held my breath, hoping he wouldn't awaken.

He rolled away from me, baring his beautiful ass for my perusal.

God, he was hot. I was going to kill Dana for having a fucking bridal luncheon today.

Oh, well. The ball was in his court now. I wouldn't be fazed if he blew me off. Maybe if I said it enough I'd start to believe it.

I leaned over and brushed my lips against his cheek. His whiskers teased me, making my core throb with want and desire again. I had to get out of here before I rolled him over and slid myself on top of him.

At the bedroom door, I glanced over my shoulder one last time to study the man who'd saved me. His breathing was soft. I watched as his massive chest rose and fell with each inhalation. The entire act felt so erotic and sensual. With my Poseidon, everything felt fueled by desire. I turned on my heel and raced for the front door.

I frantically hunted for my shoes on the small stoop outside. Then I remembered, we'd come through the back door. I didn't have any more time to spare so I scooped up the black flip-flops sitting on the porch, which were obviously mens, and three sizes too big for me. At this point, I'd be lucky to make it to the brunch on time as it was, let alone go back to my villa to shower and change.

I lifted my dress and ran for the beach. I looked first left, then right, as I tried to remember where the resort was. Apparently, a night of smoking hot monkey sex had wiped away my sense of direction.

Taking a chance, I dashed to the right, sand flinging up behind me as I dug my feet into the fine powder.

I was going to be late, and I knew there was no time to change my clothes. But, if I showed up in the same dress as last night with my just-fucked hair, everyone would know I'd been a skank last night. What could I tell them?

My thoughts went to my stepmother, Caroline. If she thought I was resorting to my old ways, she'd be devastated. And I would be heartbroken to disappoint her again.

"Geneva!" someone shouted out as I rounded the corner of the resort.

My eyes cut toward the sound, and I saw Dana waving her hand in the air like she was directing a jumbo jet in for landing. My gaze darted right and left, making sure no one else was around before I dashed straight for her.

"What the fuck?" Dana laughed, looking me up and down.

"Holy hell," Hindley called out, stepping from behind Dana.

"What?" I asked as if I were clueless.

"Obviously, you used all the condoms I gave you last night." Dana raised one perfectly groomed brow as she crossed her arms over her enormous breasts.

"No, I didn't," I squeaked out, as if appalled.

"Then show them to me." She held out her hand, palm side up.

Oh, shit. Dana was a player, or had been a player until she'd met Peter, who'd been raised a devout Mormon. His upbringing hadn't allowed him the type of frolicking that women like Dana and I engaged in. Peter knew all about Dana's sordid past going into their relationship, but it didn't bother him. He loved her anyway, knowing that, for Dana, sex had been a coping skill.

Unlike Dana, I'd used sex to gain attention from men, using them, manipulating them for my own gain. It pained me to remember a time in my life when I'd thought so little of myself that I used my body for my own gain.

"Oooo, someone got thoroughly fucked last night." Peter's baby sister, Victoria, giggled as she emerged from behind Hindley.

"What the hell?" I asked.

Peter's sister, Tori, and I had really bonded over the last month. She was a true spitfire in her own right. She'd just completed her bachelor's degree in California and was spending a lot of time in Austin to be near her niece and nephews.

I watched as her long, naturally platinum blond hair blew in the wind, her face scrunching up into that teasing expression I already knew so well.

"No, I didn't get fucked," I said.

"Holy shit!" Dana exclaimed, leaning in to sniff me like a cadaver dog. "You smell like sex and semen. There's no way you're going into my brunch like that, you skank."

Dana's words hit me hard. She was teasing, but I didn't want any of them to think I was using sex as a manipulation tool again.

"I'm just teasing, girl." Dana giggled, punching me in the arm. "I'm actually jealous. I'm an old, married woman now so I have to live vicariously through you."

"Me, too," Hindley added, sounding genuinely excited for me.

"Tell us *everything*." Tori clasped her hands and brought them to her chest as she bounced in eager anticipation.

"No way," I whispered.

"Either you tell us what the fuck happened and *who* it happened with, or I'm dragging your smelly ass into that restaurant and announcing what you did," Dana threatened.

"You wouldn't," I said, eyes narrowed.

"Nah, I wouldn't do that to ya. I'm just teasing. But we do want the details," Dana said.

I looked at the three of them, their eyes wide with eagerness as they nodded.

"Okay, look. Can I go back to my villa and shower really quick? Then I'll tell you guys everything after the brunch. If you promise not to tell anyone."

"Scout's honor," Hindley answered first, running her fingers across her lips like she was zipping them closed before holding up two fingers in allegiance.

"Go." Dana pushed on my arm. "People are already here. Go clean all that come off your snoodgie, then get back here and tell us what the hell you did to create that big-ass smile on your face. It's obviously going to be a permanent expression for the rest of our time here in Hawaii."

I touched my lips. There actually was a big, fat fucking grin on my face. Poseidon had put it there. Even though I tried to convince myself last night had been a one-time vacation fuck, I hoped like hell he'd put it there again. Tonight.

CHAPTER 8

GENEVA

FUCKER! That was the one word rolling around in my head the entire day. Fucker! I didn't know why I was surprised that the Fucker hadn't called me all day. Yes, I'd changed his name from Poseidon to Fucker.

Sitting at my table situated smack dab in the middle of Dana's wedding reception, I fumbled with the napkin in my lap as I thought back over last night's events. I was pissed that I was so irritated.

I'm sure he fucked a different chick every week as a cast of new, unsuspecting sluts fell victim to him upon their arrival to his tropical island paradise. The poor women would, no doubt, spread their legs wide, begging him to fulfill their island fantasies.

Kind of like you?

Yeah, like me. I mean, shit, look around. This whole resort gig was a player's dream—fuck the chicks senseless for a week, then send them packing and never hear from them again.

I thought I'd prepared myself to handle the fact that this was just a vacation fuck for him. Obviously, not so much.

Only minutes after Dana's bridal luncheon had ended earlier today, she, Hindley and Tori had cornered me, demanding all the details from last night. All three had been overwhelmed and excited to know Poseidon had been the man starring in my island fantasy.

Dana had even compared my night of red-hot sex to that of a chapter straight from my "porno novels," as she called them.

She was right, though. My night with Poseidon had been a page-turner come to life. And now, here I sat, a pathetic loser, pining over what could have been.

"Still no call?" Hindley dragged a chair over to sit next to me.

I shook my head, refusing to ruin the moment for the guests, who actually did have someone to love them tonight.

"It's cool." I shrugged, trying to appear unaffected. "It was one night. I knew that going in."

"Yeah, that's what Peter said." Dana pulled up a chair on the other side of me.

"What?" I shrieked. "You told Peter about my night with Poseidon?"

"Me?" She pointed to herself. "Hell no, skank, I got your back, always."

I clapped a hand over my thundering heart as Dana continued.

"Remember when Sam had that really bad seizure a few months ago, and you called me?" Dana asked.

I nodded my head. Dana's brother Sam suffered from seizures because of his cerebral palsy.

"That night when I got back home, Peter was waiting up for me," Dana said. "I hadn't told him anything about my life up until that point, but that night I knew I had to. I was worn out and tired, and he said something that made my heart begin to melt for the first time in almost ten years."

"What?" I asked, hanging on her every word.

"He said, 'Let me love you, Dana, just for one night.'"

"Oh my God." Hindley fanned herself. "You never told me he said that to you."

"Look, that's beautiful and all," I said, interrupting their

Nicholas Sparks moment, "but what does it have to do with me and this situation?"

Dana cleared her throat and swept her hand across the vast room we were sitting in as the staff cleared the way to prepare for the ensuing luau.

"What?" I asked.

"I gave Peter one night, one night to love me. And look what I got back."

I scanned the large area packed with wedding guests gathered around the stage.

Peter stood on the dance floor, his sons on either side of him as a young Hawaiian woman worked with them on their dance moves.

Peter's mother, Barbara, swung Lilly whose head was tilted back while she looked up at the stars and squealed with delight.

My eyes welled with tears when I saw my father take Caroline in his embrace.

"Guess your one night turned out better than mine." I snorted. I didn't want to be the selfish bitch I was so prone to being, but the sarcasm slipped out despite my best efforts.

"Come on, the luau's about to start." Dana grabbed my hand. "Let's get a shot at the bar, and then go shake our asses off with these hot hula dancers."

Bar? Oh, shit! What if Poseidon was bartending? I stopped in my tracks.

"What?" Dana asked.

"What if he's working tonight? Here. At the bar."

"Then you're gonna shake those fuckin' money-makers you call boobs right in front of this asshole's face." She nodded her head once in solidarity. "Then you're gonna hula those saucy hips of yours and make him wish he could tap that fine ass again."

I laughed out loud at Dana's suggestion, but had to admit, it sounded like a damn good way to get over the fucker.

"No drinks for me," Hindley said, patting her belly.

"I'm in!" Tori shouted, coming from nowhere and leading the three of us to the bar.

"Three mai tais please, sir." Dana banged her hand on the wooden bar like she was a regular.

I anxiously peered up at the bartender and blew out a sigh of relief when I realized he wasn't Poseidon—I mean, Fucker.

Dana quickly scanned the bar as well and nodded in satisfaction. "Looks like fuckwad isn't here. You're in the clear." She smiled, elbowing me in the arm.

Dana really was a great friend to have in your corner, especially in times like these, when you felt your heart breaking ever so slightly from the sting of rejection.

The bartender prepared our drinks, staring a little too long at me for my liking. God, I hoped he didn't recognize me as one of the random chicks that Poseidon fucked on a weekly basis. What if the asshole was running his mouth off to the staff about his latest conquest?

"Didn't you sing last night?" the bartender asked with a small smile.

"Yep," Dana answered for me. "She killed it. She always does." She winked at me.

My confidence slowly rose thanks to this tiny pixie, who I adored. Fuck Poseidon. It had been a vacation fuck for me, too. With the girls' help, and the sting of the rum in my drink, I was feeling stronger than ever.

Dana interlocked our arms as we all strolled back to the table. She smiled up at me in support, her deep dimples lighting up her face.

"Here's to one night." Dana smiled, holding up her glass.

I rolled my eyes, but, in reality, I was truly happy for Dana and the one night that had turned into a lifetime of nights for her and Peter. Putting her heart on the line by sharing her secrets with him had paid off, not only for them, but for their children, too. She deserved this. We all hoisted up our glasses, Hindley's filled with water, and clinked them together.

"To one night." I replaced my sullen face with a smile similar to the one I'd worn earlier this morning when I'd slipped out of Poseidon's bed. I'd only had one night with him, but, if I were being honest, it really had been one of the best nights of my life. And truly we hadn't promised anything more.

"That was such a beautiful ceremony, Dana." Tori plopped her elbows on the table, her chin resting on her upturned palms as she sighed. She was a hopeless romantic.

"It really was," I added. "Perfect. Just like the two of you."

I thought of today's festivities. Peter and Dana started their commitment ceremony shortly before sunset, the rays casting an amber glow on the ocean. The moment had been magical, something I'd only seen in movies.

Dana and Peter had stood in ankle deep water, her long dress pooling in the ocean as they professed and promised their eternal love to one another. The children had been gathered around them, Peter holding Levi because of his fear of the water. A native officiate recited their vows, and all five had become part of the ceremony. It was a magnificent event, and by the time Peter and Dana were pronounced committed again as husband and wife, with a new family, not a dry eye remained among us.

Suddenly, the lights dimmed, and the stage lights burned bright.

"Luau time." Dana rubbed her hands together.

"Mind if I borrow my bride," Peter called from behind us, his long arm wrapping around Dana's tiny waist, hoisting her up with ease.

"My drink!" she screamed, reaching out for her mai tai.

I laughed at her priorities, or lack thereof. Given the choice between a strong man like Peter and a mixed drink, I'd pick the man every time.

He whispered something in her ear, and her entire body went

limp, her eyes glazing over in that sexually perverted way that was beginning to disgust me.

Knowing she was about two seconds away from turning around and fucking Peter senseless, I reached over and picked up her drink, shoving it between the two of them, breaking their connection.

"I want to hula with you," a deep voice growled.

I turned and saw Rory staring down at Hindley. I wasn't surprised to find the same fuck-filled lust glazing over Hindley's eyes. Rory wrapped his long fingers around her bare shoulders, giving them a slight squeeze before peppering her neck with obscene kisses.

Assholes! I sat in my own pity party, sucking down the last of my drink.

"Looks like it's just us two tonight." Tori laughed. "Come on." She grabbed my hand. "Let's go hula."

The mai tai was starting to kick in and my mind said, *fuck it*. I pushed back my chair, determined to have a good time tonight at Dana's reception. I would tuck away last night's memories into my spank bank vault.

"It is what it is," my father always said. I hated that saying with a purple passion, but tonight the words were true. Last night was what it was, an amazing time with an amazing man, a memory I'd treasure always.

A light breeze blew my short, flowing skirt across my legs, the wind caressing my skin. I felt like a goddess as tendrils of my pinned-up hair wisped across my face. The rum was warming my skin. I found my place next to Tori on the dance floor, trying to keep up with the beautiful dancer on the stage as she showed us the steps to the island dance.

"Left hip out," she spoke seductively. "Full circle around."

I saw her hips rotate like well oiled gears, and I was happy I had a little alcohol in me to loosen up my muscles.

"Then right hip out," she said.

The instructor was adorned in a bright pink headdress with

wooden accents, and her skirt was a flowing mix of grass and tassels that rested on her hips as she swayed to and fro with every movement. It was intoxicating and erotic. For a second, I thought I might actually be a lesbian.

"You're doing an amazing job." Her voice boomed through the sound system.

I looked around the floor and noticed everyone staring at me. My eyes found their way back to the stage, surprised to find the instructor looking directly at me.

"Why don't you join us on stage?" She waved toward me. Four other women appeared from nowhere, dancing beside the hula temptress. All four were adorned in the same grass skirts and headdress.

I violently shook my head in refusal, regretting the movement as I felt the room sway. Several years ago, yeah, the old Geneva would have had her ass up on the stage, front and center. But now I tried to stay out of the spotlight.

I'd found, over the years, that the light of center stage always cast a shadow that got me in trouble.

"Oh, no thank you," I said.

"What do you think, everyone?" The hula goddess asked the other guests. "Shouldn't she come up here and dance with us like a true islander?"

Everyone clapped and shouted their response.

Suddenly, Dana's voice carried above the masses and the luau music. "Fuck yeah!" she shouted.

All eyes cut to Dana.

She slapped her hand across her mouth, her eyes going wide as she scanned the room.

We all knew Dana had a foul mouth, but given the fact she was a mom now, we'd hoped she'd work hard on censoring herself. Some things take time, though, and Dana's potty mouth was definitely one that would take a long time to tame.

The crowd burst into laughter, including Peter's mother.

I snorted at my friend's antics. "Fuck it," I whispered under my breath to Tori. "I'm gonna do it."

"Yay!" She jumped up and down, clapping her hands like an idiot.

The hula instructor stretched out her arm, offering me her hand and hoisted me onto the stage.

As I stood among the native dancers, who were clad in their skirts and coconut bikini tops, suddenly I wondered if I was doing the right thing.

"Let's get you dressed first," the instructor said, producing another outfit that looked exactly like the other dancers.

"Oh, uh, no. I'm good." I stiff-armed her, waving my hand to shoo her away.

She motioned for one of the dancers.

The petite woman sidled up next to me and wrapped an arm around my waist. She shuffled me back stage, then all but shoved me into what appeared to be a closet, offering me no choice but to change.

I held up the costume, shaking my head, wondering how in the fuck I had gotten myself into this. Oh, well.

It is what it is.

I slid my chiffon dress over my head and unsnapped my bra, trying to figure out how the hell the coconut top worked. Obviously the two shells went over my boobs so I started there, proud that I finally got it tied tight enough to ensure my tits wouldn't pop out while on stage. The skirt was easier to figure out, but much heavier than I thought it would be.

"Ready yet?" The dancer banged on the door.

"I can't get the skirt hooked."

"Come out, I'll help you," she said.

Slowly opening the door, I looked in either direction, not quite sure what I was expecting.

Her eyes grew wide as she surveyed me from head to toe. "Turn around." She cinched the skirt tight around my hips. "It's heavy so that it will fall onto your hips easier." She put her hands on either side of my waist and shook me vigorously until the skirt fell into its natural position. "It will help with the swaying motion and make you look even sexier."

The way she said the last statement led me to believe that, perhaps, looking sexier to her was not the way I wanted to appear.

"You look unbelievable." She smiled.

Oh, yeah, there was no doubt this girl was a carpet muncher for sure, but it didn't bother me. Given the fact that Poseidon had knocked me down a peg or two on the self-esteem ladder, it was nice to be admired by anyone.

She grasped my hand and pulled me back to the stage.

The lights were bright and blinding. I shielded my eyes with my hands as my pupils adjusted from the darkened closet. The vibrations of the beating drums behind me had my skin pulsating. An assortment of instruments played along, creating a symphony of music that made it almost impossible *not* to sway your entire body.

Cat calls and whistles echoed throughout the open air. A few actually came from behind me, obviously members of the band. I felt my skin heat, and not from the stage lights.

"What's your name?" the instructor asked into the microphone.

Where the fuck had a microphone come from?

My eyes finally adjusted to the stage lights, and I was able to look beyond the platform. The crowd had grown three times its size. I thought this was a private event, just for Dana's wedding party, but from the looks of it, others from the resort had joined in the merriment.

Fuck! I stood in silence, paralyzed. I hated being in front of large crowds now. I knew it went against everything people assumed about my outgoing nature, but it was true.

"Geneva!" Dana shouted from the mass of people. "Her name's Geneva."

Great, now everyone in the resort would know who the fuck I was.

"Didn't you sing in the bar last night?" the instructor asked.

I didn't think it was possible to turn any redder than I already was, but I was wrong. My body burned with embarrassment.

"Fuck yeah, she did!" I heard someone shout from the crowd. The voice was unfamiliar. "She was awesome!"

Oh, God, it was official. I was going to die from embarrassment right here on the stage in Kauai. I could think of worse places, though. And considering I'd had an evening filled with amazing sex the night before, I was okay to die on stage right now if that truly was my fate.

"Well," the instructor smiled, sensing my panic, "we won't make you sing. Let's dance."

I exhaled in relief. Dancing. I could do dancing.

"Now," the beautiful islander began, "it's just like you were doing down on the floor. Hip right."

I thrust my hip to the right.

"Roll a circle."

I mimicked her movements, as best I could.

"Hip left," she continued.

I followed her movements.

"Wonderful."

A smile tugged at my lips at her words of praise. In the past it had been unlike me to give two shits about what anyone thought of me, or my actions.

A delicious island breeze swept through my grass skirt, clearing the mistakes of the past. As the wind whipped around the strands falling around my legs, I was suddenly grateful for the barely-there mini skirt that came with the ridiculous hula outfit. At least it covered my underwear. Barely.

The wind infused me with a newfound courage, allowing me to let go of my racing thoughts and give up control as my body swayed to the beat of the island drums. Before long, I was swept away in the moment. My hips came to life, moving in rhythm with the other dancers.

I was lost in the moment, and it felt amazing. There were no traces of fear or anxiety anywhere in my awareness. I was living in the moment, my body immersed in my own world of erotic movements.

Whistles and catcalls echoed in the crowd, but they didn't deter me, they actually spurred me on. My movements became more aggressive, more exaggerated, like the rest of the seasoned dancers on stage with me. I was doing this shit and doing it well.

The instructor stretched out her arms, moving them in a wave like motion and I followed along, as did the other girls, my hips never missing a beat.

"Go, Geneva!" Dana shouted.

I felt like a rock star, a goddess among mortals. The feeling was exhilarating and I never wanted it to end.

The instructor tossed the microphone to the side, the beat of the music suddenly increasing. Sweat was streaming down my back and my legs were getting shaky. I loved the feeling of the island hula, but I feared if I didn't stop soon, I'd pass out.

It was clear from the smile on the instructor's face she had no intentions of letting me go. Oh, shit! Was she a lesbo, too?

Her hips gyrated vigorously as she turned and put her backside on display for all the crowd to see.

Oh, double shit. I had a big ass. I knew it. Everyone did. They always commented on my ba-donk-a-donk ass, as Dana called it. The fucking tassels and wooden ornaments hanging from my hips would only make my ghetto booty look even bigger. Fuck it. I was here in Hawaii with some of my best friends, sharing in memories that would last a lifetime.

Rowdy shouts of obscene affections from the other resort guests, who had joined our wedding luau, echoed through the open-air space, but I wasn't offended by their jeering. In fact, I kind of liked it.

After Poseidon had pulled a "one-and-done" on me today, it was nice to know there were others out in the crowd who might service me tonight.

Service me? Where had that come from?

Well, if a show was what this rowdy crowd wanted to see, then that was what I was going to give them.

Pivoting on my bare feet, I stuck out my ass toward the audience, shaking it like a seasoned hula dancer. I felt invigorated and invincible. Thankfully, another island breeze swept through my skirt, cooling my skin that was now covered with sweat. Reaching up to brush away a stray piece of hair from my updo, my eyes focused on the band.

I choked on the air that was now anything *but* cool as I stared at the person in front of me. There, sitting behind one of the big drums, beating on the skin with a large mallet in each of his humongous man-hands, was Poseidon. Fucker. *That* fucker.

Wait, he was a bartender, wasn't he? I thought I'd been in the clear tonight. *Obviously, you thought wrong.* Here the fucker sat, right in front of me, beating on his drum, his expression menacing, as if I'd killed his dog. What the hell was that look for?

Choreographing my own dance, I quickly turned to face the audience, jutting my butt toward him. That probably wasn't the best idea, considering my huge ass and the disturbing way I knew it was jiggling now.

With no warning, the beating stopped, and the other dancers went still. All but me. My dumb ass just kept moving like the idiot I was proving myself to be.

"Oh, yeah!" a random voice shouted from behind me—someone from the band. It wasn't Poseidon, and part of me loved the fact that someone else found me attractive enough to shout it out.

Was that why Poseidon had been pissed?

He had no right to be. I'd given him the opportunity to contact me. It had been his decision to blow me off. Fuck it.

I continued dancing my hula like I was the shit, no music or other dancers needed. The crowd created a rhythm for me with their clapping and stomping, and soon the band joined back in until, with one last thrust of my hips, I came to an abrupt stop. There was silence for about three seconds and I feared I might have totally fucked up Dana's reception.

The entire crowd erupted with cheers, whistling, shouting words of encouragement and clapping, the kind usually reserved for rock concerts.

Feeling emboldened by the crowd's praises, I spun on my heels and stared directly at Fucker, snapping my hands up and shooting him not one, but two middle fingers before exiting, stage right.

The best thing about the future is that it comes one day at a time.
- Abraham Lincoln

CHAPTER 9

BERK

"DID that chick just flip you off, man?" Okie asked as he beat on the tribal drum in front of him.

My hand kept a steady rhythm on my own drum as I tried not to break through the taut material I was hammering on. Each beat sounded eerily similar to the pounding in my chest.

I was pissed, like *really* pissed, and burning hot with a fever that had nothing to do with the stage lights or the temperature outside.

"What the hell, Berk?" My sister Palla danced over toward me, cleverly disguising herself within the band so she wouldn't draw attention to her absence at center stage. She was the hostess of this particular luau.

My sister and I hated the luau gigs more than any job we had at my family's resort. We would both rather clean up vomit from the bathroom floor of any guest bungalow than be up on stage, her wiggling her hips in front of drunk men, and me having to stand behind her and watch. Do you know how sick it is for a brother to have to endure that kind of shit?

"Yeah, man," Okie asked again, "what the hell was that?"

I shrugged, hoping my nonchalance would rid them both of their curiosity. My head was banging louder than the drum in front of me.

Why in the hell would she flip me off? *She* was the one who snuck out this morning without even waking me up to say, "Goodbye. Thanks for the lay. I had an awesome fuck."

Maybe her abrupt disappearance wouldn't have stung my male ego so bad if it hadn't been one of the best sexual experiences of my life. The chick was limber and could contort herself into any position I molded her into.

I cursed myself silently when my dick swelled just thinking about her hot body twisted up around me in my dinky shower.

That was it. It had to be. She was totally turned off by my sparse dwelling. She was probably used to a palatial house with manservants attending her every need. That didn't explain why she was mad at me, though. Mad enough to flip me off, on stage, at her own friend's wedding reception.

"Well, you better go make it right, Berk." My sister's eyes narrowed as she slammed her fist on her hip. "She and her family are spending a shit ton of money here this week, and, if Tutu finds out you pissed one of them off, she's gonna knock you all the way back to Colorado."

My body stiffened at the mention of Colorado. My hands stopped mid-beat, paralyzed as every nerve ending caught fire.

Palla stared me up and down, her light brown eyes wide with regret. "Sorry," she whispered.

I didn't answer, afraid of the words that threatened to explode from within me.

"But seriously, Berk," she continued, oblivious to the war raging inside me, "you need to go make it right."

My eyes cut back to hers, feeling the warmth and sincerity radiating from her. I loved my baby sister and would do anything for her, just like I knew she would me. But I had no desire to chase after some chick who had only used me for a vacation fuck. I couldn't explain that to Palla, though, or she'd kick my ass.

"Go." She nodded her head, glaring at me with her caramel-colored eyes that were just a shade lighter than mine. Her long, black hair blew wildly in the wind as she worked to keep the strands under control.

I remained silent but nodded once in acknowledgment.

Palla turned on her heel, dancing back to the front of the stage, pulling another unsuspecting guest onto the stage to join the island dance.

"Dude, seriously." Okie nudged my arm as he kept perfect beat on his drum set. "You better go. You do *not* want Tutu on your ass."

His comment brought the first smile to my face since I'd woken up to an empty bed twelve hours ago, the scent of Geneva's feminine desire torturing me.

Tutu was our grandmother. She was petite, standing less than five feet tall, which meant I towered over her at six feet three.

I was the tallest in my family, because I wasn't one hundred percent Hawaiian like the rest of my mother's family. Her brothers and sisters had married other islanders. My mother Kalani was a rebel, though, falling in love with a "haole," or foreigner, a derogatory native Hawaiian term for white people.

My grandparents had been against the union at first, but soon warmed to the charms of John Rigby. My parents had remained happily married for over thirty-four years now, proving that yes, you could make a life with a haole, and create beautiful "hapas", or half-breeds like me and my brother and sister.

"Berk!" Okie shouted above the beating of the drums and the other instruments of the luau band. "Go!"

"What if I don't want to?" I pouted like an errant child.

"Oh my God, did you fuck her?"

"No." I jerked back, trying to feign offense.

"Whatever, man. Just go. You did something to piss that chick off, and you don't want Tutu to find out. Especially if you screwed her."

I rolled my eyes, trying to feign innocence, but Okie was right. If Tutu found out I had screwed one of the guests, she would have my head. She was a small woman, but strong as nails.

Anyone unlucky enough to cross her path usually lived to regret it.

"Fine," I huffed as I stepped away from the drum and took off the ridiculous headdress. I was only here because Mano, our lead drummer, sprained his hand in a surfing accident earlier in the day. I think he probably wacked off one too many times, if you asked me, but no one did so I didn't say shit to my uncle when he'd called me late this afternoon and asked me to fill in.

"Take her clothes," Okie called after me. "They're in the back closet."

Yeah, right, I was going to take her clothes to her. She could parade around all night in that stupid-ass hula dancer get up for all I cared. Actually, I found myself caring, a lot. She was hot as fuck in it, and it pissed me off, royally, that my cock was starting to harden again, remembering her luscious hips swaying side to side, watching in fascination as the plumes on her skirt jetted out and the tassels slapped her ass as she popped her hips—

Stop!

I needed to find the girl, apologize if necessary to keep Tutu off my ass. What the hell did I have to apologize for though? She left me. Alone. I reminded myself that we weren't supposed to sleep with the guests. So yeah, an apology it was.

My feet hit the sand at the side of the stage with a thud, then I walked toward the main bar. Gazing past the crowd of people pushing toward the stage and gawking at my sister, I spotted the girl in question.

Her name is Geneva. Whatever.

She was comfortably stationed at the bar, still clad in her hula garb, surrounded by dudes. What the fuck? I stalked her from afar, like a pervert, as one of the guys pushed a shot glass into her hands.

Her face erupted in a smile that lit up the room like the full moon overhead. She opened her mouth and gently set the glass against her full lips. Her head cocked back in one swoop, and I stared as her long, slim throat swallowed the drink whole.

Visions of that same mouth wrapped around my dick last night, swallowing *me* whole, invaded my mind. *Stop!*

All the men high-fived one another. It was painfully obvious to me they were trying to get her drunk. My stomach lurched and my skin lit on fire as my hands fisted. I drew in a deep breath, trying to calm my racing heart before I smashed something, namely one of the fuck faces trying to get her smashed.

I needed to be cool though. I reminded myself that these assholes were guests, too. Tutu would kick my ass for fighting with anyone, especially a guest.

My mind yelled in warning. *Stay away!* Something deep within me told me Geneva was in danger, though. Maybe not yet, but soon.

Stalking toward the bar like a lion hunting his prey, I parted the men with ease, thanks to my bulky size and bare chest.

Geneva slowly turned her head at the commotion I was making.

When her blue eyes collided with mine, all I could remember was her naked body on top of mine, riding me like a giant wave of pleasure.

Her head had been tilted back as she sat on me, impaled by my dick, her eyes half hooded as she rubbed on her breasts. I pictured her bobbing up and down on me, riding me so hard I thought I was going to die. Fuck. Now my dick was hard as stone.

"What the hell do you want?" she slurred.

I pressed my lips against her ear. "How many of these have you had?" I growled.

Her body shuddered in response.

Mine followed suit, and my dick pushed out of my teeny loin cloth underneath my ridiculous grass skirt.

"None of your business," she said, trying to sound unaffected, but the desire in her eyes told me otherwise. She wanted me.

But if she wanted me, why had she left me this morning without a good-bye?

"Ma'am," I said, wrapping my arm around her waist and dragging her off the bar stool, "you need to change back into your regular clothes." I hoped my explanation would appease, not only Geneva, but these three monkey dudes now drinking in her gorgeous body from head to toe. I was surprised to see Geneva willingly come with me.

Her arm wrapped around my shoulders for support as her coconut top rubbed against my bare chest. Gazing down at Geneva, I could honestly say I'd never seen a hula costume look so good on anyone.

"Be sure to come back, sweetheart!" one of the douche bags shouted.

What a fucking moron, calling some chick you didn't even know a sweetheart. *Didn't you call her sweetheart a few times last night while you were bangin' the shit out of her?* I believe the term I used was "sweet ass".

Watching Geneva's hips sway back and forth as she walked away from me, I was happily reminded of why I'd given her the nickname.

"Where do you think you're going, Mai Tai?" A petite woman stopped my forward motion, holding up her tiny hand to my chest. She was the bride. I recognized her from the luau.

I was immediately intimidated by the pint-sized woman and had no good reason why.

Two more women with lighter hair, like Geneva's, joined the petite ringleader, and suddenly I felt ambushed—and terrified. All three had their brows raised and heads half-cocked, waiting for my next words, which, judging by their expressions, could very well be my last if I didn't pacify them.

"Umm," I stumbled with my words, "she forgot her clothes backstage."

The three women surveyed me from head to toe.

A flush of red spread through my body as my core temperature rose. They were protecting one of their own and they recognized me as a threat to her. "She needs to return the costume," I said, my voice a quivering disaster.

"Oh." The little one smirked. She was smart, not easily fooled by a jackass like me, but I knew she was going to let me pass. "Is this him?" She cut her eyes to Geneva.

Geneva's own eyes were wide with shock, as if her parents had found a bag of weed under her mattress. Instantly, she sobered, her body going stiff. She nodded once, her silent gesture answering more than the one question her friend had just asked.

The women glared at me, their laser stares threatening to disintegrate me. Geneva had obviously told them about our night together.

My normally strong legs went limp as all four women stared at me, that gleam in their eye matching the one an executioner had right before he dropped the guillotine on a convicted murderer. They were about to crucify me, and I had no idea why, but I knew I had to get the fuck out of here before all four of them went ballistic —and my grandmother found out.

I slid my hand into Geneva's and gave her a slight squeeze before pulling her with me as I strode past the women.

Geneva yelped in surprise, but it didn't stop me. Not even the sardonic laughter of the little pixie bride slowed my resolve. I was gonna get this girl back into her clothes and find out what the fuck was going on before Tutu found out what I'd done and killed me herself.

"What the hell is your problem!" Geneva yelled as she tried to pull away from me.

I tightened my hold on her hand and stalked up the backstage stairs, making a beeline for the small closet she'd changed in. After yanking the door open, I tossed her inside, crowded in and slammed the door shut behind me —locking it.

"What the fuck?" she yelled. "You can't keep me in here. I'll scream 'rape' if you don't let me go." The girl was a wildcat, her eyes darting back and forth between mine, not in fear but anger.

"Why did you leave me this morning without saying good-bye?" I asked.

"What?" she screeched, backing up and bumping into the wall. The closet was almost as small as my shower so we were nearly touching one another.

"I said," leaning in, my eyes narrowing, "why did you leave this morning? Why didn't you even say good-bye to me? Is that asking too much from the rich girl?" My words were sarcastic and meant to sting.

Her blue eyes went wide.

Obviously, my tactic was working. "Or am I just some vacation fuck to you? Is that what you do at home? Fuck a dude then slink out in the middle of the night like a—"

A thunderous smack rang through the tiny room a fraction of a second before searing pain shot across my face. What the fuck? She'd slapped me. And probably for good reason. I'd accused her of being a slut.

"You have some nerve, you asshole," she hissed. "I left you? You think *I* left *you*?" she mocked. "I think you have that backward, shithead."

I backed up as far as I could in the tiny closet, rubbing my face, which still stung from her assault.

"What are you talking about?"

"What am I talking about?" She laughed. "I left you a fucking note, genius. Told you to call me—which you never did. So, I guess I'm *your* vacation fuck."

"You left a note?"

She was beyond pissed now, so my words didn't even register. Her chest was heaving so hard from anger that I had to divert my gaze from her full breasts.

"You probably do this shit every week," she continued, "giving these horny, mainland chicks the same stupid ass lines, using your Polynesian good looks just to lure them into bed. 'Wanna ride my board,'" she mocked in a deep voice, trying to mimic my own. "I bet these chicks roll in here week after week, a different fuck for you, maybe even every day, for all I know. How nice for you, you cock-sucking douche bag."

Oh, shit, she was beyond pissed. She was seething mad.

"Now let me the fuck out of here before I kick you in the nut sack and ruin the rest of your, 'I'm gonna fuck a new tourist every day,' little scheme you've got going on here." She shoved me in the chest as hard as she could with both forearms, trying to bulldoze past me.

"You left a note?" I asked again, confused by her revelation.

"Yes, you fuckwad. *You're* the asshat who left me hanging. You screwed *me*, and then walked away. So, get your fucking giant, Poseidon man-beast of a body out of my way so I can—"

My lips crashed down on hers, silencing her instantly as I wrapped my hands around her face, dragging her closer.

She fought, pulling at my wrists with her tiny hands, but it was no use. She was right, I was a beast of a man, and there was no way I was letting her go. Not now that I'd discovered she thought *I* had been the one to blow *her* off.

She'd left me a note. Every ounce of anger in my body dissolved with her confession.

Slowly, her body succumbed to my desires. Her lips parted and allowed me access to everything inside her. Her moans were my invitation.

I slid one hand down her bare back, stopping just at the edge of the grass skirt, pulling her into my hips so she could feel just how sorry I was.

"I didn't know you left a note," I murmured against her lips.

My words had the opposite effect of what I'd imagined. She pushed away from me, and I realized she was much stronger than I gave her credit for. Wiping at her lips with the back of her hand, as if to rid herself of some horrible disease I'd just passed on, she backed into the wall behind her.

"Well, I did. You didn't call. So, if you'll get out of this mop closet and let me change, I'll leave the costume and be on my way."

I stalked her the few inches left between us, pinning her to the wall with my hips, watching as her eyes dilated. She wanted me, but she was just being stubborn because I'd hurt her pride.

"I'm sorry," I spoke softly against her cheek, my lips rubbing softly against her skin. I could feel her body dissolving into mine with every exhalation. "What did your note say?" I breathed into her ear, smiling against her skin when I felt her arms drop in silent surrender.

"Umm." She wobbled.

I wrapped my arm around her waist to hold her steady. "Did you tell me you'd be back again?" I whispered, praying that was what her note actually said.

"Yes," she whispered breathlessly.

"What else did it say?" I smattered her face with light kisses, awaiting her answer.

Her eyes fluttered closed.

I brushed the soft skin of her lids with my lips.

"Well," she said in a breathy sigh.

The coconut shells from her costume were mashed into my bare chest. I could feel each shallow inhalation as her bare abdomen collided with mine. She still wanted me, and that drove me crazy with desire.

I pressed my dick between her legs, begging her to divulge the contents of her note.

She gasped as the outline of my rock-hard dick rubbed along the barely-there grass skirt. Her breathing ramped up as her lips magically found my neck.

Oh, fuck!

"It said thank you," she murmured against my skin.

I pulled back slightly to gauge her reaction, wondering if it was a "thank you" like, "Thank you for getting my cat down from a tree," or more like, "Thank you for giving me the time of my life."

Her eyes were closed, her thick lashes splayed across her cheeks like fans, her jaw lax and her mouth partially open. This was definitely a thank you of the latter kind.

I slid my hands around her neck, pushing against her jaw with my thumbs as her head fell back, leaving her throat exposed for my tasting. Her moans assured me she was completely all right with my caress.

"What else did your note say?" I asked, licking across her jaw, sucking just under her ear, the spot I knew from our passionate night together lit her on fire.

"I can't think with you doing that," she panted.

I begrudgingly pulled away, giving her the distance she needed to continue.

Her eyes opened, the pupils wide inside her bright blue orbs. Her breathing was evening out as she braced her hands against the walls on either side of her. There was no question I had affected her.

"What else did your note say, Geneva?" I crossed my hands behind my back, leaning casually against the wall. I had to make sure that this was what she wanted, too. If her note said "Thanks for the fuck, it was good, have a nice life," then I'd leave her alone for the rest of her stay. *And if it didn't say that?* I wasn't willing to go there right now.

"It said, thank you for a wonderful evening, one of the best of my life." Her last words were just above a whisper and she hung her head in what appeared like shame.

I placed a finger under her jaw, gently lifting her face so I could peer into her beautiful eyes. "Is that all it said?"

She shook her head, still acting shy and coy. The entire scene seemed amusing and so unlike the Geneva from last night.

"What else did you say?"

"I gave you all my information, my villa number and my full name." Hurt and betrayal sprung to life within her eyes as she yanked her head away from my hold.

"Geneva," I said, stepping toward her, tugging her head back so it was in line with mine. "I never got your note. I swear."

"You probably wouldn't have called me anyway, so it's just as well, right?" She laughed nervously.

"I would have called you the second I read it." I spoke with all the sincerity in my heart. "I missed you the minute I woke up this morning and found you'd left."

Her big blue eyes went wide at my confession, but it was the truth.

I'd felt like a piece of me was missing this morning when I discovered she'd gone without a word of farewell.

"I would have talked to you for hours and never let you hang up the phone, even though your friend was getting married today," I continued. My heart rate spiked when a small smile tugged at her lips. "I would have met you anywhere on the island and smattered you with kisses. I would have begged you to come back with me."

My words surprised even *me* with their truthfulness and honesty. I wanted Geneva. I would have spent the entire day with her if she had let me. And if my tutu wouldn't have beat the shit out of me.

"Really?" Her eyes filled with tears that I didn't understand.

Instead of using words, I let my body speak for me. I slowly pushed her against the wall again, my lips brushing against her soft ear, still adorned with those giant diamond studs. This time, though, I wasn't intimidated by her outward appearance of wealth. Something told me Geneva wasn't nearly as pretentious as I'd once thought.

"Really," I breathed against her tanned skin.

Her hands cupped my cheeks and pushed my face away from hers.

My chest tightened with fear. Maybe this wasn't what she wanted, despite her earlier reaction to my affections.

"I'm sorry," she said. Her eyes flashed with a multitude of emotions—regret, remorse, guilt. But for what? For spending the night with me? "I'm sorry I called you bad names and shot you the finger on stage."

Relief flooded me and I laughed at the memory. "Actually, I believe you gave me a double bird shot."

Her light giggles filled the tiny closet and her eyes told me everything I'd wondered about all day. Our time together yesterday hadn't been just a vacation fuck. It had been one of the best nights of both our lives.

"Want to get out of here?" I nodded toward the door.

"Just let me change first." She looked down at her clothing, or lack thereof.

"Oh, no. You're coming back with me. In that outfit." My eyes roamed over her gorgeous body. "We're having our own luau tonight, Geneva."

"Well, if I can't change, you can't either," she said, perusing me from head to toe.

My eyes followed hers and I laughed. I looked like a Hawaiian fire dancer or something, bare chest, painted-on tattoos on my upper body, my own grass skirt hanging loosely on my hips.

"Oh, yes." She smiled, wrapping her hands around my hips, and snuggling them to the warm juncture between her legs. "We're going to have our own luau tonight. Complete with my very own island drummer boy." She giggled.

CHAPTER 10
BERK

"Did you take my shoes this morning?" I gazed down at my front porch. Her silence gave me my answer, but I wanted to see her adorable, guilt-ridden face. I glanced behind me as I turned the knob and pushed open the door, not surprised to see her nervous smirk. "You owe me." I laughed, stepping aside to let her pass.

She walked into my living room, perusing the area, taking in every nuance. A few tendrils of hair escaped her updo and blew across her face with the island breeze that wafted through the open windows of my home. Her hair teased me, begging to be caught and tamed into submission, like the woman it was attached to.

"I love your place," she spoke softly, her hand running gently over the back of my couch as she studied a hand-carved statue on my end table.

"Really?"

"Yes, really?" She grinned, turning to look at me. "Why do you seem so surprised?"

"I just figured you were more of an upscale kind of girl."

"Not anymore." Her eyes cut to the floor as she fumbled with her hands. It was obvious there was more to her story, but she wasn't going to talk about it.

"Do you want some cake?" I asked, changing the subject. I walked toward the kitchen bar and set the cardboard container down on the counter.

"How did you steal Dana and Peter's wedding cake?" She giggled.

Something in my midsection stirred from the sound. "I didn't *steal* it." I gave her a knowing wink and surveyed her amazing body that was still adorned in the hula outfit. "I just took your piece."

"It looks like you took half of the bottom tier." She chuckled, strutting toward the counter like she lived here with me. "It looks amazing."

"Oh, it is." I pulled the massive piece of cake out of the box and set it on a plate. "It's my tutu's recipe, handed down to her from generations."

"Tutu?" Her brow furrowed in an adorable way that made her seem more vulnerable.

"Sorry. Tutu means grandmother in the native Hawaiian language."

"Tutu," she smiled, "I like it."

I liked the way it rolled off her tongue and had to cast my eyes away from her sultry lips and think of some bland image to stop the raging hard-on threatening to split my grass skirt wide open. I pulled two forks from the drawer next to the sink.

"Oh, yum," she moaned, her eyes devouring the cake before I even had the chance to hand her the fork.

I pulled the plate back, holding onto the forks. "Oh, no," I warned as if she were in trouble.

"What?" Her face scrunched up and she pouted like a small child who'd just been informed that Christmas would be cancelled this year due to her unruly behavior.

"This cake is *very* good." I dug a fork deep into the multi-layers before bringing it up to my mouth. "You'll need to *earn* a bite of my grandmother's cake." Casually and purposefully, I opened my mouth wide and slid the fork full of cake over my waiting tongue. I slowly wrapped my lips around the tines and pulled the fork out of my mouth, moaning the entire time.

I watched in satisfaction as her eyes grew wide and she squirmed.

"It's *soooo* good," I mumbled through my mouthful of cake. "You have to earn a piece."

"But you didn't do anything for your piece," she whined.

"Oh, I worked *very* hard for mine. I beat on a drum all night and had to watch a hot girl shake her ass in front of me. There wasn't a fucking thing I could do but sit there and dream about having her again."

She shrugged one shoulder, her lips puckering before splitting into a prideful smile. "So, what can *I* do to earn a piece?"

Her deep, raspy voice rang with eroticism that nearly had me chunking the cake over my shoulder and pulling her over the bar to fuck her right there on my kitchen counter.

"Well." I rolled my eyes up to the ceiling as I scratched my forehead in jest. I widened my eyes as I thought of what I wanted. "I think I want to see another hula dance."

Her body tensed and she pulled away from the bar. "What? No way," she said sheepishly.

I was sure Geneva had been a lot of things in her life, but shy didn't strike me as one of them. Her reaction baffled me.

"It's just me." I moved closer. "And this cake is *soooo* good. It will be worth it. I promise."

She narrowed her eyes in a menacing glare that brought zero fear to me.

I dug my fork into the moist, chocolate cake for another bite, but held it out to her, tempting her. I *really* wanted to see her shake her ass for me one more time.

"Fine," she huffed, "but then you have to dance for me."

"No way." I chuckled, shoving the bite into *my* mouth instead.

"Then I won't dance for you." She jutted her hip and slammed a fist against it, raising one brow in defiance.

This was not going the way I'd intended. I was usually the one in control of every situation in my life. As much as I didn't want to relinquish it now, I wanted to see her dance more than I wanted to be in control.

"Fine," I huffed. I reached for a napkin to wipe my mouth, but a crosswind swept through the kitchen and lifted the pile. The stack flew across the dining area, littering the room with napkins.

Suddenly it hit me. "Where did you leave my note, the one you said you left for me this morning?"

"Here," she tapped on the bar, "on the counter."

"What did you write it on?"

"A napkin? Why?" Her eyes shot wide as we both realized what had happened earlier today.

"A cross breeze must have blown your note off the counter." I walked to the mass of napkins on the floor, squatted down, and dug through the stack until I found one ink-stained and folded in half. A feeling of shame washed over me. I was officially the biggest prick on the planet.

"Was this your note?" I held up the folded napkin.

"Yes." She bent and tried to snatch it from my hand.

"Oh, no." I laughed, tucking it into my body. "You left this for me to read, and I'm going to read it."

"That was before."

"Before what?"

She didn't answer but straightened and backed up a step.

I unfolded the napkin and let her written words speak for her.

I'm sorry. I don't know how to title this because I don't even know your name. But it feels like I've known you forever. Thank you for last night, it was amazing. Love, Geneva

.   .   .

The rest of the note listed her contact information, but the words lost focus as my eyes glazed over. The only thing my befuddled mind could remember was her declaration of eternity—*It feels like I've known you forever.*

Slowly I stood, turning to face Geneva.

She was on the opposite side of my small dining table, her eyes wide with what looked like worry.

"Berk," I spoke softly.

"What?" She cocked her head.

"Berk," I repeated. "My name is Berk."

A smile as big as the Pacific Ocean spread across her face, as if she'd found the last word to solve the *New York Times* crossword puzzle.

I silently chuckled, knowing something as simple as revealing my name had put it there. Geneva wasn't the uppity rich girl I'd thought she was when I first met her.

"Berk," she repeated. "I like that. Is it Hawaiian?"

"No, hardly. It's a long story."

"I have all night." She winked and shrugged one shoulder suggestively.

"Oh, no, you don't." I walked to the kitchen and placed the note securely in a drawer. "I asked for a dance first. We can talk later."

She rolled her eyes, but the smile tugging at her sumptuous lips guaranteed she would make good on her promise.

"Fine," she sighed, "one dance. Then cake. Then you'll tell me about your name."

"Deal." I winked.

"Where do you want me to dance?"

I motioned toward the living area just a few feet away.

"Will you turn down the lights?" she asked, rubbing her chin on her bare shoulder.

"Why?"

She shrugged, her eyes staring anywhere but at me.

This was obviously important to her so I didn't argue. I *really* wanted to see this girl shake her ass again.

I flipped off the light in the kitchen, leaving one lone lamp shining above the dining table. The glow from the chandelier above cast a shroud of darkness across the living area that I hoped would make her feel more comfortable.

The light reflected off her caramel-colored skin. My eyes were transfixed, glued to Geneva's body, sending a spark of desire across my skin. She was intoxicating and I wondered if I would be able to make it a full minute watching her body gyrate for me without popping off a wad through my grass skirt.

"Sit." She extended her arm, pointing to my small love seat as if she owned the place.

Willingly, I obliged, snuggling into the sofa, preparing for the show of my life.

She pushed the small coffee table back, giving herself more room, or so I thought. After she'd secured its new position, she stepped up on the table. She was going to use it as her stage.

Holy hell!

"Do you want some music?" I gulped, praying she'd say no. It would be impossible for me to stand up right now, let alone walk over to the radio with the raging boner inside my grass skirt.

"Nope." She smirked. "I have all the music I need right here." She tapped her temple with a dainty finger.

Slowly, she let her finger trail down her cheek, gently tracing her jawline and caressing her throat before it disappeared behind her back, along with the other hand. Her hips seemed to take on a life of their own as they swayed to and fro, the grass of her skirt moving seductively with every toss of her body.

"You said the cake is really good, right?" she asked, her voice breathy, like Marilyn Monroe.

All I could do was nod my head as I watched this seductive temptress shake her hips on my table.

She danced and shimmied until her back was facing me. "Then I better make this a good dance, right?"

God, her voice, her skin, that ass. I was not going to last.

Her nimble fingers made quick work of the string to her coconut bikini top. She tugged on the straps and slowly pulled the shells completely over her head, tossing them onto the floor with a thud.

My dick was so hard I could pound nails into steel.

Looking at me over her shoulder, she stared me, her bare back more seductive and arousing than anything I'd seen in a long time. The white lines of her bikini top were evident on her sun-kissed skin.

With her back facing me, I watched like a horny teenager at a strip club as her long, lean arms finally released her breasts and made snake-like movements. She popped her hips from side to side. The tassels along the waist of her skirt drew my attention to her shapely ass.

She'd put a spell on me, cast me in a trance, her movements so seductive.

She thrust her hips from side to side, the effect rippling through me like waves in the ocean.

Her body picked up speed, dipping lower, moving toward the surface of the table to the point where I thought she might actually fall over. Her fingers dug into her hair and released the pins, letting it cascade down her neck in a way that had every nerve ending in my body on fire.

Her dance was better than any hula I'd ever seen before, a combination of my native dance mixed with a stage show from a stripper club. My cock was about to explode.

One arm wrapped around her breasts and I ogled her as she slowly turned to face me, her hips swaying from side to side. The grass skirt made a whooshing sound as the tassels moved in a rhythmic dance that had me completely enthralled. Her tiny, pink-toed foot slipped past the edge of the table as she stepped down, her legs coming to stand directly between mine.

I spread mine wide, anticipating her arrival.

Geneva's eyes darted to my midsection, my raging boner now on prominent display. I wasn't going to do a damn thing to hide it. Hell, at this point, it would be virtually impossible to anyway.

She worked her hips from side to side, lowering her body until she was on her knees, her face level with my dick. One arm was still slung over her breasts, unfortunately. Her tongue parted her lips, licking at them before her eyes finally gazed up at me.

I was caught in her hypnotic spell, unable and unwilling to look away.

The gentle breeze chose that moment to capture her golden blonde hair and blow it across her face. She brushed it away with her hands, releasing her breasts.

I stared as her nipples puckered in the cool night air.

Fuck.

Slowly she placed both palms on my knees, spreading them wide as she inched closer to me.

"Do I get a piece of cake now?" She smirked, licking her lips.

Oh, fuck me running. All the blood in my body surged to my cock like a tidal wave, the pounding ache keeping perfect time with each beat of my heart. I couldn't think, I couldn't talk. Hell, I couldn't move. I barely managed to nod.

She pushed off my knees and stood, making her way to the kitchen.

What the fuck? I wanted to shout her name, ask what the hell she was doing, but I was paralyzed.

Then she was back, the plate of cake now in her hands. Her bare breasts bounced with every step.

God, her puckered, caramel nipples were calling out for attention. I'd never been more aroused in my life.

She stopped and bent over the table, sticking her sweet ass in my face as she set the plate down like she had all the time in the world.

Aggghhh! I had half a mind to bolt up and shove my dick inside her right then and there for tempting me. But I'd poked the lioness with my earlier teasing, and this was my punishment.

She turned. "What's wrong, Berk?"

My name rolled off her tongue like water off a freshly waxed car. I'd never heard her speak my name in desire, and suddenly, the only thing I wanted more than to sink myself deep inside her was to hear her scream out my name in a fevered frenzy all night long.

"You look like you're in pain." She half laughed. "Is everything okay? Down there." She nodded toward my dick. "Is there something I can do to help you?"

This girl was bad, *really* bad, but that was what made her good.

"Let's get this off you." She knelt and ran her hands up my thighs, parting my grass skirt.

I couldn't wait for her. I reached behind myself to undo the knot at the waist, my fingers fumbling like a high school boy about to have sex for the first time.

"Let me." Her blue eyes rolled up to meet mine, her face bathed in a sheen of sweat and desire. She was getting me back for eating cake in front of her. She was torturing me, and not an ounce of me was upset about it.

My skirt finally gave way, and I lifted my hips as she tugged on the costume and boxer briefs underneath that had kept my dick from poking through the grass layers. The cool breeze drifting through the room took hold of my naked body and I sighed in contentment. My entire body was thrumming with an intensity I'd had yet to experience in my life.

"May I have some cake now? Berk." She spoke in a low, raspy voice, throwing my name in for effect.

It was working.

I nodded once and watched as she turned to scoop up a handful of cake, then faced me again. She brought the chocolate dessert to her mouth and licked the icing, her blue eyes never leaving mine.

A small smirk lifted her lips as she closed her eyes and moaned in delight. "Oh, you're right. Berk. It's delicious." Slowly she brought her hand down between my legs, her palm still full of cake.

What the fuck was she about to do? Oh, holy shit! My eyes rolled back and my head fell onto the couch when the cool frosting made contact with my dick.

Her hand didn't stop as she smeared the entire piece all over me, my cock now covered completely with the delicious dessert. I waited, knowing any moment she would indeed take her first bite, just as she'd promised.

Geneva's warm tongue licked at my balls until she moved up to the base of my engorged cock, sliding it all the way up to the tip as if I were a lollipop.

My body trembled. I squeezed the cushions beside me, trying to hold off the orgasm threatening to rip through me at any minute.

"I want to eat my cake, Berk." She drew out my name again. "Don't come yet or I'll stop." Her head bowed, her golden hair covering my stomach as her mouth took me in.

Oh, fuck!

Her tongue danced around me as her mouth continued its assault, her head bobbing up and down like a fucking seesaw in the park.

I had to stop looking at her because it was driving me crazy. Instead, I closed my eyes and dug my fingers into the couch, trying to think of something neutral so I could draw this out as long as possible.

God, she felt so good wrapped around me. I could hear her sucking noises and it was all I could do not to blow inside of her.

Breathe, man, breathe.

I took deep breaths in through my nose, blowing them slowly through my gritted teeth, absorbing every ounce of goodness Geneva was giving me.

Suddenly, her bare teeth grazed along my skin and that was it. I exploded inside her mouth, no warning for her or for me. I bucked upright, afraid I might gag her but unable to stop myself.

Her hands wrapped under my thighs and drew me in deeper, her moans vibrating against me, causing my orgasm to rock on for what seemed like hours.

I tried to push her away, the sensations of her mouth too much for me to bear. Her movements were becoming painful, but she wouldn't relent as I continued to spill inside her. God, it felt amazing to be tucked inside her warm, delicious mouth.

Realizing she wasn't going to stop, I relaxed into the sofa, allowing her to suck and stroke me to the end.

"Fuck, Geneva." I finally breathed out when I felt her lips pull away.

"Thank you for the cake. Berk," she said with a husky, sexy tone.

My eyes opened and her face slowly came into focus. Her mouth was covered with chocolate icing and cake.

Her lips parted and her white teeth gleamed with an innocent smile. She'd been anything *but* innocent.

I yanked her body up and onto mine, devouring her mouth with a need unlike any other I'd ever experienced. I licked at the leftover icing and sucked her lips clean. God, chocolate mixed with Geneva tasted like heaven. I didn't think I would ever get my fill of this girl.

Faith is taking the first step even when you don't see the whole staircase.
- Martin Luther King, Jr.

CHAPTER 11
GENEVA

I bolted up with a start. Someone was yelling. Had it been in my dreams? My eyes darted right and left trying to figure out where I was. It was still dark outside, but the moon cast a glow inside the room through the open windows surrounding me.

"No, I'm coming back!" someone shouted.

I glanced beside me. Shit, it was Berk. He was screaming. His legs flailed within the twisted mass of sheets as if he were running in place.

"I'll be right there, I swear!" he wailed. "Daddy's coming!"

Daddy? What the fuck?

"Berk!" I shouted, shaking his huge shoulders.

"Jaime, no! Wait, I'm coming."

Jaime? Who the hell was Jaime?

"Jaime, wait! No! Jaime!" he wailed as if in physical pain.

My stomach knotted in fear. "Berk!" I yelled, wrapping my hands around his shoulders. I shook him even harder.

He flailed, violently, and sweat covered his entire body.

I feared he might fall off the small bed and take me with him.

Suddenly, his hands wrapped around my waist and yanked me

into his embrace, squeezing me so tight I thought he might break my ribs.

"Oh, God, Jaime. Thank God," he sighed.

I tried to pull out of his hold, but it was impossible with the iron grip he had around me.

"Berk!" I shouted. "Wake up!" I hit his chest, trying to loosen his hold.

Without warning, he tossed me aside and bolted straight up in bed. His eyes shot wide in what looked like fear as he frantically searched the room.

"What? Where is she?" He panted for his next breath. "What the fuck?" He raked his fingers through his damp hair.

"Berk," I pleaded. I sat up, trying to balance myself beside him. "Berk, it's me. Geneva."

He looked at me, but I didn't recognize him. He grimaced, his forehead creased with worry. Every square inch of him was marred with fear and anxiety. He reached out with shaky hands and grabbed my face, his eyes darting frantically between mine.

"Berk," I whispered, wrapping my hands around his. "You're okay, it was just a dream."

His face softened, his eyes recovering from the dark blanket that had enveloped them as his body slumped in relief. "Geneva?" My name sounded like a plea.

"Yes. It's me, Berk."

He let out a heavy sigh, but tension still sat heavy on his shoulders.

"You had a bad dream," I explained.

He nodded as if finally understanding, then cast his eyes to the bed.

I wasn't sure how to broach the subject of his nightmare but given the fact he'd titled himself as 'Daddy' *and* screamed out another woman's name, I thought it best to clarify sooner rather than later.

"What happened? You were screaming, 'Jaime, Jaime,' over and over."

His head whipped around to face me, his eyes narrowed as if I'd insulted him. This had been a horrible nightmare that had held him prisoner. I couldn't help but believe it wasn't his first. Nor his last.

"Berk," I whispered. He was obviously wounded and scared. The only thing I wanted to do was to take him in my arms and comfort him. I pushed onto my knees, reaching out to touch him.

He pulled away as if I'd hurt him.

"Berk," I called to him again, my hand rubbing lightly on his arm. "It's okay. You're here with me."

His eyes cut to mine, shrouded in darkness again. They were full of rage and fury.

Berk untangled his legs from the mess of sheets and bolted out of bed.

I watched his gloriously naked body stalk from the room. I sat in stunned silence, not sure if I should go after him or let him cool down. My mind battled internally, but in the end, I went with my gut, knowing my mythical, underwater god was hurting and needed help.

I padded down the hall in search of the man who was already coming to mean too much to me.

He was in the bathroom, his huge hands gripping the counter as his head hung low in defeat.

Walking up behind him, I leaned against his back and wrapped my arms around his trim waist.

He flinched.

I held him tighter, infusing him with all my strength, giving him the comfort I knew he needed right now. It took several seconds, but eventually his body relaxed into my embrace.

Silence was golden to Berk. I'd already learned that from our short time together. So, I gave it to him. Slowly releasing my hold around his waist, I backed away and placed my hand between his shoulder blades, rubbing in soothing circles the way my mother used to do for me after I'd had a bad dream.

It killed me not to ask questions about what he'd just experienced in his dream. Not to ask if he had a child or who this Jaime person was. Berk needed time. I got that. Better than most probably. I knew I'd stand here, all day if need be, to bring him down from whatever awful cliff he was dangling from.

"I need to take a shower, do you mind?" he finally spoke.

My eyes connected with his in the mirror.

His usually amber colored eyes were still a shade darker, his pupils dilated. He was lost, hanging precariously close to some type of free fall that could be his own demise.

His dismissal stung my pride. I pulled away and left the room, closing the door behind me to give him the space he needed.

The shower turned on and I realized I was unlikely to reach him. His dreams had taken him to a dark, remote place. Did I even want to rescue him? This was turning into something deeper, too much drama for just a vacation fuck. But then, it never really had been that for me.

Was Berk really a father? Did he have kids here on the island? Or worse yet, had he spawned on the mainland and never saw them? And who was Jaime? Was that his wife, his girlfriend? His daughter? All these were major game changers, even if what was between us was just a fling. I didn't do married guys, never had. And I didn't even want the drama of a dead-beat dad.

Instead of dwelling on the past five minutes and driving myself completely crazy, I went in search of my clothes in the living room. Shit! All I'd had on was that stupid hula outfit. I couldn't traipse back to the resort in that.

My eyes focused on the patio as I stood in the living room. The sun was barely rising. From my vantage point I could see a hint of the blue waters as the waves crashed against one another, rolling across the sand. The cool breeze floating through the open windows of Berk's house reminded me that I was still naked.

I gathered up a small throw from the back of the sofa and wrapped it tightly around my shoulders. I walked through the patio door and stood on the porch, letting the sounds of the ocean's tide calm my racing heart.

I gazed out over the beautiful tropical scene before me. This was paradise, a place anyone could fall in love with. The setting was picturesque and serene, yet I had a sense of unease, as if the bottom were about to fall out from under me.

This was way too much drama. I didn't do drama, not any more. I needed to leave before I got in too deep. As I gazed out over the beach, the realization hit me. I was already in way over my head.

Making my way back inside, I threw off the blanket and grabbed the grass skirt from the floor where I'd thrown it last night.

God, last night. It had been another magical night of seriously hot sex with Berk. He was an amazing person and worked so hard to take care of me in every way, as if I were something precious and he needed to show me.

He'd been generous with his lovemaking, and my heart ached for the misery he was going through. Should I offer him the same type of comfort?

Even though I wanted to stay, his earlier actions indicated he needed to be alone to process what had happened in his dream. I got that. I needed to leave and give him space.

I went into his bedroom to search for a top that would, at least, let me walk through the lobby of the resort without looking like an idiot. I found a small closet and pulled a T-shirt from the hanger. It had the island resort logo on the front. Tugging it over my head, I could smell Berk surrounding me, touching my skin, covering me completely.

I headed toward the bathroom to tell him good-bye. I twisted the knob but found it was locked.

He had shut me out.

I needed to leave before I turned this whole affair into something it wasn't. He didn't owe me anything. This was a vacation fuck.

Yeah, keep telling yourself that and I'm sure it will be much *easier when you leave.*

Stalking through the small house, I passed the wad of napkins that were still pooled along the wall of the dining room. I wondered if, perhaps, I should leave another note, but decided against it. I wasn't sneaking out this time. He'd asked me for space and I needed to give it to him.

I pulled the front door closed behind me and I noticed another pair of his sandals on the porch. I laughed silently at his comment last night.

You owe me.

Me making good on my debt probably wouldn't happen. The chances of seeing Berk again were slim at this point. Something had spooked him, and I couldn't help but feel I had been the trigger.

I dragged my feet along the sand, its grains cooler now in the early dawn. It rubbed between my toes as I made my way back to the resort. As the building came into view, I looked down at my clothing—a long grass skirt and an over-sized T-shirt that hung almost to my knees. I was thankful no one was on the shore to challenge my strange attire.

I cast my gaze behind me one more time, looking down the long strip of beach that separated me from Poseidon. His home wasn't even visible, but I could smell him on my shirt. Somewhere down the beach was a man who was haunted.

I passed through the lobby, mostly unnoticed due to the early morning hour. When I stood at the door to my villa, I realized I didn't have my room card. "Shit!" Now I would have to go back to the lobby and do the walk of shame. Trudging back to the main entrance, I hung my head, trying to hide my embarrassment.

"Excuse me," I called to the woman standing behind the counter with her back to me.

She turned to face me. "Yes, may I help you?"

I stood stark still. Shit, she was the girl from the luau last night.

"Oh, hello, Geneva." She smiled. "You did an amazing job last night."

"Uh," I stumbled. "Thank you. You were an amazing teacher."

She tilted her head and smiled. "Thanks." She stared at me for several moments. "May I help you?"

"I, um, yes. I seem to have locked myself out of my villa."

She peered over the counter at my outfit, one brow raised in question.

I looked down at my attire, horrified at what I was wearing. "I'm sorry about leaving with the outfit. I'll be happy to pay you for it."

"Oh, no, don't worry." She chuckled as if she knew something I didn't. "We left your dress and shoes in your room last night since you forgot them at the luau. I hope that's all right."

I flushed forty shades of red. As if she knew *exactly* what I'd done last night.

"Oh, yes, that's fine. You didn't have to do that, though."

"It was no bother." She banged on the keys of her computer, then pulled out another room card and ran it through a machine. "Here you go, you're all set." She slid the card along the marble counter.

"Thanks, um…I'm sorry, I don't know your name."

"Oh, it's Palla." She pointed to her nametag.

"That's a beautiful name."

"Thank you."

"Thanks again for the replacement card." I smiled, waving it in the air. I hoped my words sounded genuine. It was hard to tell, I was so embarrassed by my outfit.

"Please let us know if there's anything else you need."

"Will do." I pivoted on my bare feet and scurried out of the lobby, my eyes focused on the floor to avoid further scrutiny.

At my door, I swiped the new card, but the lock beeped and

turned red. "Dammit," I whispered. Swiping it again, the lock beeped another time, the flashing red light mocking me.

"Geneva," someone whispered behind me.

I jumped, startled by his deep growl. I didn't need to turn around to know who it was, but I did anyway. I wanted to see his gorgeous face one more time.

"Here," he said, taking the card from my hand and flipping it around. He slid it through the lock with ease and the light turned green. "You had it turned around wrong." He depressed the door handle and pushed it open, waving his hand in front of me.

I stared up at his honey-colored eyes, grateful to find them lighter now. Perhaps his demons had passed.

"May I come in?" he asked.

I backed into the room, holding the door open.

He strolled in, his huge form eclipsed by the massive size of my villa.

Slowly closing the door behind me, I leaned up against it, waiting and watching as he turned. The rough and tough, confident Berk of the past few days had been replaced by a man who'd been shattered at some point in his life.

His hair was still damp from his shower, or maybe from his exertions from following after me.

"What happened, Berk?" I asked quietly. If I had any sense, I wouldn't have let him into my room. But history had proven I had very little logic. Somewhere between the first time I saw Poseidon step out of the ocean and now, I'd grown to care for this beast of a man.

He remained quiet. Berk was a man of thought, not of impulsiveness like me. He planned every word that came from his mouth. Unlike me.

"Do you have children, Berk?"

His eyes cut to mine, pain etched on his face. "No," he said quietly. "Why would you ask?"

"Because you shouted out 'Daddy's coming' in your dream."

His eyes grew wide in surprise.

Had he been busted? Was he lying to me?

As if sensing my disbelief, he moved closer. "I don't have any children, Geneva."

I nodded once, assured that he was telling the truth. Berk wasn't a liar.

"Who's Jaime?" I asked.

His face washed white as his jaw clenched.

"You called out her name several times while you were freaking out in bed."

"Jaime was my wife," he confessed, his eyes rolling up to the ceiling.

"*Was* your wife? So, you're not married? Now?"

He shook his head, his long hair moving wildly around his shoulders.

My body sagged in relief.

He closed the small gap between us.

"It's no big deal, Berk. I'm divorced, too." I didn't want him to feel guilty. He must still have feelings for her if he dreamed about her, though. I never dreamed about Stan.

"I'm not divorced, Geneva," he whispered.

"But you said you weren't married." My eyes darted between his, panic washing through my veins.

"I'm not, any more."

Then it hit me like a dead fish in the face. His wife had died. That was why he'd been calling out for her in his dreams. Berk was a widower.

"She died?"

He nodded once.

"Oh my God, Berk, I'm so sorry," I whispered, covering my mouth with my hand.

He slid his fingers around my neck, drawing my face close to his. "Please stop running from me."

"What?" His request was a completely bizarre response given the fact that he just told me his wife was dead.

Before I could open my mouth to explain I *hadn't* run, his soft lips brushed against mine. My breath caught at his masculine scent from the body wash that hung in his shower. The one we'd rubbed into a deep lather all over each other last night after my wedding cake dance.

"You keep running away from me. You've left me. Twice now," he murmured against my lips, his voice barely audible.

Left him? This was just a vacation fuck for him, wasn't it?

His tongue slowly traced my lips, soft at first, then adding more pressure, trying to coax me to let him inside.

"Berk." I pulled away, about to explain, but my eyes focused on his beautiful rose-tinted lips and words escaped me.

"Please, Geneva," he begged. "I need you."

He wanted to escape the past. I recognized the look I'd worn for years after I'd nearly destroyed Hindley and my family with my selfish actions. I knew the torment associated with past regrets and how much they could cripple you if you let them.

I wanted to be Berk's escape, even if only for a few more days. I wanted him to be *my* escape, a memory to hold on to when the bad ones invaded my thoughts, like they always did.

He'd had a nightmare about his dead wife. I had nightmares about my dead mother and the people I'd harassed and wounded since her passing. We both needed to forget.

I grasped his face, pulling him closer to me. "Then take me," I whispered.

His eyes shot wide with surprise before he whisked me up in his muscular arms with ease. I was tall, so most guys couldn't swoop me up like the heroes in the romance novels did.

"Berk," I whispered in his ear as he searched my villa as if it were his first time inside.

Maybe this wasn't a regular occurrence for him. Maybe he didn't screw a new chick every week.

"Over there." I motioned with my head.

Berk whisked us both toward the farthest end of the villa, then kicked open my bedroom door. His lips curved into a delicious, predatory smile that made my insides clench with desire.

"What?" I asked.

"You're completely naked under my shirt."

I gazed down and saw that his massive shirt had actually ridden up around my waist, and my grass skirt was parted, exposing my bare lady parts. "Oh my God!" I yelled, tugging at the hem.

Berk tossed me on the bed and pinned my hands to my sides, preventing me from covering myself. His warm breath and soft lips soundly connected below my bellybutton as he released my hands and dragged the grass skirt down my hips, tossing it aside.

The early morning breeze wafted through my open-air bedroom and across my sensitive skin.

Berk slid his massive hands under my hips, cupping my ass. His tongue moved lower, making delicious circles on my hypersensitive skin.

"Berk." I squirmed under his hold, knowing exactly where he was headed.

"Hmmmm?" he buzzed against my skin.

Oh, fuck. I really wanted to talk more about his nightmare, but anytime his lips touched any part of me, all sane thought left my mind. This time was no different. He had me under his spell.

His lips and tongue skimmed lightly across my aching skin as he moved lower. He hovered over my most sensitive area, holding me captive.

"Do you know what I love?" he asked softly.

"What?" I panted.

"I love this line." His finger traced just above my finely groomed patch of hair.

My body convulsed at his touch, unaware that he'd released his hold on my ass.

"What line?" I pushed myself up on stiff arms and gazed down at his long black hair. It hung past his broad shoulders, shoulders that now had my legs spread wide.

"This line," he repeated. His fingers traced along my bare abdomen.

"My tan line?"

"Mmmm, hmmm," he buzzed on my skin as he placed light kisses along the line where my golden skin suddenly turned paler.

"Why do you love that line?" My voice quivered from the touch of his skilled fingers.

His light brown eyes rolled up to meet mine. He was seeing through to my soul.

My chest seized in pain. I didn't want anyone to see that much of me, least of all a man who was directly in front of my hoo-hah.

"Because everyone sees this." He dragged his finger along the tanned skin of my abdomen, sending goose bumps across my skin. His touch left a trail of fire that burned as he moved lower. "But right here," he stopped his forward motion, "no one gets to see this." He blew along the pale skin, and my body lit up like a rocket, my hips squirming. "No one but me," he whispered.

I shivered from his magical touch.

"Everyone on the beach gets to see *some* of you." His face surveyed my entire body as he spoke. "But only I get to see *all* of you." He smiled wickedly, pulling on my patch of hair.

My legs clenched around his shoulders, trying to relieve the throbbing between my legs.

Berk smiled up at me, his beautiful lips parted to reveal teeth that glowed against his olive skin. He enjoyed having such a sensual effect on me.

I lowered my body back down, closing my eyes and preparing for the exquisite, sensual assault I knew was coming.

"Sit up," he said.

I went up on my elbows and peered down at this god-like creature splayed between my legs.

"I want you to watch me make you come, Geneva."

Oh, fuck.

"Sit *all* the way up," Berk demanded in a tone that was more forceful than I'd ever heard him use.

Without hesitation, I sat up fully, which was totally unlike me. No one told me what to do, especially a man. But this man was different.

Berk wrapped his arms under my thighs and dragged my body so close to the edge of the bed, I thought I might fall off. Sensing my fear, he draped my thighs over his shoulders to balance me.

I latched onto his thick hair with one hand as he buried his head between my thighs, his warm tongue diving inside me. I gasped, and my eyes shot wide.

Watching Berk attack me with his mouth was hotter than anything I'd ever seen. A sharp tingle hit me directly where his tongue pushed against me. Holy fuck, this was hot. I was paralyzed by his movements, by his beauty, by his tongue. That fucking tongue was now fucking me.

My body sizzled, scorched by the flame of his skillful mouth. He gave the perfect amount of pressure that had my body taut with sexual tension. Watching him make love to me with his mouth sent me to a whole other dimension.

My head fell back as his tongue danced along me, skirting my nerve endings to the point of pain.

Suddenly he pulled away.

The cool breeze washed over my slick center as disappointment from the loss of his touch filled me. My eyes popped wide, wondering what had happened. What had caused my Poseidon to stop his ministrations? My eyes connected with his own, which were darker now, his expression one of pure lust and desire.

"I told you to watch me, Geneva."

Wait, he'd been buried between my legs, so how the hell did he know I had stopped watching?

"If you don't do what I say, I'll stop."

I heard his words but was unable to fully comprehend what he was saying. I was still deliciously high from the thorough workout his tongue had provided.

"Can you do that? Geneva?" His breath caressed my center.

I nearly came right then and there. "What?" I whispered, my mind a jumbled mess of pre-orgasmic moosh. I didn't know what he was talking about, but I knew I'd do anything, *anything* this man demanded just to have his mouth back on me.

He cocked a brow.

Unable to speak, my desire for him robbing me of my voice, I nodded once.

"Good." His lips curled into a devious smile, his sideways grin sending shivers through every part of me.

Without taking his eyes off of me, his tongue slid out from between his plump lips. It was long and hard, like his dick, and I knew he was going to fuck me with it. And I was going to let him.

More than that, I was going to watch, and that anticipation nearly pushed me over the edge before he even touched me.

CHAPTER 12

GENEVA

"I HATE TO DO THIS," I said, rolling over in my bed to face Berk. I rubbed my hand down his massive chest then slowly circled his bellybutton.

"Hate to do what? Run out on me again?" He chuckled, but I heard the anxiety in his voice.

"First, I didn't run out. You told me you needed time so I gave it to you."

He nodded once, grabbing my hand and bringing it to his mouth for a light kiss.

"Plus, running out would be pretty hard to do now, considering this is *my* villa."

He flipped me onto my back, his body hovering over me like a military aircraft about to attack. His massive dick skated across my over-sensitized core.

This guy had just macked my muff—hard—sending my body into outer space with the intense orgasm brought on with just his mouth. Then, minutes afterward, he'd rendered me speechless again with another round of mind-numbing, earth-shattering sex, so good, my body was still tingling. How was it possible for him to want more?

I skimmed my fingers over his strong jaw now littered with early morning stubble, digging my hands into his thick, black hair. I loved his hair. But it was his face, with its strong bone structure, hinting at his island heritage, that I couldn't get enough of.

"Kiss me," I whispered.

Without a moment's hesitation, he lowered himself and brushed my lips with his in the sweetest, most loving caress I'd ever experienced.

This was no longer just a vacation fuck, for either one of us, and that realization scared the shit out of me. I was falling for this guy. But he lived thousands of miles away and had a deceased wife, which meant he had issues out the ass. Our pseudo-relationship was a no-go. Besides, my stay on *Fantasy Island* was slowly coming to an end.

"What's wrong?" he asked so sweetly, his face wrinkled with confusion and concern.

"I don't have much time left here on the island," I sighed. Better to get this shit out in the open and decide where we were going from here.

He rolled off, lying beside me. I missed his warmth when it disappeared, much like I would our time together.

"How much longer are you here?" He asked the question as if it had never occurred to him that I wouldn't stay here for the rest of my life.

"Dana, my friend who just got married," I explained, "she and her husband, Peter, leave this morning for a short honeymoon. The rest of us are watching their three children while they're gone."

"So, how much longer will you be here?" he asked again, this time more firmly.

"They'll be gone for a couple of days, then we all leave the day after they get back." I was purposely vague about my dates.

"You all have to leave together?" There was optimism in his voice.

I lay quietly, unsure how to respond. Part of me wanted to stay, use this beautiful island as an escape. "I have a job I have to get back to, Berk."

His eyes darted around the room as if searching for something to make his exit easier. If I were being honest, I'd admit this was for the best, though. I'd be leaving in a few days anyway, so why not end this now.

"Yeah, I uh...need to get going." He stumbled over his words as he threw back the covers, then swung his legs over the bed.

"Okay," I squeaked out.

"I'll call you later. Maybe we can do something this evening." His expression told a different story. He was shutting me out again.

I knew, in my heart, he wouldn't call me, and something deep inside me ached. No, it broke, like really broke, hard.

So much for a vacation fuck.

How could this, whatever it was between Berk and me, have turned into something more, much more, in such a short amount of time?

Berk was spooked—hell, we both were. But it was better this way. I needed to separate now and not become more involved than I already had.

Before I could bat an eye, he was dressed and heading out of my bedroom.

I scooped up the top sheet and wrapped it around my body, following him to the living room. "Yeah, maybe later," I answered quietly.

He gazed over his shoulder at me for a moment, then opened the door and gracefully walked away.

I trudged back into the bedroom and fell onto the mattress, curling up on the pillow where his head had rested.

Yeah, this was for the best.

I rolled over and tucked the pillow close to my body. Drawing in a deep breath, I was assaulted by his scent. If this was for the best, then why did I feel so bad?

CHAPTER 13
GENEVA

I REALLY WASN'T surprised when I didn't hear from Berk for the rest of the day. Walking along the beach after dinner, I still couldn't help but search for the mythical god whose face flashed in my mind.

I sat in my villa all alone that evening, listening to the waves as they crashed into the cliffs below. My breathing was labored as my thoughts of a darker time pushed their way to the forefront of my mind. They were memories I wanted to forget. Memories that, just like Berk, sometimes woke me up at night, leaving me a terrified mess.

No matter how hard I tried, the memories grabbed hold and dragged me back in time…

~

The waif of a woman lying in her bed had my seven-year-old body frozen. It was my mother. No one had to tell me she was dying. I could see her wasting away before my eyes.

"Hi, Gen," she whispered in a raspy voice, each syllable she uttered labored and exhausting. Her thick blonde hair that matched my own had long since fallen out, replaced by stringy, dull wisps that she refused to cover with a wig. Instead, she had a bright blue scarf artfully twisted around her head, the ends flowing over her shoulder.

"Hi, Mommy." I tried to smile, but the truth was, I was afraid of her, afraid that if I touched her, her disease might spread to me. Death might capture me, too.

It was a silly thought, but something that worried a kid. No one had bothered to explain the real facts about how breast cancer worked, that it wasn't contagious.

My father, bless his heart, had been in complete denial. The process of my mother's inevitable death had been overwhelming for him. I longed for information, yet he had been unwilling, or unable to explain anything to me.

"Come lay with me, Genny girl." My mother patted the bed.

I hesitated.

"It's all right, baby, you won't hurt me."

It wasn't *her* that my infantile mind was worried about. In the end, my desire to be close to her won out over the fear—*what if*—in my mind. I crawled into my mother's lap and cuddled up close to her.

"Mommy loves you *so* much. You know that, right, Gen?"

All I could do was nod. The words were choked in my throat as I held back tears.

"And you're such a sweet girl, working hard to help Daddy take care of me."

I'd tried to numb myself to the pain, but hearing my mother's words of love and affirmation was causing me to lose it. I fought back the sobs, to shield her from the pain I knew she would experience if she recognized the agony I was in. Pain, which would upset her and rob her of the precious energy she had so very little of, already.

"It's okay to cry, sweetie, you know that?" She rubbed my back to soothe me, even in the midst of her *own* pain and suffering. That was what mothers did. "Sometimes Mommy cries, too."

I bolted up, afraid I'd caused her more heartache. "You can't cry, Mommy." My statement was a plea, begging her to conserve her energy while we waited for a cure I was convinced would come at any moment.

Every night, I knelt beside my bed, my own knees going numb as I begged God not to take my mother away from me. I was only seven, for Christ's sake. I needed her in my life—for the *rest* of my life.

"Crying is good for you, Geneva," she spoke softly. "It wipes away all the bad thoughts in your head and makes room for the good ones."

I didn't believe her. She was lying, saying things that moms *had* to say. If I cried, it would make her cry. And if she cried, she'd die sooner. In that moment, I vowed never to cry in front of her again.

With the memories of my mother fading, I fell back against the couch in my villa and looked out onto the patio. My mother would have loved Hawaii. She always loved quiet, peaceful places.

In her last few days of life, I had tried to give that to her— bringing her flowers and pictures of the ocean, singing her favorite songs while her body lay unconscious. I had truly believed if I loved her enough and brought her the things she enjoyed most in life, she'd wake up and never leave me.

In the end, it hadn't worked. No matter what I had done as a child, I hadn't been able to save the one person in this world who loved me more than her own life. My efforts had been in vain, and something inside me had changed, even at seven years old.

I calloused my own personality, refusing to feel any pain, knowing I'd never work that hard to save another person ever again. Why should I? They would only die in the end, and my hopes would be in vain. God was not a fan of granting wishes to a seven-year-old girl.

When I lost my mother, a part of me died, too—my soul, the person I once was, the *real* Geneva. Even now, I wondered where that Genny girl had gone, that girl my mother loved so much but still left all alone to fend for herself over the years. Did that old version of Gen even exist after all these years?

No. She didn't.

That Gen had died the same fateful day as my mother, leaving behind a broken girl who tried to hurt others before they ever had a chance to hurt her.

I curled up into a ball on the couch, pushing away the pain, not surprised to feel the warm tears rolling down my face. As much as I had willed myself never to cry again after my mother's death, I still did sometimes.

As I slowly drifted off to sleep, I thought of Berk and wondered what he was doing tonight.

My heart ached for the suffering he'd endured, losing his wife. Maybe like me, he was still trying to escape the ghosts that haunted him.

Even though he'd left abruptly, I understood why, but I still missed him. Deep inside, I wished he were here with me tonight. I treasured what short time we'd had together, but I reminded myself it was just that, a fleeting moment. Regardless of our circumstances, I still wished him well and hoped that tonight, wherever he was, peace would fill his dreams.

CHAPTER 14

GENEVA

"This seat taken, gorgeous?"

I pushed back my shades and sat up in my lounger by the pool, gazing up at the hottie standing above me. His firm body cast a shadow over me. I peered over at the seat beside me and pulled it close, saddling it to mine.

"Only by you, handsome." I winked.

Leif plopped down beside me, handing me some fruity cocktail as he straddled his chair. "I bet you say that to all the gay guys." He laughed.

"Only the hot ones." I giggled. Leif definitely qualified as a hottie. "Where have you been? I haven't seen you around the resort the past few days."

He waggled his brows.

"Oh, nice." I extended my fist and he bumped it with his own. "Is he here?" My gaze darted around the pool.

"Nope, he left this morning."

"So, you sent him packing." I took a sip of the fruity mixed drink.

"Hey," he nudged my shoulder, "don't judge. I hear you're knocking boots with some island local."

My face washed red.

"Well, there's something you don't see every day." Leif reared back in his lounger and propped his feet over mine.

"What?" I scooted my feet over, making room for him.

"Geneva Barton blushing."

"F off, dill hole."

"F?" He laughed. "What's up with the censorship?"

I motioned toward the pool with my head, pointing to where my stepmother was bouncing Lilly up and down in a round floaty. "We're taking care of the kids. Dana and Peter are still gone."

"Okay. Well, it sounds like you're doing a much better job filtering your mouth than Buttercup." He smiled, a dazzling expression that I was sure made every gay guy, and straight girl, within twenty yards drop their underwear.

"Yes, *Buttercup* is having a hard time taming her tongue," I said.

I smiled at Leif's term of endearment for Dana. She loved the flower and had several tattoos on her body of the flower.

"Yeah, but I bet Peter is enjoying taming that tongue of hers."

Leif and I bellowed with laughter. I could only imagine what Dana and Peter were doing on their mini-honeymoon.

"Uh oh," Leif said, sliding his shades down his nose, staring across the pool.

"What?" I sat up, frantically searching the pool, afraid something had happened to Lilly or Caroline.

"Mr. Hotty Lifeguard does *not* seem pleased with me."

I followed Leif's gaze, surprised to see Berk's contorted face staring right at us. Oh, shit!

Another man dressed in the same lifeguard attire as Berk, and just as big, stood beside him, whispering in his ear. Berk's eyes never left me, his glare menacing.

"Looks like you have two admirers fighting over you." Leif laughed.

"Whatever." I reached under my lounger and grabbed my beach bag, readying myself for a hasty exit. "Will you keep an eye on my mom and Lilly?" I stood and stuffed my belongings into my bag.

"Oh, shit, here he comes," Leif whispered.

"What?" Panic raced through me as I frantically searched for an exit. I had been silly to think I wouldn't see Berk again. He worked at the frigging resort for goodness' sake.

"What's up?" Leif sat up, staring at me. "Is everything okay?"

"It's fine." I didn't want to explain my "relationship" with Berk to any of my family or friends. "I'll call you later and we can have dinner."

He nodded, seemingly appeased by my answer.

I darted around his lounger, practically running, but then tripped over my shoe.

"Whoa." Berk's deep voice rumbled close to my ear as his hand latched around my elbow, keeping me upright.

His touch paralyzed me. I was ensnared by his very presence. That was what a mythical god like Poseidon would do to mere mortals like me.

"Are you all right?" Berk asked as he drew me close.

I had to break free from his grip. I couldn't chance being this close to him. Physically or emotionally.

"Geneva?"

I didn't want to look at him. I knew his eyes would be just as powerful as his touch. Having no ounce of will power in my body, I peeked over my shades and dared to look at him.

Mistake.

His amber eyes pierced through me. His face was riddled with confusion, as if he were trying to figure me out, like I was a puzzle to be solved.

"Yes?" I asked, trying to keep my voice steady.

"I was just wondering…" he stammered, looking over his shoulder at Leif, who was gawking.

"Yes?" I finally answered.

"Can we talk?"

"I thought that's what you were doing now."

"I mean somewhere private," he said.

"I don't think that's a good idea, Berk."

"Why?" He frowned.

"We said our good-byes earlier in my room," I answered. "Let's just leave it at that and part ways now."

He surveyed me from head to toe.

I gazed down and noticed I hadn't put on my cover-up. I was still clad in my hot pink and black, polka dotted bikini.

"I was wondering if you had plans this evening?" His voice was deep and full of desire.

I stared at him in disbelief. "Berk," I leaned in closer, "I think it's better that we break this off before..." I stumbled with my words, not knowing what to say next.

"I'm sorry about ..." Now he was fumbling, too. We were two bumbling idiots.

I laughed.

"What?" He cocked his head.

"You and I are a mess." I shook my head, still laughing.

"Yeah, we kind of are." He smiled.

My bikini nearly disintegrated. Fuck.

"Look, you said you still had a few more days here in Kauai, right?"

Where was he going with this? I tilted my head, puzzled.

"I'll pick you up at six." His words were matter-of-fact.

"That's a statement, Berk, not a request." I narrowed my eyes in disapproval.

"Yes, it is." He crossed his arms over his massive chest, just daring me to protest. Every muscle in his uncovered torso flexed at will.

Fuck me, this dude was hot.

"I'm free!" Leif yelled from his vantage point nearby.

Berk turned to look at his would-be admirer.

I gave Leif the bird from behind Berk's back and mouthed,

"Fuck off."

Leif held up his hands in surrender, laughing. "Fine. Have him all to yourself."

Berk turned back to face me. "Is he with you?"

"Unfortunately, yes."

"And, I'm assuming he's gay?"

I nodded.

"Oh, thank God." Berk slumped in relief, his hands falling to his sides.

"Why?"

"I thought you had hooked up with a new guy already."

"You seriously think I'm that slutty?" I wasn't sure if I should be offended or flattered.

"No, it's just..." he scrambled for his next words.

"Just what?" I cocked a brow, folding my arms across my chest now.

"Well, the other day, our first night together, you said you weren't a slut, *any more*."

It was the truth. I had said I was a slut. Unfolding my arms, I slid my hand over Berk's strong jaw. "That was a long time ago, Berk. I'm not the same girl any more."

His hand slid over mine as he leaned into my touch. "Then come with me tonight. I'll pick you up at six?"

This time, it was a request.

"Okay." I grinned.

He pulled my hand from his face and kissed my palm, his lips lingering on my heated skin.

I stared at his chiseled abs and arms, my eyes glassy with desire.

Leaning toward me, he brushed his cheek against mine. His mouth gently caressed my ear, sending a shiver down my spine. "Pack a bag," he whispered.

And just like that, he was gone, leaving me with soaked bikini bottoms, nipples harder than the coral reefs offshore, and three pairs of eyes and three gaping mouths, all staring at me in bewilderment —Leif, Caroline, *and* Lilly.

My body washed crimson with an unusual display of embarrassment. I had a lot of explaining to do, but it wouldn't be here, and it wouldn't be now.

"I'll call you later," I said to no one in particular as I tossed my bag over my shoulder, heading in the exact opposite direction of Berk. I had a lot of explaining to do, especially to myself.

This is just a vacation fuck. This is just a vacation fuck.

Nope, repeating it to myself still didn't make me believe it.

All I could do now was hold on and enjoy the short time I had left with my Poseidon. Skipping away from the pool, a smile broke out on my face. Yep, I was in deep. And I was screwed.

~

Guilt is perhaps the most painful companion of death.
- Coco Chanel

~

CHAPTER 15

BERK

"WHAT THE FUCK are you doing, dude?" Rhen asked as I hefted my surfboard down the beach. I couldn't answer him because I didn't know what the fuck I was doing. At all.

Geneva was supposed to be a one-night fling, maybe two tops. But I couldn't get her out of my head—or my heart—and the thought scared the shit out of me. It gripped my ball sack and twisted my nuts in a vise until I almost cried. I was so spooked by my feelings that I had to run away from her yesterday morning for fear of telling her how I really felt.

"Okie said he saw you at the pool, flirting with some married chick and her kids. Is that true?"

"Married chick?" I laughed. "It's her very gay friend, not her husband, you idiot."

"Yeah, well, he said you're gonna be the idiot if Tutu finds out you're fucking around with some married chick from the resort."

"She's not fucking married."

"But you're not denying you're screwing around with her."

I should deny it, but the truth was, Rhen and I were brothers. He knew me better than anyone. He understood the demons that still haunted me.

"Who is she then?" he asked.

"You remember that chick from the luau?"

"Holy shit, that chick who flipped you off on stage, with not one, but *two* birds? I love this girl already."

I shook my head. It was a mistake to reveal so much to my brother. He had a mouth bigger than the Grand Canyon.

"So, you like her, huh, dude?"

My feet abruptly stopped, unable to take another step as I looked out over the beautiful Pacific Ocean. The waves were high today. We'd be able to get in some good rides before our shift at the resort.

"It's okay," Rhen said. "You know you don't have to live in misery the rest of your life just because you lost them."

"Stop," I demanded, refusing to look at him, fearful of what he would see inside me.

"Does she know? About Jaime and Alana?"

I cringed at the sound of their names. I'd worked hard in my life never to say them out loud again, never to think about them. If I pushed them to the back of my mind, then it was like their deaths didn't matter, like I wasn't the one responsible.

Drawing in a deep breath, knowing I'd never escape Rhen's scrutiny, I blew it out. Rhen was the *only* person I ever confided in, but even he didn't know the depths of my despair. Luckily for both of us, he never pushed me. I hoped this would be one of those times.

"I'm assuming your silence means she does know. I can't believe you told her, man. You *never* talk about them."

He was right. My family on the island knew better than to ask me about my wife and daughter. They understood I had escaped to my native roots to forget about their tragic deaths almost three years ago. Where the media had been relentless in their questioning of the "accident," my family had remained quiet, letting me lick my wounds. Wounds that were still gaping and infected three years later.

"I didn't have a choice. I had a nightmare and screamed out Jaime's name," I said.

"Holy shit, man. What did she say?"

"Of course, she was concerned, more concerned about me. She tried to calm me down, make sure I was okay."

"What did you say?"

"You sound like a teenager playing the telephone game." I tried to lighten the mood.

"What was this nightmare about?" Rhen completely ignored my comment.

Only Rhen knew about my reoccurring nightmares. And a temptress blonde who had me feeling things I never thought I would again. The guilt from my past had been unbearable. That was why I'd run away from Geneva yesterday morning. She was getting close enough to see the real me, the monster that lived inside.

As much as I knew how short-lived our torrid affair was, I still found it impossible to stay away from her. She was making me feel good, and I wasn't sure if I liked that or not. But even I was smart enough to know that once she found out the truth, the real truth about what had happened to my family, she'd bolt.

"I screamed out something about 'Daddy will save you.' While I was still half asleep, I grabbed her, thinking she was fucking Jaime. I latched on to her so hard I'm pretty sure I bruised her."

"Oh, fuck." Rhen shook his head. He knew I hadn't been with anyone since Jaime's and Alana's deaths.

A genuine smile broke out on my face as I looked out over the ocean that Alana loved so much. She'd been named after my sister, who'd died shortly after her birth.

When Jaime and I found out we were expecting a girl, it had been her suggestion that we name our daughter, Alana, after my sister. I'd fallen in love with the idea almost as quickly as I'd fallen in love with Jaime, when I'd first seen her skiing the slopes in Aspen during the X Games, almost ten years ago.

"So, you told her about both of them, Jaime *and* Alana?" Rhen asked.

"No, I didn't tell her about Alana."

"But you said you screamed out 'Daddy', didn't you?"

"Yeah, but I just brushed it aside. She asked me if I had any children, but I told her no."

Rhen raised his eyebrows in suspicion.

"What? It's the truth."

He nodded once, but his narrowed eyes indicated he wasn't happy with my omission.

"Whatever, man," I said. "She's only here for a few more days, so it doesn't matter anyway, right?"

"Doesn't matter?" He laughed. "You haven't talked about Jaime and Alana in almost three years, Berk."

My heart seized with pain at his glossing over of the duration of my agony. Two years, ten months and four days to be exact.

"Oh my God, please tell me you're not still counting the exact days, are you?" Rhen shook his head and sighed.

"Fuck you, Rhen!" I yelled. "You try losing your whole goddamn world and see if it's not a date that's forever branded into your heart with a fucking, fiery, red-hot iron of steel, you asshole."

Rhen didn't deserve my anger. He'd been my rock throughout my ordeal. But he often got the brunt of my emotional outbursts, the few I allowed myself.

No one understood. No one ever would. Even though I felt like if anyone could, it would be Geneva. I sensed she'd have empathy if I opened up. That would *never* happen, though. She'd be gone in a few days and I'd be damned if I'd expose that much of my heart to her. I'd never given *anyone* as much of me as Jaime and Alana had, ever. And I never would again.

My spirit had been shattered, my heart split in two when they died. I would never find anyone to put the pieces of my fractured spirit back together in a way that would make me feel alive again.

"Let's surf," I said, tossing my board into the water and sliding on top. I paddled out into the deep blue sea as fast as I could, my arms burning with exertion. Not even the roar of the sea was enough to silence the demons that haunted me.

CHAPTER 16

BERK

A NERVOUS TENSION twisted my stomach when my shift ended at the resort as I anticipated my evening with Geneva.

She was making me feel again. Even though it scared the shit out of me, there was a part of me that loved it. For the first time in a long time, I felt alive. She'd be gone soon, though, so I had to make the most of the time we had left.

Lifting my hand to the door of her room, I drew in a deep, steadying breath before finally tapping it a few times. I waited. And waited. Shit.

As she opened the door my pulse raced.

She stood in the doorway posed like a runway model. The sun behind her cast a glow, outlining her hourglass figure like a celestial being.

I tilted my head to offset the glare of the sun and focused on her face. Her big blue eyes shone as bright as the sun, her full lips curved in a slight smile, showcasing her perfect teeth. But it was the aura surrounding her, her warmth that made her stunning. The few days I had left would have to be enough, but everything inside told me it wouldn't be.

"Are you ready?" I asked.

Her nose wrinkled as her lips tightened into a skeptical frown.

The look of trepidation on her face made me smile. I liked being in control of her future.

"I wasn't sure what to wear," she finally answered, lowering her head to peruse her body. She was wearing a form fitting tank top that accentuated the perfect rise of her breasts and a sarong type wrap. The slit on one side revealed the long, lean leg that I remembered wrapping around me tightly many times during the last few days.

My dick swelled at the sight of her—an annoying reaction that was becoming a habit anytime I was in her presence.

"You look beautiful." I smiled.

Her head jerked up, her eyes locked on mine in surprise, as if she wasn't sure if I were telling the truth.

"Really, Geneva," I answered her silent question. "Do you have your bag?"

"Over there." She nodded toward a guest chair in the living area.

I stood patiently, waiting for her to let me inside, but she seemed cautious. Shit, this was it. She was going to say no and I couldn't let that happen. Without wasting another second debating my next move, I slid my arm under hers while my other hand sunk into the thick hair at the nape of her neck, pulling her mouth toward mine. Just before our lips connected, I gave her what I knew she needed.

"I'm sorry about shutting you out," I said. "And I'm really sorry that I stayed away. Will you forgive me and let me show you my island tonight?"

Her lips turned downward in a slight frown. For a moment, I thought she was going to kick me out, but fuck that. I had her in a strong hold, and she wasn't going anywhere this time.

Her slender arms wrapped around my neck as her fingers dug into my hair, tugging slightly. It was her way of punishing me—making me wait, and I loved it.

Needing no further validation, I lowered my head and brushed my lips against hers. I needed to keep this kiss tame if we were going to leave her room in time for what I had planned. I broke our embrace quickly.

I was surprised to see her eyes still closed, her lips curved in a rueful smile.

Twitching in my midsection commenced—as usual. I moved past her, knowing if we didn't leave soon, we never would. Tonight was special to me and, since her time on the island was short-lived, I didn't want to waste it in her villa.

Scooping up her bag, I jostled the heavy tote on my shoulder and gave her a questioning glance.

"I wasn't sure what to pack," she said cautiously. She didn't trust me. She wouldn't unless I made things right.

That was okay. I'd been a shit for shutting her out and not talking to her after my nightmare. I had needed time to process it all, and I would have never been able to do that in her presence. Geneva was responsible for making me feel again. I had to figure out what all those emotions were before I could share them with her.

"As long as you have a bathing suit, you'll be fine." I smiled. "Well, actually, you don't even need that." I winked.

She raised her brow in apprehension, obviously knowing she'd need a little more clothing.

I tugged on the strap of her bag. "Feels like you've got a lot more. Did you bring a pair of shorts and a shirt? I've got towels."

She nodded quietly, and the gleam in her eyes spoke of things to come. She still wanted me, which meant I had a second chance.

"No hair dryer or girlie crap, though, right?" I asked.

Her eyes went wide and a sheepish expression washed across her face. She looked like she'd been caught with pornographic material. Slowly, she unzipped her bag that still hung loosely on my shoulder. She carefully removed a massive blow dryer, curling iron, and some apparatus that looked like a painful torturing device.

I chuckled.

"What?" Her eyes narrowed in warning. "A girl can't exist without hair care products."

"Your hair is beautiful, Geneva." I smiled, reaching out to run my fingers through her silken mane.

She shuddered.

I'd affected her. I hadn't affected anyone in a long time.

"No makeup?" she asked.

I shook my head. "No, Geneva. The only thing I need is you." My statement caught us both by surprise.

She stiffened at my comment.

"I just need you, not all the other stuff that you *think* turns you into you."

The look of confusion on her face told me she wasn't used to words of affection or adoration. It was a surprise to me, and I wondered why she was so uncomfortable.

She reached into her bag, removing a few more items. Holding up a pair of shorts and a top, a toothbrush, paste, and a hairbrush, she turned toward me. Her golden brows raised in a way that I'd already learned how to read. This was sarcastic Geneva—a side of her that I found not only endearing, but necessary for my own survival.

"Is this enough?" She cocked her head questioningly.

I nodded.

"Well, I don't need this big ole thing then." She slid the bag from my shoulder and stuffed her items into a small beach bag sitting by the door. She straightened, holding her small tote in front of me. "All packed." She smirked with a devilish twinkle in her eyes.

She was going for sarcasm with her comment, but she missed the mark. She actually looked hot as hell.

"Let's go then." I grabbed her hand and pulled her behind me, leading her through the doorway. "Do you have your key?"

Peering over my shoulder, I saw her draw the plastic card from behind her back, waving it in her hand.

"I'll take that." I reached out and took the card from her grasp, stuffing it in my pocket.

She stared at me, eyes wide.

"You're not leaving me again, Geneva." I smiled, letting the door close and tugging on her hand, heading for the exit.

"You ran out on *me*, Berk." Her tone was serious. This was not good.

I stopped in the hallway and turned to face her. "Not tonight. Neither one of us will run, okay?"

She smiled. "I can just get another key card," she threatened.

"No, you can't."

"I'll go to the front desk. They've already given me one replacement key."

"They've already been notified not to give you another key without ID. Since I know for a fact, your ID is *inside*, you're mine for the next twenty-four hours."

"Twenty-four hours!" she shrieked. "But, no one knows where I am, they'll be worried."

"They know." I ducked my head to hide my smirk. I'd already talked to her mom this afternoon, reassuring her that Geneva would be fine if she came with me. I wasn't a serial killer. I only wanted to take her on a camping trip on the other side of the island. Show her the real beauty of my native homeland.

Surprisingly, her mother thought it was a wonderful idea and had sent me on my way, even giving me tips on how to calm Geneva when she freaked out, like now. Ignoring Geneva was the best thing to do, according to her mom.

"Berk," she pleaded, yanking on her hand to stop us.

I just laughed out loud, knowing it was in vain.

When she planted her feet, I nearly yanked her arm out of its socket. Turning to face her, my lips twisted in mock annoyance. "I'll pick you up and carry you if I have to, Geneva, but either way, you're coming with me. And neither one of us is running away. Not this time."

Her mouth fell open, and her brows raised high.

Knowing I couldn't force her, I stepped back from my domineering stance. "After you." I extended my hand down the corridor that led to the back exit.

She walked past me, surveying me from head to toe, her eyes narrowed in reprimand. A small smirk touched her lips, though. She wanted to come.

I reached out and swatted her delicious ass, the sound echoing through the interior hall behind us.

She twirled around and pointed her finger at me. "Watch it, Berk, or I won't go." Her smile was in stark contrast to her words.

I rushed her, bending down, then scooping her around the hips and throwing her over my shoulder in a fireman's hold.

"Berk!" she screamed, swatting at my ass as I sauntered through the exit. Her cries slowly turned into giggles.

Her mom had been right. Not only did Geneva need this little escape into my piece of heaven, she wanted it.

CHAPTER 17

BERK

"OH MY GOD, Berk, this is amazing." Geneva's mouth gaped. Her awe-struck expression was the only assurance I needed to know my semi-kidnapping of her had been the right thing to do.

I gazed out over the beach as small waves crashed into the shore. The lush, jungle foliage we'd meandered through gave us a sense of the tropical paradise surrounding us. Flowers of varying shades, sizes, and fragrances flourished here. This land truly was heaven on earth.

I'd taken Geneva to the north shore of Kauai, mainly because of its seclusion, but also because of the smaller waves here. I wanted her out on my board, and I knew she'd be intimidated by the massive waves along the coastline of my house.

She was captivated as she peered up and down the beach as if it were her first time on a tropical island. "Is this land part of the resort?"

"No, this is public property."

"Where is everyone? It's totally deserted." She stood near the water's edge, her skirt wafting in the air with each breath of wind as her golden hair swirled around her face. She turned to face me and pulled back her hair, revealing flawless skin and blue eyes—and a smile that would stop a tanker ship, even in the dead of night. She was gorgeous, and I knew it came from the inside.

A tightness grasped my chest.

In the glow of the setting sun, I sensed the shadows that lurked deep inside her. Geneva Barton had her own demons. Maybe that was what drew me to her.

"Berk," she called, bringing me out of my turbulent thoughts.

"I guess everyone's at work." I smiled. Locals never frequented this area of the island because the waves were too small for surfing, and today I was grateful. That was what I'd been counting on. I wanted one night of seclusion with Geneva, praying that, together, we could both forget about our pasts and just live in the moment. No distractions. No worries. No reminders.

"What are we doing here?" Her voice was apprehensive, as if she just realized she might have escaped into a remote area with a man she didn't know at all.

I had to assure her that she was safe.

Dropping our bags on the sand, I stalked toward her, taking her hand in mine and leading her out into the water until it brushed over our feet. The warm tide washed over us both bringing me a sense of calm.

"I just thought we could use a break," I finally answered. "From everything." Cutting my gaze toward her, I was surprised to see her eyes closed and her face lifted toward the sky. I watched as her beautiful breasts lifted with a deep inhale, holding it in tight before blowing it through her soft, plump lips.

"Okay," she whispered. Her eyes fluttered open and cut to mine. Her face was glowing in the evening light.

Judging from the sun's position in the sky, I knew I needed to ready our camp. I led her back to the edge of the tropical forest, squatting down near our bags.

"Where are we spending the night?" She searched up and down the beach.

I kept my attention on the task at hand, mainly because I feared her response. "Here," I answered quietly.

"What!" she shouted.

No surprise.

"As in here, on the beach?" she shrieked.

I ventured a gaze, my heart seizing with apprehension.

Her dainty finger pointed to the sand below her feet. "As in *right* here." Her shrill voice told me everything I feared. She was not happy with our accommodations.

She'd get over it, eventually. Ignoring her was probably my best chance at survival.

"We need to hurry up before the sun sets. If you help me, it will go faster."

She surprised me by staying quiet and reaching over to sort out the contents of our tent. "I'm not really a camping kind of girl," she mumbled.

"You'll be fine. It's amazing out here at night."

She gazed over at me. The smile on her face said it all. She would stay.

Fifteen minutes later, with our tent secure, Geneva stepped back and admired her work.

"Not bad," she said, placing her fisted hands on her hips in approval.

"I'm going to go grab the firewood from the truck."

"I can start a fire ring, I guess." She was trying.

I gave her a small smile and brushed her cheek with the back of my hand. "Sounds good."

Carrying the wood back from the truck, I was surprised to find that she'd actually made a very sturdy ring with rocks from the shore. I tossed the wood inside and stacked the logs, then set it ablaze.

The sun was deep on the horizon now. The kaleidoscope of purples, magentas, and deep oranges captured my attention and left me in awe, as it always did.

This was a scene I would never tire of and was one of the reasons I'd stayed in Kauai as long as I had. It was the closest place in the world to heaven, a way for me to be nearer to Jaime and Alana, more than anywhere else on earth.

"What's wrong?" Geneva's voice broke my trance.

I was grateful for her intrusion. I only wanted to think about the here and now, about the woman sitting next to me, who had me thinking of a future again for the first time in years.

"Oh, nothing. Just enjoying the view."

"It's breathtaking," she sighed, her eyes roaming over the horizon, lost in the colors of the setting sun.

My eyes drank in her alluring form. "Are you hungry?"

"A little."

"I brought some stuff to grill on the fire."

"Really?" She sounded surprised.

"Of course." I pulled the small skewers of chicken and vegetables that I'd made earlier out of the cooler and set them on the wire rack inside the fire ring. "These will take a while. Do you want to go for a swim?"

"Should I change in the tent?" Her timid tone had me smiling.

Her reaction to my question seemed so out of character for the confident girl I'd spent the last few days with.

I raised my brow. "Seriously?" I laughed.

She clutched her suit to her chest as if I were about to take it away. "What?" Her brows pinched together as she tightened her lips.

"Not only have I *seen* every square inch of your body, I've caressed it, kissed it, and I'm pretty sure licked it."

She gazed down at her hands, which were fumbling with the straps of her bikini, her face flushing crimson as small giggles erupted from deep within her. Her timidity seemed so out of character for the bold, brave Geneva I knew.

"I know, but still." She shrugged, tilting her head.

"Fine." I yanked off my shirt and walked toward the water. "I won't look," I called over my shoulder. "I promise." As much as I wanted to peek behind me for one glance at her naked body, I knew she'd probably pummel me if I did.

Instead, I stalked out into the ocean. As the waves beat against me, I tried to stop the memories of my wife and daughter that threatened to flood my mind and push their way into the here and now. I stood in place, letting the water wash over me. I needed cleansing, from the inside out.

"Hey," Geneva whispered from behind. Her arms wrapped around my waist. It was the first physical contact we'd made since I had flipped her over my shoulder and placed her in my truck.

"Hey, yourself. That was fast." I smiled.

She rested her cheek on my back as we moved with the water. "Not much to put on." She laughed.

I gazed over my shoulder at her.

Her eyes were wide and staring up at me, a sweet smile touching her mouth.

Covering her hands with mine as if they would save me, I walked us deeper into the ocean.

"Mmmm," she buzzed against my back.

My erection came to life, despite the coolness of the water.

"The water feels amazing," she purred, wiggling her hips against my back. "And so do you." Her hands pulled away from mine as she rubbed circles across my chest with her fingers, moving up toward my shoulders.

Oh, shit. My dick was hardening at lightning speed. My lids slowly closed as I balanced us against the drifting tide of the ocean. Our bodies moved in unison, an erotic dance in the water. I was lost in her.

Her soft words and kind actions indicated that, perhaps, she'd forgotten about the shitty way I'd left her yesterday, dismissing the fact that I'd not contacted her at all. I couldn't ignore it, though. I needed to say something to clear the air.

Opening my eyes, I studied the sky. The sun was escaping into the horizon, much like my time with Geneva. "I'm sorry about yesterday," I finally spoke. The silence between us was deafening, maddening. I had no idea what she was thinking.

"Why did you run?" Her voice was barely audible against the pounding of the waves.

What could I tell her? The truth? That I was beginning to feel things with her that I hadn't in a very long time, and it scared the ever-loving shit out of me? No, I couldn't tell her that.

Her soft hands fell from my body, and instantly I felt the loss.

"Was it about your wife?"

Shit! I didn't want images of Jaime and Alana in my head right now. I wanted to forget, and Geneva had finally made that possible.

Instead of answering, I turned around in the water, my hands sliding against her cheeks to secure her as I studied her face.

Her beautiful blue eyes glowed in the flickering light of the setting sun.

My heart seized with pain. Instead of answering, I lowered my head, keeping my eyes open to gauge her response. She made no move toward me, but she didn't pull away either, so I pushed on.

When our lips finally touched, something inside me sparked. It felt like the growl of an engine roaring back to life after years of sitting idle.

Drawing her into my body, trying to sear us together to kidnap these emotions inside me, I slid one hand behind her neck, securing her lips to mine. My other hand brushed gently against her breast, skimming the skin on her taut abdomen before slipping around her waist, pulling her between my parted legs to stabilize us.

The waves were small but still held the potential for knocking us down.

She wasn't fighting me, but she wasn't participating either.

Not wanting to force her to do anything against her will, I slowly eased my grip, realizing I may have fucked this up by ignoring her completely yesterday. I had to lighten the mood.

Without another thought, I gripped her, one arm around the

waist, the other under her knees. I scooped her up above the water, my eyes silently communicating my threat. I was going to dunk her.

"You wouldn't." She challenged me, her words a statement, a warning, not a question.

Staring at her with a devious smile, I chucked her into the air.

She squealed just before she fell, helplessly, into the crashing wave.

Part of me felt sorry for her, knowing she'd probably get water up her nose, but most of me felt joy. For the first time in years, I was having fun. I didn't have much experience with that emotion.

As she emerged from the water, I quickly realized, perhaps my plan had *not* been such a good idea.

She coughed out water as her eyes grew wide, not with fear, not with anger. With revenge.

Oh, fuck! I was larger than this girl, a lot bigger, but she had it in her to totally fuck me up. Her thighs were powerful, I knew from experience. A smile escaped before I could contain it as I remembered her legs tightening around me in the throes of passion over the last few days. One thing I knew for sure. If Geneva Barton made her mind up to hurt me, she may very well be able to do it.

I galloped over the small waves crashing against my back, running toward, what I thought might be the safety of the shore. My large mass made it difficult to run in the water even though I was an avid swimmer and surfer.

Within no time, she'd reached me, her hands shoving me square between my shoulder blades.

The force was so great that my body fell forward, and I lost my footing in the sand. As I tumbled into the beautiful blue water, I twisted around and reached for Geneva. Securing her tiny waist in my grip, I brought her along for the ride.

Her body fell with mine, landing directly on top of me as we crashed into the water. It was surreal and magical all at once, feeling Geneva's body against mine as we rode out the wave underneath the water.

We both emerged from the water, flinging our heads back as we pushed hair and water from our faces. My eyes connected with hers, fearing she might be seriously pissed.

Instead, she burst into laughter, jumping into my arms.

I grabbed her and held her firmly in place.

"Thank you," she whispered against my ear.

"For what?"

"For making me laugh again. Really laugh."

Geneva and I were soldiers in a war against a silent enemy. Yeah, our time was fleeting, but somewhere inside, I knew I'd treasure my memories with her forever. She was slowly bringing me back to the land of the living.

CHAPTER 18

BERK

"THIS IS AMAZING," Geneva moaned, in between her bites of the chicken kabobs I'd removed from the fire. Her sounds usually came during the throes of passion when she was under me.

My cock twitched as I thought of the possibilities tonight held.

"You made this?" she asked.

I shrugged, unable to take full credit.

"What?" She licked her lips.

My dick swelled even more. "Well, I put everything on the skewer."

"But?" She dabbed at her mouth with a napkin. It was a natural response for someone regal and refined.

Geneva had many sides to her, sides I wouldn't be able to experience before she left Hawaii. I swallowed hard, trying to push the thought to the back of my mind.

"What's wrong?" Her brow furrowed as she reached out to touch my knee.

My body tingled from her touch. The heat of her skin on mine sent shockwaves of pleasure scouring across my skin.

"How much longer are you here?" I asked.

"I don't want to think about that tonight." She sucked on each fingertip. "I want to know how the hell you got this chicken to taste so good." She closed her eyes and continued to lap each finger.

I stared as her full lips slid up each knuckle. Blood roared in my ears, and my desire for her threatened to bust the seam of my board shorts. I drew in a deep breath, trying to tame my raging boner.

"The recipe for the rub is my grandmother's," I finally answered. If anything would rid me of my massive hard-on, it would be images of my grandmother. If she knew I was out here with a guest, she would have *me* on a skewer for sure.

"Does your tutu live here in Hawaii?"

"Yes, Tutu lives here on the island."

She nodded her head but her gaze seemed to still hold questions.

"So, your grandmother's Hawaiian, right?"

She was asking a lot of questions, delving into my family. Where was she going with this?

"Yes." There was an awkward pause as I awaited for more inter-rogation.

"Was your wife from Hawaii?"

And there it was. Questions about my past life. Questions I *never* answered. To anyone.

"Are you done?" I stood and took her plate, not waiting for a response.

"I'm sorry. I didn't mean to upset you."

I gazed over my shoulder as I dumped our trash into the bag I'd brought with us.

Geneva's head hung low, and she fumbled with her fingers.

As much as it pained me to talk about my life before I moved back to Hawaii, I knew I had to with Geneva. She was leaving in a few days, anyway, so what harm could come of it?

I didn't answer my own question. I knew *exactly* what harm might come of it. That was why I never talked about my past life.

I kneeled down on our blanket, leaving space between us. "No, my wife wasn't Hawaiian."

"You're not one hundred percent Hawaiian, are you?"

"My mother is Hawaiian, my father is white. I'm what they call a 'hapa.'"

"A what?"

"A hapa. It's what people call someone whose half Hawaiian and half white."

"That sounds racist and derogatory." Her voice was stern as she crossed her arms over her chest. Her face was hardened, her jaw clenched tight. She was offended, for me. And she was passionate about something, determined. I could see it in her narrowed eyes. Geneva was an advocate, a fighter, and I was drawn to her even more.

"It's all right, Geneva." I smiled at her protective nature. "It's what I am."

She balled her fists and drew in a deep breath.

Had I offended her? "What's wrong?"

"I abhor derogatory names. I can't stand when people use words to categorize a whole section of society, to make them feel less than they are—as if a person's worth in life is measured by some elitist system created by ignorant people who penalize a person just for being born a certain way."

Oh, shit. This had *nothing* to do with me being a *hapa*. Something else, entirely, was happening, and I wasn't sure I wanted to know.

I scooted closer to her on the blanket, wiping away one lone tear that trailed down her flawless face. "What's wrong, Geneva? This is about way more than me being a *hapa*."

Her blue eyes cut to mine, darkening now with a warning look. "Don't use that word again. Not in front of me. It may be acceptable to you and your culture, but it's not to me."

"Okay," I whispered, brushing back a piece of hair clinging to her rose-tinted lips. "What's wrong, though?"

She tucked her knees underneath her bottom and tossed the skewer back toward the fire ring.

This was Geneva shutting down, and I did *not* want that to

happen. Not tonight. My time with her was limited.

"Hey." My fingers grazed her bare shoulder, but she remained like stone. My heart sank as I realized not even my touch would bring her back.

Pushing off the blanket, I stood and jogged to the Jeep. I lifted my surfboard from the top and secured it under my arm, sprinting back to our campsite.

"Let's go riding." It was a statement, not a request.

Her eyes cut to mine. The tears were gone, but she was still hurt, wounded in some silent way.

All I could think about was easing her pain.

"Berk, it's dark already." She cast her eyes toward the sky that was littered with stars.

It was the *perfect* time to surf if you were experienced. But surfing wasn't what I had in mind.

"You'll be all right. Trust me." I nodded reassuringly toward the water and flashed her what I hoped was a panty-dropping smile.

She slowly rose from the blanket, her returning grin making my *own* shorts want to drop.

Her long, lean legs strode toward me.

I forced images of Rhen and Okie into my mind as I tried to keep my threatening hard-on in check. Seeing her luscious body, her muscular legs, her taut stomach, her perfectly sized tits in that barely-there bikini was too much, though. Mr. Chubby was throbbing. I needed the cool water to calm him down.

As Geneva strolled closer, I grabbed her hand and dragged her out into the surf. Her small yelp made me smile, but she didn't protest. I knew what I had in mind for her and if I did it right, there'd be a lot more screaming in her future.

"These waves are kind of small for surfing, aren't they?" she asked bashfully. The slight tremble of her body told me she was nervous thinking about surfing in the dark.

I didn't want to ruin my surprise. "You'll be all right, Gen."

Her body froze and she yanked her hand from mine.

What the fuck just happened? "What's wrong?" Laying the surf-board down in the water, I held on to it with one hand as I reached back for her waist.

She was lost in a trance, and I couldn't believe I was losing her, again.

Instead of giving her a chance to answer, I clutched her around the waist and hoisted her up out of the water.

"Berk!" she yelled.

I plopped her ass down on the board like an unruly child in a high chair.

"Berk!" she screamed again, clutching my shoulders as she tried to balance herself on the board. "I don't know what I'm doing." Panic rang from every word as she clutched at me, her fingers digging into my shoulders for support.

At least she wasn't pulling away.

"Just straddle the board and balance. You'll be fine." I rubbed her thighs to offer assurance. I drove us further into the water, careful to guide the board over the waves so she wouldn't fall.

She smiled down at me.

"What?" I asked, thankful to feel her body relax.

"You called me Gen."

"I'm sorry."

"No, it's okay. It's just..."

Shit, I'd fucked this up and didn't even know it. I put my hand over her taut stomach. "Lie back."

She tilted her head as her eyes scrutinized me. "How is this supposed to help me learn to surf?" She laughed nervously.

"Who said anything about surfing?" I smirked and gave her a playful wink.

"What are you up to, Berk—" Her grip on my shoulders tight-ened, and her eyes darted back and forth between mine.

"What?"

"I don't even know your last name." She seemed confused and overwhelmed. "Oh, God, I'm such a slut."

I laughed at her comment. "It's Rigby."

"Rigby," she repeated.

I pushed her further out into the ocean until the water was above my waist. I gazed out over the water. The sun had set long ago, leaving a blanket of dark blue sky and ocean.

I squared the surfboard perpendicular to the beach, the nose side pointing toward the vast, blue ocean ahead of us, as I stood at the other end, my back to the shore, water waist high.

I spread her legs further apart.

She trembled at my touch.

"Lie back," I said, taking her hand in mine.

She obeyed my instructions, slowly reclining back. Her body was splayed across my board, and her breasts swayed naturally with the rise and fall of each wave.

I could barely stay in the water because my desire to jump on top of her and drive into her deep was so primal. This was for Geneva, though. She needed this, and I was going to give it to her.

"I can't believe all the stars in the sky," she said. Her eyes were cast above her. "You don't see them all in the city like this."

I wanted to ask where she was from. My sister told me it was Texas, and I knew I could pry more if I really wanted to know. But tonight was about tonight, no past, no future—only the present.

"That's the Summer Triangle." I pointed up to the stars.

"Where?"

"That bright star right there," I answered, "that's Altair. It's part of the Aquila constellation." I looked down at her.

Her eyes searched the night sky for the pattern.

"Aquila means eagle in Latin. He was the bird who carried Zeus's thunderbolt in Greek mythology," I said.

Her gaze returned to mine, her head tilted with a puzzled look on her face.

"What?" I asked.

She shook her head but gave me a small smile, returning her gaze to the sky.

"That's Deneb." I moved my finger over, still pointing toward the sky. "It's part of the Cygnus constellation."

"What does Cygnus mean?" Her eyes stayed riveted to the stars overhead, studying them intently.

"It means swan in Latin." Taking her silence as my cue to proceed, I did. "And there," I moved my finger over diagonally, "that's Vega. It's part of the Lyra constellation."

"That's Latin for lyre," she spoke softly. "I know what that one means. I love the harp." She seemed lost in her own thoughts, memories of something special wiping across her face as a huge smile appeared.

"You can see the three brightest stars of each constellation form an invisible triangle." I stood silent, watching her eyes dart between all the stars as she tried to piece the constellations together. "Back before GPS and computerized navigation, people used these stars to direct ships and planes and other traveling vessels. That's why it's called the Navigator's triangle."

Geneva pushed up onto her elbows, staring at me as if I were a loon.

"What?" I asked.

"How do you know so much about the stars?"

I shrugged my shoulders. I loved astronomy. Always had. "I don't know. I've always had a fascination for the stars, I guess. And I love the symbolism of Greek mythology mixed with real world science."

"That's funny." She laughed under her breath.

"What is?"

"It's just that, when I first saw you," she hesitated.

"What?"

"I didn't know your name."

"And?"

"And, so I nicknamed you Poseidon." She giggled.

"Poseidon, huh?" I raised a brow and joined in her laughter. If I were going to be any mythical creature, Poseidon would definitely be my choice.

"What?" She swatted at me playfully. "You looked like a friggin' Greek god coming out of the water that day."

My heart swelled and my pride nearly burst at her words of affection and confessed desire. I knew what she did to *my* body, but to hear I had the same effect on her gave me a newfound sense of determination.

"Lay back down," I growled.

"What?" Her voice broke and I could tell she was worried she'd offended me.

"I have something I want to show you." I smiled with an evil gleam in my eye.

"More constellations?"

"Yes," I laughed under my breath, "you'll be seeing more stars."

Without questioning me further, she lowered herself onto my board, her eyes cast up toward the heavens as she drank in the night sky's majesty. She was just as mythical and beautiful as any constellation I'd ever seen.

I scooted my palms underneath her rear end and dragged her until her hips were on the very edge of my board, flush with my chest, her head pointed toward the nose.

"What are you doing?" she squeaked out.

"Shhh. Just watch the stars," I said. I pushed her legs wider apart and latched on to the underside of the board, helping guide it over the lapping waves. Geneva's body floated effortlessly, as if she were another layer of the sea. God, it was erotic to watch her.

Slowly running one hand up her thigh, I made my way to the edge of her bathing suit thankful she had on a string bikini today. Tugging on the bow, I was discouraged to find it was double knotted. I'd tied many a rope in my day sailing, surfing, and fishing on the island. These knots would prove no problem for my dexterous hands.

"Berk, what are you doing?" She asked the question but made no effort to stop me. She wanted this.

"Just focus on the stars, Geneva." I tugged on the string of her bikini. After some finagling, it finally gave way, opening up one side of her hip, revealing a tantalizing trail of lighter skin underneath. Still guiding the board over the waves, I moved my hand to the other side of her bikini bottom. This time, the knot came loose more quickly. I was almost there.

Gazing down at her, I studied her body. Her eyes were still cast heavenward, but a knowing smirk curved her delicious lips. She knew what I wanted—and she was going to let me have it.

Placing my fingertip just under the bottom edge of her top, I traced an invisible line down her abdomen, dragging it lower toward the edge of her bikini bottom.

Her breath stilled.

Oh, shit, had I done something wrong? Gazing up I found her still lying face up on the board, staring up at the sky, her mouth slightly open. Her breathing was heavy now, her chest rising and falling rapidly.

Feeling no reservations from her, I curled my finger into her bikini and dragged it down further until her familiar patch of hair appeared. This was *my* summer triangle.

I lowered my head so that my mouth was even with her opening.

Her hips rocked with every motion of the waves.

Leaning forward, I pressed my lips against hers. The smell of Geneva's desire, mixed with the salt from the ocean, was the most erotic scent I'd ever inhaled.

The rolling tide of the sea pushed her against my mouth, brought her center close to me, then far away, then back again. The ripples of the tide set a perfect rhythm as my tongue stroked her sensitive skin.

"Oh, Berk," Geneva moaned. "God, that feels amazing."

Her cries of pleasure spurred me on, but I wanted her harder than the sea was allowing. Wrapping both arms under the board and spreading her wider with my shoulders, I buried my face deep, my tongue caressing her, lapping at her, pushing her higher toward the sky, toward her release.

Her legs stiffened and her back arched off the board, and still her body rolled with each rhythmic wave.

My feet dug into the sandy bottom of the ocean floor to keep us secure. Salt water seeped into my mouth, but I didn't care. There was no way I was going to stop. I lifted her higher off the board and out of the water. My tongue delved deeper, pushing harder with deep strokes against her sensitive skin.

"Fuck, Berk!" she screamed.

I was thankful for the secluded beach. Someone might think I was hurting her.

"Oh, oh, God. Oh my God, holy fuck!" She gripped the side of the board as she shouted.

I eased my pressure, covering her with my mouth and sucking hard.

Suddenly, her hands shifted, and she dug into my long hair, pulling my face into her. She wanted more.

Every sensation was on overload for me—the night sky, the ocean breeze, the magical constellations, the ebbing tide, and now, Geneva's screams of ecstasy—it was all too much. I was about to explode merely at the strokes from the sea.

Gripping her thighs with both hands, I pushed her toward the nose of the board, until her head nearly went over the edge. I climbed on top, keeping perfect balance as I pulled down my shorts and hovered above her on the board, my hands now on either side of her head.

Her eyes went wide in surprise.

"Ready to see more stars, Geneva?" I lowered myself on top of her, my swollen dick driving inside her.

Three thrusts deep into her core were all it took to take her over the edge. She screamed out in a guttural tone that had my own release near the edge.

My muscles strained as I balanced the board underneath me.

Geneva wrapped her legs around my hips, her body rocking against mine as she sought more pressure to ride out her orgasm.

Being so connected to her, knowing she wanted me deeper inside of her was my undoing. I came inside her, hard and unrelenting, riding out the waves of my own orgasm in perfect sync with the ocean's ebb and flow. It was one of the most intense experiences of my life, and I was the one seeing stars now.

A sense of calm and peace washed over me. The suffocating band of grief and guilt that had been locked around my chest three years ago began to loosen. I was able to breathe again. But only for a brief second. Only until the moment I realized—we hadn't used a condom.

～

There are always flowers for those who want to see them.
- Henri Matisse

～

CHAPTER 19

GENEVA

"Berk." I nudged his arm with my elbow.

He sat motionless, lost in the hypnotic flames of the campfire.

"Berk," I called again.

"Hmmm," he murmured.

"Your marshmallow." I nodded toward the flaming ball engulfed in the blaze of our small campfire.

"Oh." He shrugged, unaffected by the event, pulling his skewer from the fire. I watched as he slowly blew against the marshmallow to extinguish the flames.

Part of me was totally aroused, watching his lips pucker and blow against the sweet treat. But most of me was still sad and disappointed.

He'd been distant ever since we'd returned from my "ride" on the surfboard. Oh my God, that had been something straight out of my romance novels. Actually better, incredible—the stars, the waves, his tongue. I pressed my knees together and squirmed on the blanket we were sitting on to try and relieve the ache deep between my thighs.

As soon as he realized we hadn't used a condom, he'd freaked out. As much as I tried to reassure him, I was clean and on the pill, he still seemed gripped with fear. He was angry and brooding, and I had no idea how to bring him back.

"I love burnt marshmallows." I smiled, reaching over to remove the charred, sticky goo from his skewer. Popping the burnt delicacy into my mouth, I closed my eyes to savor the flavor. "Mmmm," I moaned unconsciously.

When I opened my eyes, I saw Berk's gaze focused on my lips. This was my chance to bring him back.

Pushing onto my knees, I leaned into his body, my face even with his. Our eyes locked. I stared at him with an expression that silently assured him everything would be all right.

His light brown eyes scanned my face as if he was trying to read me, to see if I was either real, or safe, or both.

Pushing my body closer to his, I moved within inches of his lips, my eyes never leaving his. I refused to make the final move, but I was going to get as close to him as possible.

I wasn't sure what had spooked him. I knew it was more than just us forgetting a condom or worrying if we had any diseases, no matter how much we reassured each other.

I didn't want to lose him though. Not tonight. Not like this. Our time together was fleeting, and I didn't want to waste a minute of it. Especially when it was over something so irrelevant.

His hands ran up my arms.

I drew in a deep breath. It was the first physical contact he'd given me since we'd returned from our "surfing lesson." My body trembled at the touch of his skin on mine.

I was lost in everything about this guy, and the realization unnerved me. This was more than just a vacation fuck, for both of us. My limited time on the island left us no choice but to make our affair a short one, though. It was probably best I pull away now.

I sat back on my feet and pushed away from him, preparing to stand.

His huge hands wrapped around my neck, his fingers digging into my hair, latching on to me as if he were free falling, and I was the only thing that could save him. "Don't go," he whispered, his breath washing over my face.

The scent of sweet, sugary marshmallows and the chocolate bar assaulted my senses, making it impossible for me to move.

Drawing me in the fraction of an inch necessary for our lips to connect, he fastened his mouth to mine, both our eyes still open as our mouths seared together.

It only took a second for my eyes to flutter closed. I was lost in his spell anytime his lips touched my body. This man was lethal and volatile, like a giant Hawaiian volcano.

Slowly he broke our embrace, his eyes searching mine.

"What happened?" I asked.

He slid his fingers around my face. "It's nothing."

"It was definitely something, Berk."

His hands fell away.

I leaned back on my heels but kept my palms secured on his knees. I needed some type of connection to help him feel safe.

"I'm just really pissed," he finally answered.

My stomach knotted in pain. He regretted our time together. Tears stung my eyes. I stood.

His hands gripped my wrists, and he yanked me down into his lap.

I turned my head and drilled my eyes shut.

"Hey, I'm sorry. I didn't mean to hurt you." He released my wrists.

He thought he'd physically hurt me. He wrapped his arms around me and drew me in close.

I felt protected, nurtured—and for the first time in a long time, safe.

His fingers swept over my cheek while the pad of his thumb wiped away a tear that had worked its way past my lashes.

Dammit! I did *not* want to cry. I forced my eyes open.

"What's wrong?" His eyes searched mine.

"You said you were pissed," I answered. "I'm assuming at me."

"What are you talking about?" His brow creased in confusion.

"Do you regret what we did, just now, out in the water?"

His deep, rich laughter sent chills over my entire body.

"Geneva, that was one of the most amazing experiences of my life."

We sat silently as I studied his face, searching for any sign that he was only saying that to appease me. Looking into his eyes, all I saw staring back at me was an honest man, a lonely man, a hurt man. All of them confused me even more.

"I don't understand, though," I said.

His eyes wrinkled around the edges and his brows drew together.

"You say it was incredible," I started, "and yet you sat here, not talking to me, as if it was the most horrific, regrettable thing you've ever done. And then you say you're pissed."

"I'm sorry." He exhaled a heavy sigh as his shoulders slumped.

"Sorry for what?" Now I was starting to get pissed.

He tightened his grip around me, preventing my escape.

"I'm not sorry for what we did, Geneva." His tone and his expression assured me at least *that* statement was true.

"Then what are you sorry about?"

He paused for a moment, collecting his thoughts. "I'm just sorry I put you in harm's way."

"Harm's way? What are you talking about? Harm's way?"

"Having unprotected sex with you puts you in harm's way."

I twisted in his lap to look at him fully. "It only puts me in harm's way if you have some kind of sexually transmitted disease that you haven't told me about." My heart stopped, and my body stiffened, when I realized what he was saying. "You have a fucking STD, don't you?" I wiggled in his lap but his huge man hands held me down.

"I don't have an STD, Geneva, calm down."

I believed him. Not once had Berk ever struck me as a liar.

Maybe a man who disclosed very little and held things back, but not a liar.

I settled back into his lap. "Then what's your problem?"

He stared at me blankly.

"What we did in the ocean was one of the most amazing things I've ever done, too, Berk," I said. "And then we come back here and you act like it's the worst thing you ever did, like you feel guilty and wrong."

"I acted like a total man out there." He nodded toward the ocean.

"I know." I smirked, waggling my brows. "That's what I loved."

His returning smile set my heart beating again and stole my breath, all at the same time.

"I mean," he said, "I was thinking with my dick and not my head. I don't want to get you pregnant. I don't want *any* chance of you getting pregnant. Ever."

Ever? Fuck.

"So, you don't want children?" *Why in the fuck did you ask him that?* "I'm sorry, that was a dumb question. I'm only here for a few more days. I didn't mean to sound like one of those crazy stalker chicks."

His eyes went wide, and I wasn't sure why.

"No, I don't want children." His statement was cold and flat—and final.

I wanted children, one day, but it wasn't like I'd planned a future with this guy. I was only here two more days. I should be thankful there was something between us that would make this relationship a no-go.

I wiggled out of his hold, not surprised to feel him release me.

"Well, I guess it's a good thing I'm on the pill then." I laughed with a nervous smile. I was here for the moment, living in the moment. Forget about the future. There was none for Berk and me. All we had was right here, in this moment, on this amazing beach.

I stood and dusted off my hands. We needed to forget this entire conversation.

"Want to go for a swim?" I extended one hand out to help him stand.

He gazed up at me. Sorrow filled his eyes, but only for a brief moment. "Sure." He gave a half-hearted smile but grasped my hand and lifted his body until he was standing next to me. His arm snaked around my lower chest, and he scooped me into his arms and traipsed through the sand toward the rolling water.

"Berk," I admonished, slapping his shoulder.

His gait quickened as he hit the first wave with determination. The evil glint in his eyes let me know he was planning something, something I wasn't going to be completely all right with.

"Berk, you better not."

He smirked.

"Berk!" I yelled above the noise of the ocean lapping at his knees.

Before I could catch my breath, he catapulted me into the air.

My hands and feet flailed about wildly, a split second before my body slammed into the ocean. My gaze found his one last time before I sank into the water.

His face was alight with a grin, his eyes dancing with playful mischief.

My heart filled with joy as the waves took me under.

I wasn't sure where his dark thoughts had taken him earlier. I was just thankful Berk was back.

CHAPTER 20

GENEVA

I TRUDGED the final assent up the huge cliff, each step pained as my thighs burned from the exertion.

"Just a little further," Berk called over his shoulder.

"That's what you said fifteen minutes ago," I huffed, my breaths coming in short pants.

"Well, I promise, you're closer now than you were fifteen minutes ago." His rich laughter filled the deep crevices of the mountains beside us.

I had no idea why I'd agreed to come on this morning "hike." It had sounded like fun at the time. But now, as my lungs burned to catch my next breath, and my legs threatened to give out, I wasn't so sure.

I stared at the trail before me. Others had obviously traversed this path. If they could conquer this mammoth hill, surely, I could, too.

"It's the getting down part that worries me," I said under my breath.

"Oh, getting down is a lot easier." Berk's hand appeared in front of my face, offering help as I took my last few steps.

As he pulled me to the plateau of the cliff, I dragged in a ragged breath, more from awe than from exertion.

"Here we are." Berk waved his hand before us. "*Pau Hana*," he said.

"Pah-ah-hoo-ah what?" I said, gulping in much needed air.

"Are you going to be okay?" He tilted his head and stared at me.

I nodded. "What was that poo poo thing?"

He laughed. "It's *Pau Hana*," he repeated, enunciating every syllable. "It means, "our work is done" in Hawaiian. Well, loosely translated," he added.

"Well, thank God pah-hoo-hoo-hee, whatever, my job is done just getting up here."

Berk chuckled. "The islanders say this is where God rested after his work was done. He looked out over the heavens and earth and said, 'Pau Hana.'"

I stepped closer to the edge, gazing out over the shimmering blue sea. Looking to my left and right I saw the other mountains jutting up from the vast tropical forests below. "I can see why God stopped and rested. It's a hell of a walk up here."

Berk shook his head.

"It's beautiful, Berk. And peaceful," I added, drawing in a deep breath of the sea air that whipped around me.

"I used to come here a lot."

"When you were young?" I asked, finally able to catch my breath.

"Yeah, then, too."

"How long have you been back in Hawaii?" I turned away from my view of the sea and stared at him.

"Long enough," he sighed.

No more past, I reminded myself.

"Well, it's an amazing place. I can see why you'd come here."

"You haven't seen the best part. Come." He extended his hand. We walked a few yards further and he pointed to the side of another mountain.

I followed his gaze and saw a waterfall on the cliff beside us that pooled in a lagoon a hundred feet below. A beautiful rainbow arched across the spray. I stared, mesmerized by the colors.

"God's gift, his promise during the floods—a rainbow." Berk announced it as if it were the simplest fact known to man. I guess the story of Noah and the ark and the rainbow really was simple and well known.

"That's amazing, Berk. Surreal almost." I stood in stunned silence.

"You're supposed to say '*Mahalo Akua*' when you see it."

"What does that mean?"

"*Mahalo* means thank you, and *Akua* means God. Thank you, God, for your promise, for the rainbow. It's more out of reverence and respect."

I studied the cliff, watching the water as it free fell over the edge and splashed into the pool below.

"You usually only see the rainbow in the morning when the sun is in the east and shining on the waterfall." He pointed back over to the horizon opposite us.

The sun was just making its ascent into the mid-morning sky.

"That's why you woke me up so early?" I turned and smiled at him.

Berk walked up behind me, snaking his long arms around my waist. "You are definitely *not* a morning person." He kissed along my neck.

"I can wake up. For the right reasons." I giggled, bending my neck to give him more access.

"Is this the right reason?" He nodded toward the waterfall. Then his gaze swung wide over the cliff where we were standing.

A gentle breeze blew over us, drying the sheen of sweat that covered my body, causing me to tremble. Or maybe it was this spot, this moment here, with this man. It was surreal.

"*Mahalo Akua*," I said softly.

Berk kissed my neck. "*Mahalo Akua*," he repeated, bending us both at the waist. "Then you bow to the rainbow," he whispered.

As I stood bent over, wrapped in the safety of Berk's arms, I offered up my own personal thanks for the second chance in life I'd been given, thanks to the people who'd offered me forgiveness—Hindley, Rory, my dad and Caroline, among others.

Berk straightened us, and I twisted around in his arms, looking into his caramel-colored eyes. They were lighter this morning, shining in the light of the sun as it peeked over the cliffs.

"*Mahalo*, Berk." I smiled. "For bringing me here."

"*He mea iki*, Geneva."

"What?" It sounded like gibberish.

"You're welcome." He laughed. He took my hand and walked toward the edge. "That's still not the best part." His face was bright with excitement that was infectious.

I pulled back as he got within a few feet of the cliff's edge. It wasn't as tall as the one with the waterfall next to us, but I was pretty sure you'd do some serious damage if you fell over the edge.

"It's okay. I won't let you fall." He tried to reassure me. "Yet."

I jerked on his hand. "Yet? What the hell does that mean?"

"I'm not going to let you fall, Geneva." His expression hinted at more. "You won't fall. You'll jump. With me."

"The fuck I will," I half screamed, yanking my hand from his.

"Everyone does it on the island." He smiled.

My palms broke out in a sweat as my heart slammed into my chest.

"It's a rite of passage. It's symbolic." He tried to sell the idea like he was a used car salesman, convincing me to buy the biggest piece of shit car on the lot.

"Symbolic of what? That you're a dumbass?"

He chuckled, moving closer to me. "You'll be fine. People do it all the time. See the sign." He nodded toward the pole next to the edge that I hadn't noticed before.

The sign was white with a huge orange banner at the top that said "WARNING." Below that was a yellow diamond graphic with the picture of a cartoon man falling off a cliff. Directly underneath it said, "Jump at your own risk."

"What the fuck, Berk, it says *warning*!"

"It's really just an advisement."

"Well, I'm taking the government's *advisement* and staying up here." I pointed to the ground below my feet.

"Come on, Geneva," he pleaded.

"Uh uh." I shook my head. "No way."

"Where's your sense of adventure? You only live once." He smiled with that look that made my panties disintegrate. That smile that would make me do just about anything. Anything except jump off the side of a cliff.

"My senses are back down at the campsite and that's where they're gonna stay."

He moved in closer, his expression becoming serious as he stared down at me. He reached out and tucked a wayward strand of my hair behind my ear. He had his long hair pulled back in a pony-tail today, his strong features on prominent display.

He was truly a mythical creature, my Poseidon, and I'd been cast under his spell a long time ago.

Fuck!

"I think you and I deserve a second chance. I haven't jumped off the ledge since I've been back since Jaime died. It's been almost three years."

Three years? Holy shit.

"I think you've been living with the demons of your past, too," he said. "I can sense it. Maybe that's what brought us together. I don't know." He shrugged his shoulders.

How the hell could he read me so well?

"I think we *both* could use a fresh start." He stared at me, his eyes filled with promise. "We need to say *Mahalo Akua* and *ho'o-ponopono*."

"We need to say what?"

"*Ho'oponopono*. It means to set things right, to rectify everything. To cleanse and absolve. It's a meditative state." He held out his hand. "*Ho'oponopono*, Geneva." His amber eyes were filled with such genuineness and vulnerability it made my heart ache.

I stared down at his open palm. It was firm, steady, and huge. I gazed up at his face, not surprised to see a smile spread wide. Poseidon beckoned me.

Drawing a deep breath that did nothing to calm my racing heart, I said, "*Ho'oponopono*, Berk." I slipped my hand in his, intertwining our fingers as I sucked in another ragged breath and faced the rim of the cliff.

He walked us closer to the edge.

Oh, shit. My heart was beating out of my chest, and my knees shook so bad, I feared I might fall before I could ever jump.

"To second chances," he said.

I turned to look at him one more time.

"*Mahalo*, Geneva." He kissed the back of my hand, and with no further warning, swung our bodies in a forward motion as we ran toward the edge of the cliff.

This was it. The pivotal moment in my life. My one chance for a do-over.

"*Mahola*, Berk!" I yelled as our bodies jetted out over the water below. *Ho'oponopono*.

CHAPTER 21

GENEVA

"WELL, I BETTER GET GOING." Berk led me through the lobby of the resort. "I have to work tonight."

"Will I see you? Later I mean?" God, I hated the desperation in my voice.

You would think after jumping off a cliff in Hawaii I'd be made of stone, fearless. Not with Berk Rigby. With him I was vulnerable. He melted away all my defenses and that scared me. I didn't like being exposed. Besides, I was leaving. He was staying. It was a heartache waiting to happen. I'd been foolish many times in my life. Why be different now?

Suddenly Berk stopped and his body went rigid. His eyes were glued to the front desk.

Mine followed. I noticed several people lined up, but one woman stood next to the counter. I wasn't sure if she was a guest or an employee. She had light skin and dark, auburn hair, obviously not family or an islander.

She watched us intently, studying our every move. She raised one perfectly manicured eyebrow, her menacing stare indicating just how unhappy she was—with one or both of us.

Berk dropped my hand and slowly stepped away from me.

A horrible feeling hit me in the pit of my stomach.

"Berk," I called, reaching for his arm.

His trance-like gaze with the girl broke as his eyes peered down at me.

I didn't need to hear his words of rejection. So much for all the *hakuna matata* shit he rambled on about while we were on the cliff.

The hot sting of tears pressed against the back of my eyes. There was no way I was going to let him see me cry, no matter how much I cared for him. I turned on my heel and flung my bag over my shoulder, heading for my room.

"Geneva," Berk called out quietly, gently touching my shoulder as he caught up with me.

I turned to face him, praying my tears weren't visible. I didn't want Berk, or anyone, to see me so weak and vulnerable. *This is a vacation fuck. This is a vacation fuck. This is a—*

Berk's soft lips dusted my cheek. The act seemed half intimate, half familiar. Either way, it left me wanting more.

"I'll see you when I get off?" he asked.

I wanted to say no. This needed to end. Now. But knowing what was right and doing it were two completely different things. I was in too deep. Berk was a drug and I needed one more fix before I left.

"Okay," I whispered.

A beautiful smile washed across his face, his lips so full and plump. God, all I wanted to do was grab his face and pull it down and press those lips against mine. No one had to tell me that wasn't appropriate, not in the lobby of his family's resort. I sensed his involvement with me was something best kept hidden.

Making my way toward the corridor that led to my villa, I couldn't help but look back at my Poseidon one last time.

The woman at the counter was strolling toward Berk, her earlier frown replaced with a timid smile.

Berk stepped closer, taking her in his embrace and kissing her gently on the cheek, as he had with me. They stepped apart and smiled. They were familiar with one another. They were friends. Had they been lovers?

My body went taut with tension as my stomach roiled.

As if sensing my stare, they both turned toward me, their gaze colliding with mine.

Jealous anger swirled in my gut. I had to get the hell out of here before I totally broke down.

Ducking around the corner to escape their attention, I leaned up against the wall, trying to catch my breath. My heart was banging hard against my chest.

I didn't know who this woman was or what role she had played in Berk's life, but one thing was painfully clear. They had a past. And something in my gut said she was here to start a future.

No one ever told me that grief felt so much like fear.
- C.S. Lewis

CHAPTER 22

BERK

"WHAT THE HELL are you doing here, Jackie?" I seethed, staring into her familiar hazel eyes.

"Well, it's nice to see you, too, Berk," she said sarcastically.

I heard the disappointment in her voice and saw the anguish in her eyes. She was hurting, ripped to shreds by the loss of her niece and sister, and yet I'd never contacted any of them since I'd left Colorado after the funeral.

Her auburn air fell forward as her head bowed. She looked so much like Jaime, for a moment I thought she was.

"I'm sorry, Jackie," I whispered. "It's just, you took me by surprise, that's all. I haven't seen you since—"

"Since Jaime's funeral. It's been almost three years, Berk."

Funeral.

My stomach burned as if a steel toed boot had kicked me in my abdomen. As soon as Jaime's body had been lowered into the ground, I'd left Colorado. I hadn't said good-bye to anyone. Not even Jaime's parents.

"I'm her sister, Berk. You don't think I miss her, too? You don't think I grieve every day for Jaime *and* Alana?" Her voice cracked and her eyes glazed over with tears.

"I'm sorry." I reached over to kiss her cheek. I didn't need to take my shit out on Jackie. I pulled away and gave her a half-hearted smile.

Jackie's eyes lit with hopefulness, and a smile covered her face. Her gaze left mine as she looked over my shoulder.

I turned to see what she was looking at and saw Geneva staring at both of us, her eyes wide and her jaw clenched.

Shit.

Before I could stop her, Geneva darted around the corner and disappeared down the hall.

"Do you like her?" Jackie asked.

"Who?"

She nodded behind me.

I didn't want anyone knowing about my relationship with Geneva, least of all my sister-in-law. With the death of my wife, I wondered if technically Jackie was still considered a relation to me.

"That's none of your business," I said with force, squaring my shoulders.

"You're right. I'm sorry, Berk."

I cut my gaze to the marble floor. She didn't deserve my wrath, but I couldn't let my guard down.

What happened to second chances and fresh starts and ho'o-ponopono?

Maybe this was it. Maybe Jackie's presence was a sign.

"Look, Berk." Jackie's hand gripped my forearm. "I know I should have called first."

I gazed up and saw the sorrow etched across her face. Time had aged her, worn her down, too. Of course, it had.

"But I knew you wouldn't take my calls, even if I had," she said.

I nodded. It was true. I had cut myself off from Jaime's family the minute the car door slammed shut, and I bolted from the cemetery the day Jaime was buried.

"I know you think my parents blame you. But they don't, Berk."

The mention of Jackie and Jaime's parents, and the pain they lived with twisted my gut. They blamed me. Of course, they did. I hadn't taken care of their daughter in her time of need. But who could blame me.

This was all too much—Jackie's presence here, her reminders of shit from my past. I had to get the fuck out of here before my head exploded and I passed out.

"Please don't push me away, Berk."

"I'm sorry, Jackie, but I can't do this."

She stepped in closer. "Will you ever be ready, ready to come home?"

Come home? Her question echoed through my befuddled mind. Would I ever be ready to return to the mainland, to my parents, to the sport I loved?

"I don't know, Jackie. But I do know that I can't do this right now." I waved my finger between us.

"I'm not leaving, Berk."

I jerked back in surprise. "What do you mean you're not leaving?"

"I came to bring you home."

"Bring me home?"

"Yes. There are things you need to know. Things I need to tell you."

"What things?" I growled.

Jackie surveyed the lobby. "I don't want to talk here."

"Well, I have to be at work soon."

"Can we talk tomorrow?"

I drew in a ragged breath. What the hell could she possibly have to tell me? *Things you need to know.* I blew out the air in my lungs. Maybe this was just a plot to get me home. Maybe Jackie's motives weren't as pure as she'd like me to believe. Either way, I had to know.

"I can meet you here at the resort, in the bar tomorrow," I said.

"I don't want to do this at the bar. Can I meet at your place?"

she asked. "Your grandmother said you're living down the beach just a ways."

"You talked to my grandmother?" I grumbled through gritted teeth. Jackie was infiltrating my safe place, my harbor in the storm. She was a hurricane that was threatening to wipe away what little peace I had here in Hawaii.

"Berk, I don't mean to pry, it's just—"

"I've got to go." I bolted down the corridor, cutting through the dining room. I followed a path through the maze of tables until I burst through the swinging door of the kitchen. Clutching my knees with my palms, I heaved deep breaths of air.

"You all right, Kahuna?" My brother, Rhen, slapped my back.

I shook my head. As my breathing calmed, I stood, all the blood rushing out of my head, leaving me dizzy and lightheaded. I wobbled on shaky legs.

"Whoa, brother." Rhen scooted me back into a chair. "What happened? You look like you saw a ghost."

"More like the sister of a ghost," I said as I plopped down in the chair.

"What?"

"Jackie is here." My head fell back against the wall with a thud and I stared at the ceiling.

"No way."

I righted my head and stared at my brother. His eyes were wide. "Way," I answered.

"What the hell does she want?"

"She wants me to come 'home.'" I used air quotes.

Rhen's blank expression told me his thoughts. He wanted me in Colorado, too.

"She said she has something to tell me," I said.

"What?"

"I don't know. She wouldn't say. And I wasn't in any mood to hear it anyway."

"I wonder what it could be?" Rhen took the seat beside me.

The kitchen workers bustled around the prep tables as they prepared for the evening crowd.

"Shit," I said under my breath.

"What's wrong?"

"I forgot. I was supposed to work in the dining room this evening."

"What's wrong with that?" Rhen asked.

I didn't want Rhen to know how desperate I was to spend more time with Geneva. "Have you seen Okie?"

"Not since last night." Rhen waggled his brows.

"What?"

"Karaoke night."

That was code for "Okie was screwing some poor, unsuspecting tourist."

"Why do you need him?" Rhen asked.

Geneva and her family would, more than likely, be dining here tonight. There was no way I could see her. Not right now, not after Jackie's visit.

"I want him to cover my shift tonight in the dining room."

"Why are you trying to get out of working in the dining room, Berk?" Tutu's familiar Hawaiian dialect rang through the kitchen.

Shit! If my grandmother knew the truth of how far my relationship had progressed with Geneva, she'd send me packing back to Colorado faster than I could ski down a half pipe.

Tutu had never been a fan of me staying at the resort. She loved me tremendously and understood my loss. She'd lost her own husband a few years before Alana and Jaime had passed away. Her invitation to stay at the resort for a few weeks, to allow me space after their deaths, had turned into almost three years.

"I'm just not feeling well," I answered quietly.

"I heard you felt well enough to go camping yesterday," she said.

Well, fuck. It was silly of me to think Tutu didn't know every single thing that happened with her family, with the resort, hell, with the whole island of Kauai, for that matter.

With one nod of Tutu's head, Rhen vanished. His large form bolted through the swinging door. Lucky bastard.

"Walk with me, Berk."

I gulped. Everyone in my family knew that a "walk" with Tutu meant a lecture. And it was usually because you'd fucked up.

Tutu pushed through the back kitchen door that led to the tropical forest surrounding the resort.

She was small, just under five feet, with long, raven colored hair streaked with gray. She always wore it in a braid that hung loosely over her shoulder, drawing attention to her strong jaw and native island bone structure. She was regal and elegant—and meaner than a starving wild cat if she was pissed.

"How long have you been in Kauai, Berk?" she asked as we walked.

"Um, a couple of years." My answer was purposely vague—and untrue. I had the years, months, and days since Alana and Jaime's death etched in my mind.

She gazed over her shoulder with a rueful smile, raising a brow in warning.

"Maybe a little longer," I sighed.

I followed her along the familiar garden path to her private home. It was situated close enough to the resort to be accessible if someone needed her, but far enough away so she could escape as well.

She stopped just short of her front porch and turned to face me. Her face gazing up, her neck strained because of my height.

"It's time you leave, Berk." Her voice was loving but stern.

Her words hit my heart like a poisoned arrow.

"I don't mean it like that, sweetheart." She gently stroked my cheek. "I meant, Jaime and Alana would want you to move on, they would want you to live again, Berk."

I drew in a deep breath, reaching out to brace myself on the tree beside me. My family loved Jaime and Alana. They both had loved Hawaii. I wondered why I'd ever thought I could escape them here.

"I know you've met someone. Here," she added.

My hand dropped from the tree, my mind frozen with fear by her revelation. She was going to kill me, then ship my body back to Colorado.

"Berk, you misunderstand."

I ventured a gaze. The fact she wasn't strangling me already was a good sign.

Her eyes were bright, and a small smile tugged at her mouth. "You deserve to love again, Berk. You deserve to love and *be* loved again."

Her words hit me in the chest harder than a prize fighter's fist.

"This woman you've met here has changed something deep in your soul, Berk. I can see it. Your spirit is awakening. You have your glow again. It's something we've all tried to do for you for nearly three years."

"What are you talking about?"

"Berk, just because we don't speak of Jaime and Alana around you—because you've asked us not to—doesn't mean their names don't go unspoken."

I was floored that my family was talking about me and my wife and daughter behind my back.

"Berk, stop. It's not like that. We're not gossiping. We're all worried. That's why I allowed Jackie to come."

"Yes, about that." I raised a brow.

"I know, I know." She smiled, patting me on the arm. "Perhaps not one of my best decisions."

Her light laughter eased my heart.

"She cares about you, Berk. Probably too much."

"What does that mean?"

She shook her head as if she'd already shared too much.

Tutu was right, though. Jackie did care about me. Everyone did. But I'd shut the door on my past as soon as they'd closed the lid on

Jaime's casket. I'd thought lowering Alana's body into the ground had gutted me, but it was just as painful to watch my wife's body disappear below the earth.

"Jackie's a sweet girl, don't get me wrong," Tutu said. "Her heart is in the right place, but I think it may be too attached to you, if you know what I mean."

I knew what Tutu meant, but I wasn't going to acknowledge it.

Tutu stepped up on her porch and sat down in one of the rocking chairs. This side of her home faced the tropical forest, but the roar of the Pacific Ocean could still be heard from the other side of her house.

"Sit." She motioned toward the other chair.

A conversation on Tutu's porch could only mean one thing. She wanted information. Information I wasn't sure I wanted to give her.

"Jackie called and wanted to come here to the resort." Tutu pushed her toes against the floor and rocked her chair. "She said she had things to talk to you about."

I gripped the arms of my chair. "Do you know *what* things?"

"No, I don't. But she sounded devastated. Heartbroken really." Tutu turned and placed her small hand over mine. "You don't suffer alone, Berk. Always know that. Jackie's parents lost a daughter, too, you know. And a granddaughter." Tutu's dark brown eyes gazed up at me. "And I lost a granddaughter and great-granddaughter as well. You understand that type of heartache better than anyone."

Tears stung my eyes. I'd closed myself off from feelings and emotions for a long time—especially from Jaime's parents. I felt guilty for her death and couldn't help but think they blamed me in many ways, too.

"I don't know what Jackie has to say to you. I'm just hoping it's enough."

"Enough for what?"

"Enough for your warrior spirit to fight back."

I didn't know what the fuck Tutu was talking about, but that was nothing new with her. She spoke in soliloquies and riddles. It was best not to ask for explanations. Chances were, I wouldn't understand it anyway.

"So," she patted my hand, "tell me about her, this girl who has your spirit glowing again."

Her laughter surprised me.

"I'm scared, Tutu."

"Of returning home?"

I shook my head.

"Ah, of this woman? The one staying here?"

I nodded. How could I articulate the emotions Geneva was stirring inside me? Turning to look at my grandmother, I knew I didn't have to. She understood completely. She had a psychic ability that defied explanation.

"Tell you what, Berk, why don't you take the night off. Maybe spend some time with the girl. Talk a little."

"Talk." I laughed under my breath. If Tutu only knew. Actually, I'm sure she already did. "She's a resort guest, Tutu. She's strictly off limits. Your rule."

"Berk, she's the first person who's ever made you feel *anything* since Jaime and Alana's passing. She's much more than a resort guest, and you and I both know it."

I sat stock-still, stunned silent, my mouth gaping. "How did you know all of this?"

"I'm old, sweetheart, but I'm not blind. And you're not as covert with your maneuvers as you think you are. I see everything." She tapped her temple and grinned.

"Wait, are you saying you're not mad about me seeing her?"

"Go wash up, then take her to dinner."

I noticed she purposely didn't answer me.

"She's having dinner with her family tonight."

Tutu raised her brow. "Stop running, Berk. Before you know it, you'll look back and your life will be over."

"What are you saying?"

"I'm saying, sometimes things are snatched away from us for no reason at all. Not because of *anything* we have or haven't done. Just because that is life. But you shouldn't stop living it."

My eyes burned. She understood the guilt that crippled me.

"And other times, things are given to us that we don't deserve. We're afforded another opportunity, another chance. Those gifts cannot be wasted, Berk."

Tears welled in my eyes, but I made no move to wipe them away.

"You've wasted enough time here, sweetheart." She reached over and wiped away the tear that rolled down my cheek. "I love you, you know that. You're always welcome here. But not to hide."

Tutu saw everything. It was silly to think I could hide anything from her.

"Go, Berk. Enjoy what time you have left with this girl. Let yourself enjoy life again. You don't have to grieve every day for the rest of your life to prove how much you loved Jaime and Alana. We all know how much you did."

"But what happens when she leaves Hawaii, Tutu? It will be over."

"Maybe *your* time in Hawaii will be over, too."

I sank back in my chair, pondering Tutu's words. She was a mother bird, threatening to kick her grandbaby out of the nest. Mothers always knew best, didn't they?

"Maybe this woman is a gift from God," she said. "His way of saying, 'Your work here is done.' *Pau hana*, Berk."

I cut my eyes to Tutu. She knew, of course she did. She understood the hold Geneva had on me. And if her gentle smile was any indication, she was happy for me.

We sat in comfortable silence, her words covering me like a blanket.

"I think she may be a little put out with me," I confessed.

"Why?"

"I was in shock when I saw Jackie and it didn't go well."

"So, apologize," she said. "Your grandfather used to bring me vanilla milkshakes with coconut shavings sprinkled on top when he thought I was upset with him."

"Why?"

"Beats me. But it worked. A girl will *never* refuse ice cream. Trust me."

She raised her hand and stroked my face, her eyes glowing with motherly affection and love.

"I'm not saying she's the one, Berk," she continued. "And I'm certainly not going to kick you out of Kauai if this truly is where you want to spend your life. But you can't continue to hide here, losing yourself in the tropical jungles or the rolling waves of the Pacific Ocean. Jaime and Alana wouldn't want that for you. We both know that."

"Thanks, Tutu." I smiled down, brushing her cheek with a small kiss.

"For what, sweetheart?"

"For letting me get here on my own time, in my own way." She had understood that no one could rush me. Healing took time, a lot of time.

I knew I'd never *completely* get over the death of my wife and daughter. There would always be a gaping hole in my soul, which no one could fill. But maybe the pieces of my broken heart could be put back together again. It would have a different shape and a new rhythm, but at least it would have life again. And maybe even room enough for another love. Maybe Geneva could help me do that.

The thought brought a genuine smile to my face as I considered a life beyond Jaime and Alana for the first time in years. I couldn't hide any longer. I needed to start living again.

CHAPTER 23

BERK

THIS HAS GOT to be the most ridiculous thing I'd ever done in my life.

Glancing down at the vanilla milkshake adorned with coconut shavings sitting on the tray in my left hand, I had to admit—this probably did rank up there pretty high on Berk's Most Ridiculous Stunts list. I was hoping Tutu was right, that ice cream *would* make everything better.

I lifted my hand, gently tapping my knuckles against the door of Geneva's villa. I had a master key and could have easily walked in unannounced, but that would have been deceitful and not what I wanted Geneva to think of me. *Plus, someone could be in there with her.* A jealous surge of anger ran through my veins at the thought.

"I'll be right there," her singsong voice called.

Drawing in a deep breath, I closed my eyes, praying she'd still want to see me. If the look on her face from earlier was any indication, I knew I had some work to do.

The lock clicked open, and I watched as the handle lowered. My heart was racing so fast I could hear the blood rushing in my ears. I felt like a giddy teenager picking up his girlfriend for their first date.

And then it happened. Geneva slowly pulled the door open,

her sumptuous body clad in nothing but a huge terry cloth robe, compliments of the resort. My mind went blank, all thoughts lost as I stared at her. She was captivating, mesmerizing, bewitching.

"Berk," she said in surprise, her hands clutching at her robe.

Her action brought a smile to my face. I'd seen every square inch of her delectable body. Hell, I'd licked, sucked, and kissed most of it, too. And now, here she stood, trying to cover herself from my gaze.

"What are you doing here?" she asked, the annoyance in her voice hard to miss.

"Were you expecting someone else?" The words rolled out before I could even think about them. I didn't mean to sound like an arrogant, jealous asshole, but that was exactly the tone I'd used. And I was. The thought of her meeting someone else tonight had my skin on fire.

"No," she stuttered. "Well, uh…" Her voice quivered.

Oh, fuck, she *was* meeting someone.

"My friends and I were thinking about going out tonight. It's our last official night in Hawaii."

Last night? I nearly dropped the tray. "I thought you had two more days." My voice cracked and I sounded like a pathetic, pubescent boy.

"Well, I do, but Peter and Dana will be back in the morning, so tomorrow we'll all probably be busy catching up with them and packing our things."

The steel band that had tightened around my chest at her earlier statement, "last night," began to loosen. I dragged in a much-needed breath of air. She *wasn't* leaving tomorrow. But she was leaving soon.

"So, you'll still be here tomorrow night, right?" God, how pathetic did I sound? *Pretty fucking pathetic.*

"Uh, yeah. Technically."

Technically? What did that mean?

"Well, since *technically* this is your last night, I was wondering if maybe you'd like to spend it with me."

Her eyes grew wide.

"What?"

"I don't know. I guess I just thought I'd seen the last of you, earlier, when we got back."

"Why would you think that?"

Her gaze fell to the tile floor, one bare foot kicking the top of the other. Her bright pink toes looked so delicious, all I could think about was biting one.

"I saw the way you and that woman were talking earlier when I left, and I guess I just assumed maybe…"

Geneva had obviously felt the tension between Jackie and me. I wished I'd come sooner to explain myself.

"May I come in?" I changed the subject, hoping I could also change her plans for the evening.

"Um, sure, of course." She stepped back, swinging the door wide for me to enter.

As I brushed past her, my eyes scanned her face, but she wouldn't meet my gaze.

She rolled her bottom lip between her teeth. She was nervous, possibly even frightened. She was letting me into her room, but that was all. For now.

"I don't want to interrupt your plans," I said as I set the tray down on the kitchen bar.

"What's that?" She slid in beside me, her eyes roaming over the vintage malt glass.

"It's a vanilla shake."

"Why did you bring it here? I didn't order room service." The corners of her blue eyes crinkled in confusion and her lips shifted to the side in a small pucker.

"I thought I'd kind of messed up earlier." My hands were visibly shaking so I shoved them in my pockets. "So, I brought you this. To reassure you."

"Of what?"

Words weren't necessary. We were both skating around the issue. I didn't want Jackie's presence earlier to put a damper on my evening with Geneva. Especially if it was my last one with her.

Skimming around the corner of the bar, I walked into the familiar kitchen and slid open the utensil drawer, pulling out two spoons.

"For you, ma'am." I held out one spoon over the counter.

"What's this on top?" she asked, staring at the dusting of coconut shavings.

"That's coconut. Fresh coconut from here at the resort." Oh, shit. It just dawned on me. Maybe she wasn't like my tutu. Maybe she hated coconut with a passion. Or worse yet, maybe she was allergic to it.

"Do you like coconut?" I asked. *Please say yes.*

"Mmmm," she moaned.

My dick twitched at the sound. I looked up.

Her spoon was tucked inside her mouth, her plump lips closing over the base as she suckled the ice cream. Her eyes fluttered closed, and her face fell lax with pleasure. She definitely liked coconut, and I definitely *liked* watching her eat it.

"This is so good, Berk," she continued to groan.

I watched the column of her throat as she swallowed. Damn. My hard-on pushed painfully into the zipper of my shorts.

Her eyes slowly opened, as if coming down from some high. They were a dark blue now and hooded with lust, the way I'd seen them many times before. Only this time it was for fucking ice cream.

"I'm glad you like it," I squeaked out, all the blood from my body now pooled in my dick, robbing me of sight and sound—and the ability to speak properly, apparently.

Someone banged on the door, and we both jumped. The protector in me flew around the bar and headed toward the entrance.

"Don't." Geneva tugged me back. "It's my friend Tori."

Friend?

"I'll be right back," she said.

Wait? Was she saying, "I'll be right back," as in, "She's not going to be right back and I should leave," or as in, "Let me get rid of Tori so I can spend the night making sweet, sexy love to you." God, I hoped it was the latter.

Geneva swung the door open.

"Let's go, horndog!" her friend shouted.

Nope, not the latter.

"What are you still doing in your robe, wench?" Her friend continued. "Chop, chop. You need to get ready if we're gonna go live it up on our last night in Hawaii."

Last night? Live it up? Dammit, I was too late.

"You best get shaking, little momma," Tori said. "I'm ready to find some man candy."

More voices echoed from the hallway. Shit, she had a gaggle of friends. They were planning a *Girls Gone Wild* night.

A tall woman with long platinum blonde hair pushed through the door. I recognized her.

"Oh, shit." She stopped in the entrance, her face flushed red. "She's got company," she called behind her to unseen people.

"Berk, this is Tori, Peter's sister and my friend."

"Hello." I extended my hand.

"Well, hell-oh indeed." She smiled.

This girl was trouble with a capital T.

Two more people emerged from behind Tori. I recognized them both and prayed they wouldn't do the same of me. The world of extreme sports was big, but it wasn't big enough to escape fellow competitors.

"Uh, well, we'll just leave you two alone then," Tori said.

"No, wait." Geneva tried to stop her.

"Have fun, Berk." Tori winked at me. She actually winked.

The other woman stepped forward. She was Rory Gregor's wife. You had to be half dead or from another planet not to know this couple and all the trials and tragedies they'd endured over the last few years. Their story was the topic of headlines for months. They'd been to hell and back, like me. But at least they still had each other —and their precious baby girl.

They both looked at me, Hindley with a smile, Rory with a stern look of brotherly warning.

"Rory, Hindley, this is Berk." Geneva's hand moved from me over to her friends. "Berk, this is my stepsister Hindley and her husband Rory."

Sister? Brother-in-law? Shit, they were all related.

"I met you at the beach a few days ago," Hindley said.

I gave her a blank stare.

"When you offered surfing lessons to us. Well, to Geneva." She giggled as she looked over at Geneva.

I remembered that afternoon vividly. How could I forget it? Geneva had looked like a goddess that afternoon, lying on her lounger in a barely-there string bikini. I'd had to use my surfboard to hide the bulge in my board shorts when I finally worked up the nerve to approach her.

Other women had accompanied Geneva that day, but honestly, I couldn't have told you anything about them. It was Geneva who'd captured my attention that afternoon. I'd seen hundreds of girls at the resort since I'd returned, but none stopped me in the sand the way Geneva had.

"It's nice to finally meet you, Berk." Hindley smiled, extending her hand, breaking my wayward memory of Geneva stretched out on the beach.

"Uh, nice to meet you, too, Hindley," I answered, taking her hand in mine.

"So, *you're* the Greek God these chicks have been yacking about." Rory chuckled, extending his hand. "The one who's been stealing Geneva away from her family vacation." His words were playful.

So, they'd been talking about me? Geneva's family and friends?

I wasn't sure I was comfortable with that. They probably already hated me.

"It's nice to meet you all." I shook his hand. I'd grown out my hair since my return to Hawaii, and I hoped it was enough to hide my identity from Rory, a man who was a legend in extreme sports.

Rory's brows furrowed as he studied my face, his head half-cocked. "What did you say your name was?"

Fuck. Here it was. My name was not common. Most people remembered it.

"Berk," I answered quietly, hoping he hadn't heard me. I'd come to Hawaii for a reason—anonymity—and I didn't want to give that up. Not yet.

Rory held my hand and my gaze for a second longer than I was comfortable with. "Do I know you?" he asked.

"You've probably just seen him around the resort," Geneva answered for me. "His family owns it."

"Oh, wow," Hindley sighed.

"Let's go! Let's go! Let's go!" Tori shouted. "I'm ready to boogie." She held her hands high above her head as she shook her hips from side to side, bumping into Hindley and nearly knocking her over.

"All right, already." Hindley laughed as if she were used to Tori's antics. Her eyes cut to Geneva with sisterly affection and apprehension. "You guys have fun tonight." Her instructions sounded more like a warning.

"But not *too* much fun." Tori giggled, wrapping her arms around Geneva's shoulders and whispering something that had Geneva's eyes shooting wide with surprise.

"Let's go." Rory snaked his arm around his wife and tugged on Tori's arm. "Nice to meet you, man," he called back over his shoulder as they walked out the door.

Hindley gazed back to her sister, her look still filled with caution.

Geneva nodded her head, as if accepting Hindley's earlier warning. It was the silent sister language that no man was ever able to decode.

My blood ran cold, wondering what that warning may have been.

Slowly closing the door, Geneva leaned back, her hands tucked behind her as her face searched mine.

My body was drawn to her in a primal way, and I lost all control as I inched closer to her. I stopped just short, my hands planted on either side of her head against the door. She smelled like jasmine and vanilla, the fragrance of the resort's body products, and all I wanted to do was lick every square inch of her.

Her eyes darted between mine, trying to decide if she wanted to give in.

"Are you involved with her?" Geneva's voice was quiet.

"Who?" I heard the question, but all the blood from my brain was quickly traveling south.

"That girl. That woman you were talking to when we got back from camping earlier."

"Uh, no. I'm not involved with her." I didn't want to elaborate more, but I knew Geneva would push.

"Who is she?"

I wasn't willing to divulge exactly who Jackie was. Not yet. "She's a friend, I guess you'd say."

Geneva tilted her head in inquisition. "A friend like you and I are *friends*?" She raised a brow in warning.

"No," I chuckled, "definitely not *that* kind of friend, at all. Ever."

Geneva's body sagged in what I assumed was relief, but her eyes were still doubtful.

I bent my arms and leaned in closer so my lips were mere inches away from hers. "She's an old friend from Colorado, here visiting." Okay, that wasn't a lie, technically.

A small smile tugged at Geneva's lips.

Leaning in the short distance needed, I grazed my lips against hers. Our connection turned into a raging inferno, as if someone had flipped a switch that detonated a bomb. We were both lips and legs and arms, attacking one another in a carnal frenzy of need and desire. Bending to wrap my arms around her hips, I lifted her off the floor.

She wrapped her long legs around my waist as her hands dug into my hair.

I backed up, gripping her ass tighter, trying to turn us around. Instead, my knee connected with a side chair, and I yelled out in pain. I dropped Geneva into the chair as I toppled over.

Not wanting to fall on top of her, I shifted the weight of my body as I plummeted to the floor, trying to clear the teakwood coffee table. I extended my arm to brace my fall, thankful that my head missed the wooden piece of furniture. I fell, bracing myself with my hand.

"Shit!" I yelled as my wrist and hip began to throb.

"Oh my God, Berk, are you all right?"

Geneva jumped out of the chair and bent down beside me. Her robe slid open, revealing her bare legs and red lace panties underneath.

My mind was filled with images of my hand and my mouth and my tongue inside those panties, taking more from her than I deserved. The throbbing in my hip and wrist instantly ceased as my dick hardened with desire.

"Berk." She shook my shoulders, jolting me from my dreams.

The rumble of my laughter started deep in my chest and bubbled up my throat, echoing throughout the room.

"What's wrong? Are you hurt?" She was frantically rubbing up and down my body, assuring everything was still in place.

My cock twitched. God, how sick was I? Here she was, my real-life Florence Nightingale, trying to offer me medical assistance, and all I could think about was getting her naked and underneath me.

"I'm fine," I sighed, rubbing my face to rid the thoughts floating through my mind.

"Are you sure? Is your hip okay? You hit it pretty hard." The empathy in her voice and the grave expression on her face was overwhelming. She cared about me, *really* cared.

Wrapping my arm around her tiny waist, I pulled her close to me, her body nearly on top of mine. "I'm fine," I repeated. "Only my ego is bruised."

"Feels like something else is bruised, too." She giggled, rubbing up against my massive hard-on with her slender legs.

"I can't help it. It was your red lace panties that got me all hot and bothered."

"Berk." She slapped my shoulder. "I thought you were really hurt."

"I am," I said, rubbing my crotch against hers.

Her head fell back in laughter, exposing the slender column of her neck for my pleasure.

Leaning up on my other elbow, I pushed to a sitting position, squaring her on my lap. I lowered my head until my lips touched the golden skin of her throat. God, not only did she smell heavenly, she tasted divine, too.

"Oh," she moaned as her head fell to the side.

I added my tongue to the assault, licking my way up her smooth neck until I reached the base of her ear, sucking on the lobe. Experience had taught me this was a spot that would set her off. Geneva and I had known each other less than a week, but already, I knew her body almost as well as I knew my own.

In one fluid motion, I shifted us to a standing position, pulling her body flush with mine.

"Are you okay?" she asked, rubbing along my hip.

I knew she meant physically, but all I could think about was my heart and my head. They were both a mess. After talking to my tutu, I didn't know how to respond.

"So, you're leaving the day after tomorrow?" I asked, giving us some distance. "When your friends get back?"

Her eyes lowered.

Shit, I'd said the wrong thing. Ruined the moment.

"Yes," she answered, pulling away. "We're all flying out shortly after lunch."

I didn't want to believe it, but her voice sounded just as pained as her expression. She didn't want to be reminded that she was leaving soon, any more than I did. Thoughts of my own departure to the mainland had me speculating on a future with her. Maybe Geneva would agree to see me again if I returned.

I didn't want to ruin the moment and sound like a stalker, though. This had started out as a small-time affair on a tropical island for a girl on vacation and a guy lost in his own fucked up world. I didn't want to assume she wanted more. Rather than debate the arguments for why I should leave or stay in Hawaii, I turned my back and began to pick up the objects that had fallen to the floor when I fell. She didn't need to see my internal struggles.

"God, this is so good," Geneva said from behind me.

I gazed over my shoulder.

She was sitting on the bar stool, her face bathed in ecstasy as she pulled the spoon from her mouth. She was eating the milkshake again.

My own one-eyed snake was filling with venom. "I'm glad you like it." I jerked my head away from the erotic scene unfolding before me, averting my eyes to the floor as I tried to calm my sordid thoughts. Damn, what that woman did to me by just eating a fucking vanilla shake. Tutu had been right.

I focused on the task at hand, trying to clear my X-rated thoughts. Suddenly that became impossible as I stared down at the item in my hand.

It was a book, a novel. On the cover was the back of a woman, kneeling on the floor, completely nude. Her arms were tied with rope just above her elbows, her hands covering the crack of her naked ass. Her long hair was draped over one shoulder. A man wearing dress pants and no shirt rested his hand on top of her head as he dangled a whip in his other hand. *What the fuck?*

"What the hell is this?" I held up the book in my hand as I turned to face Geneva.

Her face washed over with an ashen color, the spoon in her mouth falling to the floor with a clattering thud.

"Oh, shit!" she yelled, lurching from the chair and charging after me.

I held it high above my head.

"Give it to me, Berk!" she pleaded, jumping in the air, trying to grab it from my hand.

"So, Geneva reads naughty books." A small smile spread across my face when I realized this girl had a kinky side, a *really* kinky side. The thought brought more blood to my midsection.

"Berk," she shouted, "give it back!"

"Oh, hell no." I laughed, skirting her grasp, jumping over the coffee table to escape.

"Please," she begged.

"Why I declare, Geneva," I teased in my most southern drawl, "it seems you're a dirty, dirty girl." Studying the cover, I focused on the title. "*My Master's Plan*," I read out loud. "Master?" I repeated, raising my brow.

Geneva's face was crest-fallen, all the life drained from her eyes. She was guilt-ridden and embarrassed by my discovery.

"What is this?" I asked.

She plopped down on the sofa, her fingers fanning out to shield her face, which was now redder than the delectable panties she wore under her white robe.

"Don't be embarrassed." I soothed. I plopped down on the sofa and thumbed through the pages of her porno book. I stopped at an arbitrary location and began to read out loud.

West darts around the large glass desk, gripping CC's wrist before her hand connects with the receiver, his long finger driving toward the button marked "speaker."

"Don't you dare answer my phone, West!" CC shouts.

Ignoring her pleas, like the dominant he is, she watches in horror as he depresses the button.

"I'm sorry," his deep voice informs the caller. "Ms. Jones will be tied up for the next few hours." His lips spread into a devilish grin as he removes his finger from the console, effectively ending the call before it even begins.

"This isn't your chamber," CC reminds him. "This is my fucking office. MY office, West. It's off limits, we agreed."

Slipping his hand into the pocket of his tailor fitted suit jacket, his breath quickens and his eyes darken in that familiar way she's grown to despise. CC's legs go taut as her eyes focus on the object in his hand, his other still gripping her wrist, drawing her hand behind the chair.

"Not here, West. Please," she begs. "You promised."

"I didn't promise you anything."

The hiss of his voice burns her insides with anger and need.

"And I wasn't lying, Priscilla." The long violet hued ribbon unfurls from his large hand, rolling out across her lap.

Her breathing becomes labored.

"You're going to be tied up for quite some time."

"Damn, Geneva, what the fuck are you reading?" Ashamed by my own arousal, I marked the page with my thumb as I peered over at her.

She sat quietly with her head hung low and her shoulders slumped, seemingly mortified. "Please don't read any more," she whispered.

"Are you fucking kidding me? This shit is hot. No wonder you chicks go ape-shit crazy over it."

Her head jerked up, her eyes wide at my declaration. "Don't make fun of me." She scowled, jumping from her seat to take the book.

I lurched away from her grip as I held the book high in the air. No fucking way was she going to get this book out of my hands. "What? Can't a guy get turned on by this shit, too?"

"Are you serious? You aren't making fun of me?"

"Hell no." I chuckled. "This shit is hot. I give my sister shit all the time about reading these books, the ones with the half-naked men in a semi-porn pose on the cover, jeans halfway unbuttoned. But now I know why she likes them." Opening the page I'd marked earlier, I read out loud again.

"Stop!" Geneva shouted, reaching across my chest to snatch the book away. "Don't, please." Grief cut across her face with a type of pain I hadn't seen before.

"Why?"

"I'm just…" she stammered.

"Don't be embarrassed."

"It's not like I'm a horndog or anything. I just really like this author, and this is her first BDSM book so I wanted to read it."

"BDSM? What the hell is that?" I mean, I knew what it was, but not in relation to books. Maybe it meant something different in the reader world.

"It's like *Fifty Shades of Grey*. You know, bondage, spanking." She shrugged her shoulders in an adorable way that I just couldn't resist.

"So, do you like that bondage stuff? Being tied up and spanked?" I asked playfully, but semi-serious.

She shrugged again, a crimson flush staining her cheeks. Oh, she liked it. This could be fun.

"Have you ever tried it?"

"No," she answered quickly. "Have you?"

A shy, expectant glimmer in her eyes made me laugh.

"What?"

Instead of answering, I opened the book and continued reading.

. . .

He swallows thickly, trying to contain his fury. "Tell me, Priscilla, why do you live?"

His tone is low and seemingly uncaring, but CC has grown accustomed to the edge in his voice when he's displeased.

"Answer me!" He slaps her bare thigh just below the hem of her skirt.

"I live to please you," CC whispers, ashamed of how aroused she is by his spanking. Her pussy grows wet with need.

His raised brow indicates her statement is not acceptable.

"Master," she corrects. "I live to please my Master."

"And have you pleased me, Priscilla?" He squeezes her tightened nipple through her shirt, his lips mere inches from hers.

An aching need sparks between her legs. She hates how much she wants this, the sharp sting of agony necessary to reach the erotic levels of pleasure only he can bring her body. She's grown too dependent on him, and he knows it. It was part of his master plan all along.

"No," she moans.

He yanks both arms behind her chair. The action stretches her blouse until the top two buttons pop off and fall, dancing obliviously atop the granite floor of her office.

Her nipples tingle with desire. The way this man affects her, this brooding and frightening beast, isn't surprising to her, only frustrating.

In the day-to-day chaos, CC Jones is the mistress of her domain, exacting her will over the employees of her company, including West Cumberland. But sitting in her high-rise office, their positions have changed. With one misstep, she broke their rules, and now West has all the power. He is the master, despite their surroundings. The master she wants to please.

CC instinctively knows what he wants, what he craves. He requires surrender, complete and total submission. The rules were only to be enforced in his chamber, but many things have changed over the course of the two months they've been together, including her own personal feelings for this man who dominates her—the man she wants to give herself up to, body and soul.

Now he exacts his power anywhere he desires, and it frightens her more than the whip in his hand.

"Do I like disobedience, Priscilla?"

"No."

West cracks the whip, hitting her desk and scattering papers across the floor. He leans forward, his gorgeous green eyes boring into hers. The intoxicating scent of his body builds up a fire between her legs that threatens to spontaneously combust.

He moves in closer, seemingly gentle, but she knows better. He grabs a fist full of hair, yanking her head back so she is staring up at him. His face is beautiful but brutal, the pulsing in his neck indicating how out of control he is.

"No, what, Pricilla?" he grits through clenched teeth.

"No...Master," she whispers.

His dark eyes twinkle in satisfaction and desire, lust pooling in the depths of his innermost being.

Master does not like disobedience. He does not tolerate disrespect, regardless of how powerful or wealthy Priscilla Jones may be. To him, she is just another sub, and that's the way she wants it. There will be consequences, of that she is assured. There always are.

This time, CC will be prepared.

"Holy shit, Geneva," I sighed, falling back into the plush cushions behind me.

"What?" Her eyes were wide as if fearing my reaction to her erotic novel.

"That was like, seriously hot. I totally didn't expect to get turned on reading about some chick getting slapped while she's tied up."

"But?"

"But I did. Does that make me a bad person?" I chuckled nervously.

"Does it make me one?" Her eyes locked on mine. They were darker, more demanding, her pupils dilated and pooling with desire. She wanted this. This was her fantasy. And I wanted to give it to her.

You never know how strong you are until being strong is the only choice you have.
- Bob Marley

CHAPTER 24

GENEVA

"Do you trust me?" Berk asked, his voice low and controlled.

I'd never felt safer in my life. "Yes," I answered.

His eyes melted like caramelized sugar, and a warm smile spread across his supple lips. His jaw clenched, accentuating his masculinity and God-like features.

My body tingled in anticipation.

He stood, book securely held in one hand, as he reached for me with the other.

Not knowing what to expect and not really caring at this point, I slipped my hand into his, allowing him to ease me up off the sofa. I was a fly caught in his web, his hypnotic spell woven around me.

Leading me to the bar of the kitchen, he nodded toward one of the high standing stools. "Sit." His gentle command was soft, but precise.

With my eyes glued to his, I tugged my robe securely and lowered myself onto the stool. My gaze never once broke the spell I was under.

Taking both hands, he opened the book to where he had marked it with his thumb, his body looming over me in a dominant way.

Electric sparks shot through my body as I finally understood what he was about to do.

I wasn't a submissive, and I'd never been restrained. But somehow, reading through the short passage of my book, Berk had been able to see through me. He understood that I wanted to try but somehow knowing I would only do it with someone I trusted.

Berk began to read again.

West holds CC's wrists behind her executive chair, mindful of the torque he's placing on her shoulder joints. He understands domination comes in all forms. He's made it his mission to study it intently for the past six months. It goes against his personality, but he's done it, learned the lifestyle, all for her. Being a dominant isn't his natural tendency, but he's willing to do whatever it takes to make CC his.

"Okay, wait." Berk held his place in the book and stared up at me. "So he's *not* a dominant?"

"West is in love with CC, always has been," I explain. "A year ago CC's husband passed away. He was a lot older than CC, but they were in love. They'd built an empire together and now she's the sole owner, a very powerful woman running a huge corporation. Secretly she's always dreamed of being dominated, though."

"Okay?"

"West works for her. He's her company's chief technology officer, part of her executive team. He discovered some searches on her computer one day and realized bondage and submission is what she's always craved. He researched the BDSM lifestyle and learned how to become a Dom."

"What's a Dom?"

"Sorry, a dominant is the partner who's in control. It can be the man or the woman."

"Hmmm." Berk scratched his chin with a lopsided smile.

"Anyway, West goes through some pretty intense training in the beginning of the book to learn what to do and how to act, so he can please her."

"Wow, that's a lot of work for one guy to undertake." Berk laughs.

"He loves her. You do a lot of crazy shit for love."

Berk's eyes narrowed as if asking for more of my story.

I remained silent.

Obviously understanding my wishes, he started to read again.

Controlled pain is part of her submission, but intentional injury, like some Doms pursue, is not his way. His love for CC transcends his domination, but now is not the time for him to show that. Now, he is the dominant, and she is his submissive. It's the only way CC will accept his love, if he completely dominates the world she thinks she controls.

With her wrists in his possessive hold, he expertly binds them with the satin ribbon, leaving a long tail. West remembers purple is her favorite color. She has said so many times before. Indigo represents passion and power. Today it will be a symbol of both.

Berk laid the book face-down on the bar as his eyes scanned the room. They stopped at my waist.

My gaze followed his, and I noticed the robe I was wearing had fallen open, revealing the expensive red satin bra and panty set underneath. Lingerie had been an indulgence of mine once. Even though I had no viewing audience any more, I always liked the way the sexy undergarments made me feel.

Instinctively, I knew Berk was going to spread me open. My panties dampened at the thought. I'd read enough of V.M. Wilson's book to know what would come next, what West would put CC's body through. Tonight, I was glad I'd afforded myself the luxury of at least looking my best for Berk like CC always tried to do for her dominant.

Kneeling in front of me, Berk slowly pulled the belt from my opened robe, running it through his fingers as his face morphed into the perfect dominant male. *Oh, shit!*

"Do you still trust me, Geneva?"

"Yes," I whispered, my throat grainy and dry as desert sand. It was the truth.

He gently took one wrist in his strong hand. Bringing it behind the back of my stool, he then brought the other arm. Gently, he used the belt of the robe to tie my wrists together. *Oh. My. God.*

"Is that okay?" he whispered in my ear.

A chill curled around my spine and moved down to my toes. I nodded once.

He walked around me, surveying my body. With my robe open now my breasts were on prominent display for his consumption. I was bound, unable to cover myself from his predatory gaze.

"A dominant is not supposed to ask his submissive if she's comfortable." I smiled.

He gripped my chin with his fingers, raising my face to meet his squarely before speaking. "I don't know much about this book you're reading, Geneva, or how this lifestyle works. But it sounds like this is about trust, not pain. It's obvious there is nothing West would do to ever hurt this woman beyond what she desires. I intend to treat you the same."

His words wrapped around me like a thick comforter, cocooning me in warmth and security. Just like CC, I would do whatever Berk asked me. He was right. The BDSM lifestyle was about trust. Berk wouldn't hurt me. I trusted him with this type of play. There hadn't been many people in my life who I trusted.

Berk stalked toward the table, leaving my body gaping open for the world to see. My villa was an open-air concept with the walls retracted to see the beautiful landscape surrounding the resort.

My heart raced as I thought about someone walking along the beach and seeing what we were doing inside. The thought should have scared me, but it only heightened the intensity of the scene playing out before me.

Sensing my concern, Berk walked across the room and slid the retractable wall closed, hiding us from view. Berk's job as my Dom was to know my needs, even before I did.

My heart pounded hard against my chest like the ocean waves into the rocks below. A slight breeze from the open windows blew across my exposed skin, puckering my nipples.

Standing in front of me, Berk's eyes drank in my body. The moment was so erotic I nearly came from his perusal alone. He had that much power over me.

He began to read again.

West walks around, surveying his handiwork. Satisfied with his job, he leans over her body with one hand on the arm of her executive chair while the other covers her delicate thigh. Extending one long finger, he traces the hem of her skirt, crawling up her leg until he reaches the border of her lace-topped silk stocking. His dick twitches as his hand reaches soft skin just above the edge.

Moving further up her leg, he watches intently as the anger in CC's eyes begins to dissolve. No matter what she says, she always longs for his touch. It's his magic wand, and he intends to wave it to cast his spell on her.

Watching as her eyes smolder with desire, he gives a wry smile, sensing that her anger is waning. He's invaded her professional world, but he doesn't care. It was the last place CC felt in control. He has to break her completely to capture her and make her his.

West stops abruptly when his hand reaches the apex of her thighs and his disappointment at the material covering her pussy infuriates him.

"What the fuck are these, Priscilla?" He watches the contours

of her delicate throat as she swallows. "I've told you I don't want you wearing anything but a garter and stockings. I want your sweet pussy accessible to me at all times, anytime, anywhere."

"This is my office, West." Her voice is strained as she tries to keep the last shred of control she thinks she has.

"Who?" he asks, slapping her thigh.

"Master," she chokes out.

"I don't give a shit if it's the goddamn White House, and you're having dinner with the fucking president. If I tell you to do something..." He yanks on her hair, bringing her face directly in front of his to make sure he has her undivided attention.

She needs to let go of herself, of all her control. She needs to understand exactly who's in control now. If he wants her, he must break her, no matter how much it breaks him.

"If I tell you to do something, Priscilla, what do you do?"

"I..." She wavers as fear seizes her voice.

Good. Power is good. "Yes?" West growls.

"I do it," she blurts out.

"Do you understand that simple, fucking concept, CC?" West speaks succinctly, adding her nickname to garner her full attention.

"Yes," she whimpers in defeat, her eyes lowering.

"Yes, what?"

Yanking on her hair again, he waits until her gaze finds his. His brows rise, awaiting her correct response.

"Yes, Master."

"Good submissive, my darling," West coos, releasing her hair and stroking gently on the hair he's just pulled taut around his hand.

His long fingers caress her face as he trails them over her chin and down the contours of her smooth neck. His hand moves further down her chest, until one rests on the edge of her lace bra, dipping inside until he touches the already peaked nipple.

Her small moan is his undoing, and he nearly drops to his knees to bring her the pleasure he knows she craves. But this is a lesson she has to learn. She is not in control. Anywhere.

Abruptly removing his finger, ending his deviant assault, West yanks on the ribbon behind her, whipping CC's chair around as he drags it over to the floor-to-ceiling wall of her corner office.

Berk peered down at me over the top of the book, his large hand reaching out as one lone finger made contact with my breastbone.

I watched as his eyes smoldered and his finger trailed down toward the top of my lacy bra.

"God, you're beautiful," he whispered, his eyes hungrily drinking me in. "Do you have any idea?"

"I used to." I didn't even know where those words came from as they rolled out of my mouth. Berk's wrinkled brow told me he was confused, but I didn't want to offer more. Not when I had no idea what I was saying.

"Keep reading," I said.

He raised one brow as a reminder of who was in charge tonight.

"Please keep reading, Master." I smirked.

"You don't have wheels on this chair so I'm going to leave you be." Berk's face broke with a deviant grin. He was happy I was playing along.

I liked this game. I liked Berk. I trusted him with my body, and I could tell my submission spoke to him on a level that words couldn't.

He continued reading.

"You disrespected me in the boardroom, Priscilla. What did I tell you would happen if you disrespected me in public again?" he asks.

"This is work, West. It's different, we agreed."

"No, my darling, you asked for work to be off limits. I never agreed."

Her eyes dart toward the window as she tries to focus on

anything other than West, but he needs her full attention. She's afraid.

Taking her face in his hand, West turns her head until they are nearly nose-to-nose. "I am in control of you, everywhere, Priscilla." His voice is low and threatening.

Her body shudders under his grasp. Exactly what he wants.

"I own you, Priscilla Jones. You're mine for the taking—in my chamber, in my bed, in the fucking boardroom of your own goddamn company, if I want you. You. Are. Mine."

West bears down on her lips hard, his tongue probing, prying hers open.

She fights him.

West slaps hard against her leg, just the way he knows she likes it.

She soon complies, her moans of pleasure sparking his own desire. She loves when West spanks her. She's said so before. Much to his surprise, something inside him loves it, too.

Pulling away from her, he gulps a breath of air. Her own breathing is labored. Their passion consumes every part of their bodies. West can see it in her eyes that she's questioning him again, even in the midst of his dominance over her.

"I even own your dreams. Nothing you have is yours any more, Priscilla. You just think it is. You dream of me at night. I hear you calling out for me while I fuck you hard, whether you're awake or in your dreams. I. Own. All of you, Priscilla. Don't I?"

She hesitates.

"Don't I?" West snaps.

She jumps at his words but nods once.

"Good girl," he purrs.

He understands how difficult it is for her to admit. He has wrested the last piece of control from her—her mind. He won't force the words.

One lone tear rolls over her lashes, staining her cheek.

West's heart breaks for her, but he can't show that. He is her

*dominant and this is the only way he can reach her if he wants her
forever.*

*He slides his hand down her silky leg and grasps her ankle,
pulling it back behind her chair. He loops the ribbon around her
ankle, then binds it to her wrists, watching as her legs spread wide.
Pulling her panties aside, he sees her pussy lips glisten with her
desire. He smiles confidently as he stands back and admires his
work. She is beautiful. And one day she will come to him, without
being ordered.*

Berk set the book on the bar again and stalked toward me. Placing
his hands on either side of my legs, his lips brushed against mine,
much gentler than West's would have.

I wanted to touch him, to feel his stubble underneath my hands,
but, as I tried to move, I remembered I was trussed up and bound by
this delicious man.

His lips left mine, and I moaned from the loss, trembling as they
skimmed across my jaw and down my neck, making their way
toward my breast.

I didn't remember him reading this part of the book, but, at the
moment, I really didn't give a shit. What Berk was doing, how he
was making me feel, was too good for me to care about anything
other than his body connecting with mine.

He pulled away again, too quickly to satisfy my need, and I
whimpered in disappointment.

Just as West had in the book, Berk dragged one of his large
hands down my leg until it reached my bare ankle.

"Okay?" he asked in permission.

His gesture was so kind. I knew he wanted to dominate me, but
he also wanted me to feel safe with him. And I did. I knew that
without a doubt.

I nodded my head, giving him complete control. Tucking my leg
behind me, I squirmed a bit, trying to gain my balance at this new

position. Placing my free foot out in front of me for balance, I drew in a breath as Berk fastened the remainder of the belt around my ankle.

I was bound, completely at his mercy. Tugging on my arm, I nearly fell off the chair as my foot moved with it, pushing me off balance. Shit! If I moved either arm or my leg, I realized, I'd go tumbling off the chair. I was now dependent on Berk, for everything.

With my legs spread wide, the cool ocean breeze ran across the villa and gently licked the material of my thin panties. Heat rose to the surface of my bared skin. The moment was erotic, surreal, and I suddenly realized what all the fuss about BDSM had been all along. It was fucking hot as shit, the anticipation, the not knowing, the loss of control.

The trust.

"My God," Berk sighed, focusing on my body as he stood in front of me, his eyes darker, his pupils dilated with raw desire as his tongue licked his lips.

His gaze brought a tingle that skimmed across my skin, my own panties now coated with the evidence of my need for him. I wanted him so much in this moment, to touch him and be part of him, to connect his body with mine.

He stood an arm's length away, not willing to give in to my desires as his hand skirted across the granite-topped bar. Grabbing the book, he gripped it hard. He was turned on, too, both our senses heightened as we awaited West's instructions.

My eyes moved down to his pants. The evidence of his arousal was on display, his giant Poseidon dick bulging through his shorts. His body was taut, flexed with desire, for me. Drawing in a deep breath, he continued reading the story.

CC gasps as West takes the scissors from her desk drawer. The stainless-steel blades shimmer in the afternoon sun.

"Since you can't seem to follow directions, my sweet, I'll have to take matters into my own hands." West's eyes burn through her, his desire so potent she nearly collapses. What the hell was he going to do with those scissors?

"Are you afraid?" West asks.

"Yes, Master." This time CC remembers.

West kneels before her, spreading her legs wider as he stares at the juncture that's already wet for him.

"Do you think I'll hurt you, Priscilla?" He waves the scissors in the air.

CC draws in a deep breath. For the first time since they've entered into this relationship, she's scared.

"You know your safe word," West reminds her, running the cool blade against her cheek. "And maybe this will remind you not to defy me again."

West takes the scissors and runs them up her bare thigh, just above her stockings. He slides the blades beneath the edge of her skirt.

"West, it's my skirt!" CC cries out.

His eyes collide with hers. Nothing but fury is held inside.

"Do not defy me, Priscilla. You and I both know you have a closet full of clothes just inside the bathroom here in your office."

It's true, CC does have a full wardrobe inside her massive office, but this is about more than clothes.

The scissors remain in place as West pushes up so that he's directly in front of her. "I will never push you beyond what you can handle, Priscilla. Trust me to take care of you."

She nods, the sting of tears pissing her off. Losing control of any situation has never been an option for Priscilla Whitman Jones.

Suddenly, the cold, hard steel is gone from her leg. She casts her gaze down to see that West has removed the scissors from her thigh. He knows her, knows that she is afraid but unwilling to disclose it. He truly is her dominant.

"I'm all right, Master, I promise."

"You're trembling, Priscilla. Breathe, sweetheart."

CC draws in a ragged breath, willing her heart rate to slow. Her eyes pop wide when she feels his warm breath on her leg. Gazing down, she sees West lapping at her inner thigh.

"There is more than one way to remove your panties, Priscilla. And I think I may actually enjoy this way better."

West lifts her hips, her skirt riding up around her waist, her thong panties leaving her bare ass stuck to the leather chair.

His teeth clamp onto the lace front of her underwear.

She feels the pinch of her skin.

His head shakes like a wild dog, and the familiar ripping sound echoes through her office. A small smile tugs at her mouth. It's become one of her favorite ways to be undressed by him.

The cool office air wafts over her bared lips as he pulls the lace away—with his teeth. He tucks his fingers into the elastic band and tugs with both hands, the fabric ripping easily, baring everything to him.

She is exposed, in more ways than one.

"I want you, Priscilla. All of you." West's voice is firm and serious.

For a moment she tricks herself into believing there could be more between them, more than just a relationship between a Dom and a sub. But that's silly. She could never exist in his world full time. She is falling for him, falling hard for her master. But that goes against every rule in this lifestyle. Doesn't it?

Their time together is fleeting, even though she yearns for more. More with West.

His warm tongue strokes her from ass to clit, back and forth, up and down, his fingers invading her pussy as she clenches in preparation. She can never stave off her orgasms long for her master. He is too wild, too passionate, and too skilled. He knows her body too well.

West is everything she's ever wanted in a man—strong, success-

ful, passionate. But he is a dominant, destined to move on to a new submissive when he tires of her.

She cries out when her orgasm reaches its peak, but her screams aren't all in pleasure. She hides the sobs underneath, knowing one day he will leave her. Just like everyone she loves.

Berk peered up over the book, one brow arched.

"You are *not* using scissors near my hoo hah," I said. "And these are expensive panties."

"Come on, Geneva." He set the book down and walked toward me. "Where's your sense of adventure?"

"You think your teeth can rip through these panties." I laughed.

He chomped down several times as he smiled wide. "I'm pretty strong." He moved closer, putting his hands on either side of the bar stool.

"Fine," I huffed, leaning my head back. I tried to move my arms and nearly fell out of the chair.

"Whoa." Berk caught me as I fell forward, and then righted me. "So maybe this whole BDSM thing isn't as safe as we thought." He chuckled.

"They definitely make it sound a lot sexier than it feels."

"Do you want me to untie you?"

"No."

He smiled, giving me that expression that set my panties on fire every time he gifted me with it. He wouldn't need to cut them off, I was pretty sure they'd already disintegrated.

His hands slid up my robe, spreading the terry cloth material apart as they traced the center of my panties.

"Oh, God," I moaned. The pressure was perfect, but his tongue would feel even better.

He knelt below me as he kissed my inner thigh, working his way up with little nibbles. He reached the edge of my panties, his tongue tracing the elastic band. "Okay?" he asked.

"Okay," I sighed. I could always buy more panties.

His teeth sunk in, and he pulled the lace material back, stretching the panties taut. The seams stayed intact as well as the lace. Taking a larger bite of the material, my panties now clenched tight, he shook his head like a coyote ripping apart its prey. The material didn't budge.

"What the fuck are these things made of?" he grumbled through his teeth now grinding on my red satin panties.

I giggled.

His eyes rolled up to mine and he growled in disapproval.

It only turned me on more. "Try with your hands," I suggested.

He dug his fingers inside the waistband, stretching them beyond their limit as his teeth tugged on the material. Still nothing. My panties were not shredding as easily as we'd hoped.

"What the fuck?" he said.

I laughed. Loud. Suddenly a smack echoed through the room, my outer thigh stinging, pulsating with a heated burn. "Did you just fucking hit me?" I snarled.

"You laughed at your Dom," he answered quickly.

My eyes narrowed and I cocked my head. "I'm sorry, I couldn't hear you through your mouthful of panties." I giggled.

With one final tug, he yanked on my panties. The force threw my body forward.

"Berk!" I screamed as my body fell toward him, stool and all. With my arms and legs tied, I couldn't catch myself. I crashed on top of him, both of us plummeting to the floor. My head hit Berk's, the force slamming his into the floor with a thud.

"Fuck!" he yelled.

I tugged on my foot and hands to balance myself but they were still bound behind me. "Oww!" I yelled.

"Oh my God, Geneva, are you all right?" He stood, bringing the stool and me with him as he set us upright.

My head was pounding from the impact with Berk's head. "Are *you* all right?" I asked, knowing he'd hit the tile floor hard.

He didn't answer. Instead, he raced behind me, undoing the belt.

As my arms fell free, I gripped the bar with both my hands and slid off the stool.

"Geneva, I'm so sorry."

"Berk, your head." I reached behind his neck and ran my hands through his hair. There was already swelling. "Let me get some ice." I walked around the bar and took ice from the freezer, wrapping it in a towel. I butted up next to him and pressed it against his head.

He winced. "Oww."

"Oh, God, I'm so sorry," I said.

"No, *I'm* sorry." He frowned. The guilt on his face hit my heart. "I'm the one who tied you up." He took the rag from my hand. "Here, let me." He held the ice against my forehead.

"We're a pair, aren't we?" I laughed.

"I think from now on we should probably stick to the safe sex stuff. No more bondage. Or, at least, nothing on a bar stool." He smiled, that enigmatic grin that punched me in the heart. "What the hell are those things made of anyway?" Berk tugged on my underwear, and we both broke out in laughter.

"And, did you hit me?" I raised a brow and cocked my head.

"I believe it's called role playing," he teased. "Did you like it?" His expression was expectant.

Did I? "It was kind of hot. I could see where it would work. Maybe in the confines and safety of a bed, though, like you said." I yelped as he scooped me up.

"Grab the book." He nodded toward the bar.

"What?"

"One way or another, I'm going to get those panties off you. And I want to find out what West does next."

"Are you addicted to my naughty book?" I leaned over the counter and grabbed the book.

Berk walked us into the bedroom. The sun was setting, casting a romantic glow around the room. "I'm addicted to *you*."

My body stiffened in his hold, afraid to say anything to break the intimate moment. I studied his face, committing it to memory. I was just as addicted to him. I only had one more night to get my fill of Berk Rigby—a fix that would have to last.

He pulled back the comforter and laid me on the bed, staring down at me like I was his most prized possession. It was a look straight from every romance novel I'd ever read.

He dropped the book on the side table, climbing on top of me. "How's your head?"

"It's fine. How's yours?" I reached up and stroked the back of his head.

Without answering, he grabbed a fist full of his shirt from behind and slowly pulled it over his head. His chiseled body was stunning, so powerful and strong.

I gulped at the sight of him, overcome with emotions that I didn't even know how to explain.

"What's wrong?" He tossed his shirt aside.

"You're so beautiful." I rubbed my hands over his dark chest.

"So are you." He kissed my neck, moving lower to the top of my breasts, which were heaving over my bra. Working with nimble fingers, he popped the front clasp, exposing my breasts to the cool evening air. Taking one nipple into his mouth, he rolled it with his tongue as his hand gripped the other.

"Oh, God, Berk." I dug my fingers into his hair.

"Oww!" he yelled, pulling back.

"Oh my God. Your head, I'm so sorry." I reached over for the ice but he stopped my hand mid-motion.

"We won't use ropes or belts tonight, but why don't you try to put your hands up here." He took my wrists in his hands as he knelt before me, pushing my arms up toward the headboard. "Hold on here and don't let go. Okay?" He gave me a wink. "Otherwise, I'll have to spank you."

"Maybe I want to be spanked."

With my hands still above me, he flipped me over. I screamed in surprise as he tugged my panties completely off.

"Tuck your knees underneath you and hold on to the head-board," he growled in my ear.

Holy fuck.

"Now, Geneva."

Oh, dominant Berk was here. And I was wet and ready.

"Yes, Master." I giggled.

Smack! It was loud and hard and stung like shit against my ass. But I couldn't lie. As he soothed it with his hand, the sting turned to a burn that went straight between my legs.

His finger ran through the length of me, my desire coating his finger.

"Fuck, you love this shit, don't you?" he asked.

"Yeah, I kind of do," I said, surprised by my own reaction. "Do you?"

"Yeah. I just don't want to hurt you again."

I gazed over my shoulder. His face was weary and distraught. "It's a good kind of hurt." I smiled, trying to reassure him.

"I don't have any condoms."

"I'm on the pill," I reassured him. "Took one this morning. And I'm clean."

"You know my history," he said.

He'd already told me he'd never been with anyone since his late wife, and I believed him.

"Yes," I whispered, not wanting to detract from the present moment by bringing up memories from his past. "You're clean. I know. And I trust you." I hesitated a brief moment, not wanting our moment to end. "Now get naked and do something with me. I'm hot and bothered and ready for you."

His brow furrowed. "I thought I was the Dom here."

"Then act like it."

He swatted my ass again.

"Oww!" I yelped.

His bare chest rubbed against my back as he leaned close to my ear. "You are mine, Geneva. All of you."

With no other words or warning, he slammed into me, hard. He rode me fast and strong.

Berk stole my breath. I came within seconds, screaming out his name in exaltation.

He continued to pump into me, riding out my orgasm with me, filling me completely with his ever-thickening cock.

The tension of another orgasm built to a painful peak within me.

Berk's fingers dug into my hips and yanked me against him as he slammed his giant body against me. His dick hit me at the center of my desire.

My legs quivered as my hands held tight to the headboard. Oh, God, I was going to come again.

Slowly, his fingers slipped through my legs, pressing my throbbing core, sending me over the edge. Again. I screamed out in climax.

His own orgasm hit and he released inside me, tugging on my waist and pushing further inside. Berk consumed me, body and soul.

I was his.

CC's words from the book rang through my head. I was tricking myself, thinking there was more between us than just a quick vacation fling. We belonged in different worlds, thousands of miles away, with pasts that weighted us down to the point of exhaustion. We could never be together.

CHAPTER 25

GENEVA

I RESTED my chin on Berk's chest as my fingers danced on the smooth skin of his abdomen. Peering up at his face, he seemed so far away for someone who'd just been so close to me all night. "You look lost in thought," I said, trying to lighten the mood.

"I am."

His answer shocked me, and my mind went on high alert.

"Why?" I pushed up on my arm so I could see him fully.

"I've been thinking of going back home."

That was shocking. "Are you going back to visit your parents?"

"Yes." He offered nothing more.

I withdrew my hand from his stomach.

He snatched it with his huge hand to keep it in place. "What?" he asked.

"You just seem quiet today."

Drawing in a deep breath, Berk's eyes rolled up to the sheer white canopy hanging over the bed.

The breeze moved through the material as the waves outside crashed against the shore. The entire scene was the most romantic, idyllic setting I'd ever experienced. I could see how people fell in love in Hawaii. *Love? Whoa!*

His hand slid up my arm as his body rolled toward mine, his face now directly above me. "I'm sorry."

Something in my gut tightened, and not with desire. He seemed distressed, and it didn't sit well with me.

"I'm thinking about going back to Colorado," he repeated, "for good."

Oh, shit! For good? What did that mean? *It means this isn't just a vacation fuck any more.* Was Berk saying he wanted the potential for more? Part of me was excited, but most of me was frightened by the prospect of his return. That meant revealing more of myself, more of my tainted past, and I wasn't sure that was something I was willing or able to do.

I sat up in bed, trying to free myself from Berk's hold. I needed to think, needed to collect my thoughts. Being wrapped around Berk made that impossible to do.

"What's wrong?" he asked.

"Nothing," I said, but my voice and body language betrayed me.

He reached up to toy with my hair. "I've been thinking about it a lot since I met you, actually."

Oh, shit. A bolt of fear hit me, sending a wave of anxiety pulsating through my limbs.

"What?" he asked.

I shook my head, trying to reassure him I was fine, but inside, I was anything but.

"I didn't mean to scare you." He smiled, his hand moving from my hair to wrap his fingers around my wrist.

I peered down at his dark hands. His touch was so light and gentle, not possessive like a lot of men I'd met in my life.

"It's just…" I stammered. "I wasn't expecting that."

"I'm not a stalker. I won't follow you back to Texas if that's what you're afraid of." He chuckled nervously. "I mean, I'd like to see you again."

Shit! See me again? This was *not* what I expected him to say.

His pause was intended to catch my attention. And it did.

My gaze traveled the length of his long torso, his sculpted abs, his broad chest, his shoulders, flexed, with his strong biceps and triceps and all the other 'ceps' in the world on the display for me.

"Why are you blushing?" He smirked, tugging on my arm until I'd returned next to him on the bed.

I crossed my legs, looking down at him as his other hand wrapped leisurely behind his head.

"I don't know." I blinked rapidly, picking at an invisible piece of lint on the comforter. But I did know. I didn't want him to learn about my past.

Remembering my night with Berk—how we lived out some of my novel fantasies—brought a genuine smile to my face. Yes, if I were being honest, seeing Berk again would definitely be nice. And why couldn't it just be a vacation, even on the mainland? People had fuck buddies all the time. *That's impossible with this man and you know it.*

"I didn't mean to scare you." Berk's expression was pained, his brow crinkled.

"You didn't scare me." I smiled, wanting to reassure him, even though, in my heart, he'd scared the *fuck* out of me. "It's just, I had no idea you were even thinking about returning. For good, I mean. I thought you'd pretty much made Kauai your home."

"Kauai has been my hiding spot." He pushed up on his hands and leaned against the headboard.

"Since your wife died?" My question was blunt, but I needed to know. He rarely spoke of her, and if he really was coming back to the mainland for good, and he wanted to see me again, it was something we would eventually need to address.

"Yes." His answer was distant and hollow.

I didn't want to share my past either, though, so I had to respect him. Did I want to see Berk again, outside of the resort setting, back in the contiguous forty-eight? What if he didn't like the everyday Geneva? What if he couldn't get past everything I'd done, all the people I'd hurt, the crimes I'd committed?

"I'd like to see you again," I whispered. That was the truth, and it was what he deserved. Leaning against him, I skimmed my hand across his arm.

He grabbed the nape of my neck and yanked me down across his lap, his other hand sliding around my naked waist. His face was inches from mine as he stared over me.

"Good." He smiled, his eyes lighting up his entire face. It was an expression I'd do almost anything to see every day of my life.

Every day of your life? What the hell are you talking about? As soon as he finds out what all you've done, you'll never see that smile again. Ever.

Before my mind could run away from my fears, or Berk, his soft lips melted into mine as his tongue sought refuge inside me.

Kissing Berk was one of the best things in life, something to be savored. I could definitely get used to this if he came back for good. Waking up next to Berk, sharing passionate kisses, reading smutty novels together—yeah, that would work for me.

This guy was inside me, not just physically. For the first time in a long time, I had hope. We had a lot to talk about, a lot to sort out if he truly wanted to see me again after Hawaii, but, at least, there was a chance for me—a chance at something more.

Berk broke our embrace, and I felt his heat leave my body as soon as he pulled away. "Aren't your friends due back this morning?" Disappointment marred his beautiful face.

I'd forgotten about Dana and Peter returning from their short honeymoon trip. "Yes. They should be home later this morning. We're all spending the day together. At least that's the plan." A pang of discontent hit me as I realized my last full day in Hawaii wouldn't be spent with Berk. I wiggled my brow, hoping Berk understood my comment. I could definitely be persuaded to sneak out on my family obligations to spend my last night with him.

Returning to Colorado wasn't a given. He said he was thinking about it. Had been thinking about it since he met me. Maybe Berk was opening up his heart to love again.

Love? Nope, I couldn't go there.

"Tonight's your last night, right?" he asked.

I nodded once, not wanting to talk about leaving. I had just a little over twenty-four hours left in Hawaii, and I wanted to spend every one of them with Berk. That was ridiculous, though. He had obligations. I had obligations.

"I'm working this morning out at the beach."

A brick of jealousy hit me square in the gut as I pictured Berk giving surfing lessons to hot, new female tourists.

"What?" He rubbed between my brows.

I wanted a perfect last day with him. Admitting my own insecurities would do nothing to bring that fantasy to life.

"I'll miss you," I whispered, brushing my lips with his.

"Maybe I could see you when I get off?"

"Maybe," I teased. "What time do you get off?"

"Around three-thirty. But I should be home and dressed by four."

"Would you want to have dinner?" I asked. "With my family?" Oh, fuck! Did I really just ask that? Introducing him to my family— on the last night of my vacation?

This was really going to freak him out. Plus, it probably went against some kind of written policy for the resort. Even though it was family owned and operated, it didn't take a genius to assume fraternizing with the guests was not a good thing.

Suddenly, images of Berk wrapped up in these same sheets with other women rolled through my mind. He'd all but assured me I was the first woman he'd been with since his wife, though. Hadn't he?

"I'd love to have dinner with your family, Geneva." His voice sounded hopeful.

His words brought me back from the clutches of the green monster. "Really?"

"Of course, really? Why?"

I shrugged my shoulders, not sure how to articulate my fears.

"What time are you eating?"

"I'm not sure. Probably around six or so. They tend to eat earlier with the kids and all. Kids change everything," I said with a smile.

His face went ashen, his lips pursed as his jaw clenched.

"Are you all right?" I asked.

He scanned the room and drew in a deep breath before expelling it. "Why don't I meet you back here around four? That will give both of us time to shower and dress."

I crawled toward him. "Why don't I meet you back at your place at three-thirty and we can shower together?" I waggled my brows.

I yelped as he flipped me over, his massive body trapping me underneath him. His light eyes were growing darker.

I was wet with anticipation.

"That sounds perfect, Geneva."

His lips found my neck and moved lower, past my collarbone, heading south. I pretty much gave up caring about anything other than the pleasure Berk was about to bestow on me.

"It sounds more than perfect." His low growl against my skin was my undoing.

I wrapped my arms and legs around the man-beast, trying to seal my body to his as he nestled himself between my legs. His swelling cock rubbing against me had me on the verge of yet another orgasm.

He drew back from my neck, his eyes gazing down at me, his hair falling artfully around his strong face. "I'll do anything to spend more time with you today."

There was a rawness to his voice, and to his words, that captivated me and gave me hope. Maybe he would understand all the wrongs I'd committed against my family and friends and give me a chance. Maybe this would be more than just a vacation fuck for both of us.

Either way, I didn't want to waste what precious time I had left with my Poseidon. We were in the most romantic setting on earth and I was going to take advantage of it. And him.

Digging my nails into his thick mane, I scraped along his scalp drawing his mouth to mine.

His lips parted and his tongue and his cock plunged inside me. Being filled with Berk, physically and emotionally, felt perfect.

CHAPTER 26
GENEVA

AFTER SPENDING the day with my family, I made my way down the long stretch of beach toward his home. It was just before 3:30 p.m. and I didn't want to be late.

I thought about what life would be like to *date* him if he really did return to the mainland. For the past few days, he'd just been a vacation fuck in my mind.

Yeah, keep believing that just like you believed Santa Claus was gonna plop his fat ass under your tree every year at Christmas. Disappointed much?

A band of fear tightened around my chest as I rehearsed what I'd say to Berk about my past. He needed to know. After I told him everything, how I'd drugged and seduced my own brother-in-law and nearly served time in jail, would he even want to see me again?

My thoughts drifted to Dana and Peter. They were complete opposites. Dana had a sordid past, but they'd made it work. Hell, I was here in Hawaii because they'd solidified their lives to be together. They even had a family now.

I tugged my bag higher on my shoulder. I'd packed a few things, so I could change at Berk's house—hopefully after a short, sexy shower. Our dinner with my family would be casual, but when I picked out my dress for the evening, I found myself searching for something sexy. I wanted to look good for Berk.

Nearly to Berk's home, I was lost in thought of what our last night would hold for us. Maybe we'd continue reading my book and try out more kinky stuff. Hopefully, with more finesse this time. I heard voices coming through the tropical forest near his house. It was a woman's voice. And Berk's.

I stepped closer, their words becoming clearer as I hid behind the thick foliage.

"You need to see them, Berk," the girl said.

"I don't even know if I'm going back, Jackie."

Going back where? To Colorado?

"They don't blame you," she said, desperation in her voice. "No one does. It was an accident, Berk."

Accident?

"Stop, Jackie. Just stop! This is why I left. I don't want to hear this. Not from you, not from anyone."

"I'm sorry, you're right, I know. Please forgive me." Silence rang loud through the trees.

I peeked through the leaves and saw her reaching up to stroke Berk's face.

He closed his eyes and leaned in to her touch.

Fuck!

My jaw clenched and my stomach roiled. It was the woman from the lobby yesterday. And it was obvious they were much more than just "friends," as Berk had told me.

"I saw you with her again today. Is this serious?" she asked. Her tone held no bitterness or jealousy. She actually sounded pleased.

"It's none of your business, Jackie."

"Berk, I still love you, you know that."

Oh my God, she *loved* him. But this didn't make sense. She was a friend. A friend who didn't sound jealous of the fact that he was seeing me.

"I love you, too, Jackie."

Oh. My God. My heart sank. He was in love with someone else.

"No, I'm not seeing her. She's leaving tomorrow. I'll probably never see her again."

"So, it's not serious?" she asked.

"No." He answered without hesitation.

My entire world began to spin and I thought I might vomit. I'd been nothing more than a vacation fuck for Berk. Always had been, always would be.

I turned and ran back toward the resort, sand flying behind me as I dug my feet in deep. Tears burned my eyes as the wind whipped across my face, the air burning my lungs.

By the time I reached the resort, my feet were on fire and my body was covered in sweat.

"Geneva?" Tori called out.

I turned to face her, unable to hold back the flood of tears that threatened.

"Oh my God, girl, what happened?"

"Berk," I stuttered through my sobs.

"What? Is he hurt?"

I shook my head furiously. "Please," I hiccupped, "please just get me home."

"All right, all right, sweetie. Let's get you back to your villa."

"No, not Hawaii." I clutched her shirt. "I want to go *home*."

"We are going home. Tomorrow."

"I want to leave now. Tonight."

"Have you said good-bye to Berk?"

I shook my head.

"Don't you want to?"

"No," I pleaded. "You can't tell him."

"Geneva, what in the world happened?"

I held back my sobs, covering my mouth with my hand. "I just need to leave, Tori. Tonight."

CHAPTER 27

GENEVA

I ROLLED over in my bed, slapping the alarm clock that mocked me with every shrill sound it emitted. I tugged the covers over my head, burrowing in for more sleep.

All I wanted to do was stay in bed all day. I blamed my exhaustion on jet lag, but we'd been back from Hawaii for three weeks and the real reason for my lethargy could no longer be ignored.

The truth was that I was depressed, for a multitude of reasons. How could I have done this to myself? How could I have fallen in love with a man thousands of miles away who didn't share my feelings?

"Geneva!" Tori banged on the door.

I pulled the pillow over my head to drown out her noise. Tori had recently moved in with me. She'd graduated college in California, but her new environmental studies job was still in limbo. Rather than stay in California and wait, I suggested she move in with me for a while to be near Dana, Peter, and her nephews and niece. Most days I was happy to have the company.

"Open the door, dammit. I'm not kidding, Geneva."

Today was not one of them.

She sounded super pissed. My stomach knotted with fear. What could be wrong? I sat up in bed, hyperventilating.

"Geneva," Tori threw open the door, "what the fuck is this?"

She held a plastic stick in her hand, waving it in the air as she approached my bed.

My eyes went wide when I saw what was in her hand. My head spun and my stomach lurched. I was going to be sick. I pushed past her and rushed to the bathroom, shoving up the lid just in time to puke up the empty contents of my stomach into the waiting toilet.

Tori was behind me, holding back my hair.

When my body finally quit heaving with rolling spasms, I sat back on my heels.

Tori handed me a cool, wet wash cloth. "So I guess it's true."

"What?" I rubbed my mouth and face with the rag.

She wiggled the stick in my face. "These things actually *are* over ninety-nine-point-nine percent accurate."

"Fuck you, Tori." I burst into tears, mainly because she was right. I had three more pregnancy sticks in the trash can to prove it, all of them registering the results crystal clear. As much as I'd prayed to be the point-one percent, I wasn't. It was ninety-nine-point-nine percent clear, I was pregnant. And totally screwed.

Thank you for reading
Extreme Attraction

You can read
Extreme Courage
the conclusion to Berk and Geneva's story.
Available now
Available now

Geneva Barton may have changed her ways, but she still knows how to fight. Now she has more to protect than just her reputation. The bitch may be gone, but the fighter just stepped into the ring. And this time she plans to win.

Berk Rigby has returned to Colorado after a three-year absence from the sport he loves. After winning the gold medal in snowboarding at this year's winter X Games, he should be riding high. But when a familiar face in the crowd of fans reveals some shocking news, his whole world is turned upside down. Now his future is more uncertain than ever and he's not sure he can face it.

As Berk and Geneva come together for a mutual cause, will they find the courage to love again? Or will the mistakes of their pasts drive them further apart?

Life is about second chances.
A chance to forgive himself.
A chance to redeem herself.
A chance for both to start over.

Available now

WANT TO RECEIVE A FREE EBOOK?

Join my email list and I'll send you *Extreme Beginning*, the X-Treme Love Prequel for free. It's the story of Caroline Hagen and Paul Barton. Just visit the website below and join today.

I also give away free things all the time, including ebooks and signed paperbacks (my own and from best-selling authors) and more.

You'll also receive exclusive sneak peeks and teasers of upcoming books in my series.

Visit my website and join my email list now to receive your free ebook today!

www.kaymanis.com

IF YOU ENJOYED THIS BOOK

Please:

    1. Write a review. It's so important to my work.

    2. Tell your family and friends about my books.

    3. Visit my website and sign up for my newsletter. You can also send me an email. I love to hear from my readers.

www.kaymanis.com

    4. Follow me on social media.

Facebook: www.facebook.com/kaymanisauthor2

Twitter: www.twitter.com/kaymanis

Instagram: www.instagram.com/kaymanis

JOIN MY PRIVATE FACEBOOK GROUP
THE MANIS MOB SQUAD

We support and enable those diagnosed with **MOB Disease (Mania of Books) -** a rare and debilitating disease that causes sufferers to become unable and/or unwilling to stop reading and obsessing over all things book related.

Are you a book-aholic? Do you have a One-Click addiction? Then come join this support group. We're all about fun in here, no judgment.

ALSO AVAILABLE BY KAY MANIS

X-Treme Love Series

Extreme Risk (Hindley and Rory)

Extreme Devotion (Hindley and Rory)

Extreme Sacrifice (Dana and Peter)

Extreme Trust (Dana and Peter)

Extreme Attraction (Geneva and Berk)

Extreme Courage (Geneva and Berk)

Extreme Promise (Hindley and Rory)

Extreme Gift: The New Arrival (Hindley and Rory)

Extreme Beginning: The Prequel (Caroline and Paul)

Baxter Bay

You Could Be Mine (Aiden and Olivia)

Sumner Brothers Series

Born to Be My Baby (Ben and Maggie)

Never Say Goodbye (Emmett and Elle)

Thank You for Loving Me (Max and Devlin)

With These Two Hands (Aaron and Kayleigh)

I'll Be There for You (Jake and Lina)

If That's What It Takes (Grant and Sophie)

Now and Forever (Max and Devlin)

Season of Love Short Story Series

Second Chance Heart

Dance with Me

Fall for Me

ACKNOWLEDGMENTS

I've said it before and I'll say it always—writing a book takes lots of help. I want to thank those people who have helped me make Geneva and Berk's story special.

Elizabeth Theeck, MSN, CRNP, my medical advisor – You have been my go-to girl for everything medical in all of my books. Without your help, I could not have made Geneva and Berk's story as authentic as it should be. J.P.'s arrival and survival is all thanks to you.

Connie Neal, MS, LSSP, LPC, my mental health advisor – You're not only an amazing person, you're a sister-in-law and friend. Without your advice and feedback, Berk never could have made it back to the land of the living. Thank you for reading through his therapy sessions and making sure I got it right. Here's to the *real* Dr. Neal.

Julie Deaton, my proofer – Once again you stepped in at the last minute and saved the day. You're my hero, and I'm lucky to call you friend.

Tony and Kimberly, my family – Your love and support means that I can continue to do what I love (and some days what I hate, too).

Melody Bennett, my bestie – You're the reason this whole writing thing has continued. Your willingness to read anything I write, and your absolute honest opinion mean more than you know.

Billie Jo, my mom – I lost you during the writing of this book, and for that I will always be sad. But I know you live on with Jaime and Alana. You will be in every book I write because of the creative gene you gave me. Hopefully, wherever you are, you're drinking a margarita, smoking a cigarette, and reading my books. I hope you like them.

ABOUT THE AUTHOR

Kay Manis is a funny chick who's sprinkled with a little crazy on top. Okay, let's be honest. . . there's ALOTTA crazy up there.

She writes books filled with passion, promise and purpose (with laughter and a few tears, but always an HEA).

She is a native Texan and lives with her family in Florida. When not reading or writing, you'll find Kay eating out with friends or napping with her favorite pillow (stolen from an Inn in Vermont - true story).

Please feel free to contact her at: **www.kaymanis.com**

 facebook.com/kaymanisauthor2

 x.com/kaymanis

 instagram.com/kaymanis

www.ingramcontent.com/pod-product-compliance
Lightning Source LLC
Chambersburg PA
CBHW020738250626
47155CB00003B/817